D0506339

3085264

RISK

C. K. STEAD

RISK

A novel

MACLEHOSE PRESS
QUERCUS · LONDON

First published in Great Britain in 2012 by

MacLehose Press
an imprint of Quercus
55 Baker Street
7th Floor, South Block
London W1U 8EW

A CIP catalogue record for this book is available
from the British Library.

ISBN (HB) 978 0 85705 222 3
ISBN (TPB) 978 0 85705 223 0
ISBN (Ebook) 978 1 78087 759 4

10 9 8 7 6 5 4 3 2 1

Designed and typeset in Cycles by Libanus Press, Marlborough
Printed and bound in Great Britain by Clays Ltd, St Ives plc

RISK

PROLOGUE

THE POLISH CLUB, KENSINGTON

IT WAS SEPTEMBER 2002, AND SOUTH-WEST FRANCE HAD been struck by storms and floods. Nîmes airport, from which Sam and Letty had been booked to fly, was still closed. Letty was Sam's recently acquired French daughter. More proficient than he was at using the internet, she had secured them an AirEire flight from Nice to Luton. Sam said if Letty's mother, Simone (who had never been his wife), would drive them from Uzès to Avignon they would take a train from there to Nice. But Simone insisted the floods had put her in crisis mode and she would drive them all the way.

She did that, delivered them in good time and there were airport farewells: first Simone and Letty, mother and daughter, fond and somehow efficient in the French way – lots of *mwa mwa*, left and right, and *au'voir* and *à la prochaine*; then Sam and Simone, the long-ago lovers long since parted and gone their separate ways, awkward now, even embarrassed, and unsatisfactory. There were so many questions he would have liked to ask.

And then there had been Jean-Claude, the rejected boyfriend in his black leathers, hanging about on the perimeter looking sorry for himself. Was Letty going to ignore him completely? Yes – until the last minute, before they went through into Security, when she softened a little, and while her parents watched, went over to him, kissed him on one cheek and then the other, but barely touching either – after which Sam could see by the wagging finger and the nodding head that she was telling him it was all over between them; she was getting on with her life and he must get on with his.

AirEire's advantage was said to be that it was cheap, but with the rebooking fee, and because Letty's luggage was a few grams over the impractical limit, it came up costing more than a regular flight. Predictable, and no choice really – Letty had had to take what she could find. So for the price of something better she had secured for them the sardine experience.

Sam was not a nervous traveller but he found it disturbing – so many people and so much luggage jammed into a plane that looked as though it might have been bought from the asset-stripped airline of a failed East African state and repainted to suggest that cheerfulness and colour will defeat gravity. Banana palms (perhaps) had become outsize shamrocks; there was a very big "little green man" in a tall hat over the wing, and a verse –

> To an isle in the water
> With her I would fly
> W. B. Yeats

on the fuselage.

As they boarded Sam caught, or thought he did, over, or through, or despite, the smell of diesel, a last scent of lavender from the hills, and perhaps just a faint waft of eucalypt.

They found their seats, and while the ritual warnings and instructions about "the unlikely event of an emergency" were got through in a lovely breathy Irish-English he pulled a book out of his bag to settle his mind, to focus it. *Lettres de mon moulin* by Alphonse Daudet. It was part of the programme Letty had set for him to improve his French. She had even persuaded Simone to leave in good time and divert a little between Uzès and Nice so they could take a look at Daudet's famous mill on its stony slope where the stories had been written; and to drive through Tarascon, home of Daudet's quixotic hero Tartarin.

The takeoff was long and slow – a lumbering shuddering run down a strip that seemed to go on and on, sea to the left, white apartment blocks with hills behind to the right, and then late, almost too late, the lift-off, up and out and away banking left over the sea; the slow wide arc, climbing all the time, a huge circle that crammed the windows with blue and white, the blue dotted with small craft and cut with slashes of wake, while AirEire flight 6337 lined itself up and levelled itself off, north and west for London. And there now, directly below for a few minutes, were the rock faces of the Alpes Maritimes frowning, folding and tumbling down to the Mediterranean with its hazy pale blues and dark turquoise stripes; and between mountain and sea, the terracotta littoral that was Nice and the Côte d'Azur.

Sam, who had "done" French at school and then lost most of the little it had given him, remembered Daudet's story of M. Séguin's goat – "La chèvre de M. Séguin". This nice little animal (the tone was cosy and the goat spoke fluent French) had been so determined to be free she ignored all the warnings her owner gave about the wolf, and the goats he had eaten, and escaped from the locked stable through a window. So she found again, and enjoyed, the freedom of the hills, the delicious grasses, the bluebells and foxgloves and the fast-flowing streams – until the wolf came. Then (Sam remembered it from school days, but thought of it now as if it might have contained a warning to those who break out of the stable in search of freedom) the brave little white goat with her inadequate horns fought the wolf and kept him at bay until dawn, when at last she succumbed, bloody and exhausted, and was eaten.

He chose that story. It would make his start with his new text easy. He read slowly, checking unfamiliar words in the glossary and notes. He got to the point where the goat heard a noise behind her, "*C'était le loup*" – it was the wolf – and closed his eyes.

The Luton landing when it came was a bump-down rather than a smooth glide, bringing alarmed yelps, nervous laughter and a ripple of mocking applause from the sardines. While they were hurried off by staff who had to make the turnaround quick, Sam prepared his mind for the next hurdle. Lacking the E.C. passport that would let his French daughter past the barrier without interruption, he would have to present his New Zealand "Uruwhenua" and front up to the question, "What is the purpose of your visit?"

Once he had replied, "The visit is the purpose." The questioner had been a Sikh in a burnt-umber turban and the smart reply had not aided swift passage. Sam had been stood to one side to be dealt with later by someone senior. Hadn't there been a war – two wars – with Germany in living (or only recently dead) memory? And if it was true we had all "moved on" so sides taken *then* were of no account *now*, why was *she*, H.M., still New Zealand's Big Cheese? He'd been through all this with Letty, and knew she would be waiting nervously on the other side, signalling – yes, there she was now, finger to lips and a pleading frown that said, "Please don't!" This was not the moment to ride that particular hobby horse.

"What is the purpose of your visit, Mr Nola?" The questioner this time was Euro, like himself – pure pale English, probably, or Anglo-Celt, unlovely and with wolf-like intent.

While Sam described, laboriously and in non-confrontational tones, his "present situation", that it was "under review", that he had "interim status" for his employment at Interbank America, there was a shadowy otherself explaining that he had escaped from M. Séguin's barn in order to savour freedom and the mountain grasses . . .

But the wolf wasn't listening. Those killer eyes were already on the next in the queue – a dark tan couple, anxious and discomposed, and with two small children.

"Next." The stamp came down on Sam's Uruwhenua.

"Good hunting," he said over his shoulder as he walked towards where Letty was waiting.

She hugged his arm and gave it a small reproving shake.

"I did nothing," he said in answer.

"Your face," she said.

"I can't help my face."

"Yes you can."

"Man, proud man," he quoted, "dressed in a little brief authority . . ."

"Look at them," she said, pointing to the armed police with their padded jackets and automatic weapons. "They have serious things to worry about and you want to make a fuss about their harmless questions."

Well yes, it was only a year since 9/11. "I made no fuss," he said. "And if they insist on what you call *armless kestyons*, they should be ready to put up with my legless answers."

"Legless?" Since she didn't hear her own dropped aitches she often missed his jokes about them.

Beyond the doors the next coach to Marble Arch and Victoria was already humming and stirring, eager to be on its way. Everything was on time and on target. It was one of those lovely late afternoons that seem to happen often now that the globe is warming, when the English end-of-summer simmers as it used to only in works of fiction by novelists with initials (always two) rather than forenames – P.G., E.M., D.H., L.P.

They handed their bags to the driver who had a fierce black moustache over fiercely white teeth. He grabbed at them, slung them under with what might have been an angry flourish, and barked a word Sam didn't catch. Sam turned with an enquiring look and the driver pointed, silent and displeased, to the steps up into the coach.

Letty chose their seat and took out her book. Sam got behind a copy of the *Guardian*, wrestling it around himself. The news was full of the P.M.'s latest alarms about Saddam Hussein's weapons of mass destruction and unwillingness to comply with the U.N. weapons inspectors. When Sam next looked out they were cruising swift and smooth past fields that alternated green and gold with, now and then, patches of dense woodland, heavy foliage unruffled by any breeze. He could see the driver in the mirror, one hand on the wheel and the fingers of the other smoothing his moustache, as if calming it.

The vehicle rose and fell end-to-end, a liner (land-liner) cresting the waves. Sam returned to the *Guardian*.

Afterwards he was not sure he hadn't dozed for a while; perhaps he and Letty both had. In any case he became aware of some kind of argument, an angry altercation at the front of the bus, the driver being challenged about something – possibly the route he had taken, or had failed to take – offence given on both sides, and then all at once they were in the midst of a crisis, veering off up a ramp from the main route and into a side road that led in turn into a narrow lane. They were all hurled sideways and now were racing through, brushing first one side, then the other. Bushes, hedgerows and bracken scratched at paintwork and flicked across windows. They were bouncing, thrown up out of their seats. There were complaints, shouts, "Oh I say . . ." and "Look here . . ." and "What the fuck . . ." Passengers were clinging to their seats. The driver in the mirror was angry and wild-eyed.

The lane closed in on either side. Sam could see nothing beyond hedges and shoulder-high cow-parsley. Then, in only a few seconds, the view opened on the left, the land dropping towards what might have been a stream. The coach was slowing now, approaching an old wooden five-bar gate, but not stopping. They went through it, over it into a field, almost in slow motion, the wooden bars cracking audibly under the wheels. A herd of half-grown steers lurched and bounded this way and that, avoiding the giant intruder, then turned and watched, with the kind of intelligent interest the young take in anything new, as it came to a stop under a tree.

By now there were yells of protest and complaint. The driver grabbed a small bag and his jacket. He stopped only long enough to deliver some final insult to his antagonist at the front and was gone. The late sun glinted on his oiled hair as he stopped only to fiddle with a switch out there. The door closed behind him and he disappeared back in the direction from which they had come.

"What did he say?" Sam asked the man across the aisle, but he was already deep in argument with his mobile phone.

The passengers sat looking at one another, glad the punishing ride had ended. There was indignation, but astonishment too, and even flutters of amusement. It seemed so far outside the normal order of things, they didn't know how to respond.

"Has he locked us in?" a woman asked; and then, in a slightly shriller voice, "I hope he's not going to blow us up."

All who were not yet on their feet stood up at that, and began to make moves towards the front. It took a few moments to find how to open the door. Voices were raised, there was pushing and elbowing.

As the door sighed itself open, moving out and sideways, they pushed and jostled into the lovely late-afternoon field that smelled of cow and crushed pennyroyal. One or two removed bags from the side compartments; others left them there. The sense of panic was not quite past until they were all some way from the coach, up on the crest of the hill beyond which the land dropped down to the stream. There they stopped and turned, a group of panting people feeling variously confused, foolish, embarrassed. Angry too. Indignation would soon take over again.

And there was the coach, comfortably parked under the splendid tree, the cattle gathering around as though they might be next to board.

Mobile phones were busy now. Men swished up and down through the dry summer grass, shouting into their hands. The women seemed to stay each in one place, crouching or bending forward, but also shouting needlessly. Emergency services were alerted; the bus company was called. Families, business associates, lovers, were warned that someone would be late.

A sort of William Hague with the head of a comic-book alien was saying, "Yes, my dear," – the "my dear" was full of Yorkshire irony – "as a matter of fact, I am. *Alone*. Alone with a couple of dozen other poor bastards and a herd of cows." And he clicked her dead, a man telling the improbable truth for once. How satisfying!

"Those are not cows," Sam told him.

The alien looked at him, blinked twice, and turned away.

To Letty Sam said, "They're not cows you know."

He borrowed her mobile and called his friend Charles Goddard. He and Letty were supposed to meet Charles and others for a literary reading at the Serpentine Gallery, after which there was to be supper. "We're going to be late," he said.

Charles, already at the gallery, wanted to know where he was calling from.

"We're in a field in deepest . . . I'm not sure. Possibly Hertford-shire."

"That's progress. Is it nice?"

Sam looked around. "Yes it's nice. Some corner of a foreign field that is forever England."

"Are you in England or France, Sam?"

"No no – England, definitely. But that's foreign for me. I've just come through immigration."

"You need to get yourself an E.C. passport."

"I'm working on it."

"And you're in . . . a *field*. Did you mean that?"

"We got dropped in the middle of nowhere by a furiously angry bus driver, and now we're being held hostage by a herd of cattle."

"What are you talking about, Sambo?"

Sam tried to explain. But where did you begin? "In fact," he said, "I'm not sure what happened. Something incendiary was said. Umbrage was taken."

"Umbrage." Charles savoured the word. He was laughing.

"High dudgeon in fact. But no violence. He just left us here.

You remember the Larkin poem? 'He just walked out on the whole crowd.'"

Charles interrupted: "Sorry, Sam. Have to switch off. We're moving indoors. We'll keep your places for dinner. 8 o'clock if you can make it. O.K.? *Ciao* for now. *Ciao-ciao.*"

Sam and Letty deposited their luggage at Sam's flat and took the taxi on to Exhibition Road. The Polish Club was a fine building, with a terrace looking out over gardens at the back, a splendid staircase to the upper floor ballroom, heavy-framed paintings, a bar and restaurant, with tables inside and out.

The friends, two couples, Charles and Githa, Jake and Jan, were sitting at a table at the end of a long room looking out on gardens that were fading into darkness and reflections. They had kept two places but were deep in conversation.

"The arseholes are lying, Charles. Where's your brain, you cunt."

This was Jake Latimer, an actor with an actor's voice and delivery, so it boomed among the flowers and echoed off the moulded ceilings. "We're being lied to every fucking day. They have self-correcting software. If they gap for a minute and type a truthful statement it inserts a 'not'. Tony Blair can't do a shit that's honest."

And then, because he'd caught sight of the newcomers: "Do sit down. Here – those chairs . . ."

They sat. The two women made welcoming motions but for the moment Jake was not to be stopped. He was turning to Sam now, while pointing across the table. "Our Charles believes in these fucking W.M.D.s. Unlike Blair he doesn't believe in God – which I understand and appreciate – but he believes in Saddam's weapons of mass destruction . . ."

"I didn't say that," Charles grumbled. "This is bullshit. I said anything's possible and until we know for certain . . ."

"We should *mobilise an army*? Two armies? *Ten* fucking armies."

"No, but . . ."

"We know where the *oil* is. Where are the fucking weapons?"

Charles sighed and leaned back in his chair. "How about you lay off for now, Jake? Give it a rest."

Jake looked around the table. His face expressed astonishment, indignation. "Is this the issue of the moment or fucking *what*?"

There was silence. "I've just been reading the *Guardian*," Sam said. "And yes, it's the issue of the moment."

"Thank you." Vindicated, Jake waited for his challenge about the oil to be taken up. It wasn't, so he took a different tack.

"Tell me," he said to Sam, "since you're a clever fellow – why would a nation capable of producing Rutherford and the All Blacks name themselves after a hairy fruit?"

Sam felt himself bridling. Hadn't he been supporting the prick? "We don't," he said. "Or *I* don't. And the kiwi is not a fruit. It's a bird."

"Apteryx," Githa said. "Wingless." Githa was Indian. She was slim and beautiful, quick and intelligent, with lovely dark eyes and a beautiful bow of even white teeth. Sometimes it seemed to Sam that Githa knew everything.

Jake frowned. He didn't care what a kiwi was. He cared about Iraq, and oil, and those imaginary W.M.D.s.

"When we were kids," Charles said in a tone of wanting to help, "what's now called a kiwi fruit used to be called a Chinese gooseberry."

Jake shook his head. "Good," he said. "Excellent. Thank you. I needed to know that." He poured the last of the wine around the table and raised a hand to no-one in particular, to the room at large, for more. He looked for a moment like a forlorn football player claiming he'd been fouled. There was another silence while everyone sipped.

"How was the reading?" Letty asked brightly. "Did we miss something special?"

"The reading?" It was quite dark out there now, and Jan was detained by her own reflection in the window. "It was O.K." She flicked her hair out at the sides. "Wasn't it?"

The other three nodded as if recollecting something that had happened last year. "Yes," Charles confirmed. "It was very good. Brilliant, actually."

London, Sam reflected, was a place where so many things were "brilliant" you lost track of them five minutes after they happened – during which five more brilliant things had happened, *actually*.

A waiter had seen Jake's semaphore and was hovering. Letty and Sam ordered pastas and salads and Jake another bottle of wine.

Githa said to Letty, "And Sam told Charles you were in a *field?*"

"It's true," Letty said. "We were 'ijacked."

She dropped the aitch. The story had to be told and Sam left it to her. Without the aitches it was more colourful. Now and then she made an effort and inserted one where it didn't belong. Their flight had been with HairEire; but the coach ride, careering through the lane, brushing bushes on either side, was "air-raising".

"'e was so angry," she said. "Someone said something to 'im at the front of the coach, maybe about the Koran, or 9/11 . . . I don't know what, but 'e lost 'is, you know – completely, and just left us there. And then a woman thought 'e was going to blow us to smithereens."

Sam took it up. "We waited in that field. The police came – sirens and flashing lights. A replacement driver was sent. There was an apology from the company – forms to be filled in so we could reclaim our fares. Cops did a sweep of the bus . . ."

"A sweep?" Jan said.

"Looking for explosives . . ."

"Of course," Jake said, his voice heavy with irony and disapproval. "Black moustache, swarthy skin – a Muslim terrorist. What else?"

"Muslim terrorists exist," Charles said. "Don't they? They're not little green men who come down out of frying pans or flying saucers."

Jake picked up his glass and stared at it. "I have measured out my life with frying pans." He sipped, and savoured. "We're being played upon."

He looked around at them all, one by one, inviting them to disagree. "Fear is the terrorist."

"I call it the 9/11 effect." This was Sam, over breakfast, explaining to Letty, who had stayed the night in his small spare bedroom, the change in his two friends, Jake and Charles. A year ago they had seen eye to eye on most things, politics in particular; now they could hardly talk to one another without falling out and shouting. "Both Labour supporters. But Charles has stayed loyal to Blair. Jake thinks – well, you heard it. Blair is George Bush's poodle."

"Jake's very forceful."

"Big voice, lots of swearing. When I agree with him it seems to upset him – I'm not sure why. Maybe it's my job – he probably thinks anyone who does my kind of work . . . But about Iraq and Blair, he's right of course."

Letty looked at her watch. "I have to go *mon papa*." She kissed his brow and began to clear away the dishes.

"Leave them. I've got time."

She pecked him again and headed for her room.

"Bye *au'voir*," she called a minute later from the door. "See you Friday night if you like the idea."

"I do. I like. See you then."

He leaned forward and through the window watched her emerge from the front door, down the steps, and turn right and right again towards Paddington. She paused before the second turn, getting her scarf right.

"Your Perdita," Charles had called her.

The 9/11 effect

1

SWEET THAMES . . .

AFTER GRADUATING IN LAW AND ARTS IN 1978 SAM NOLA
came to London on what New Zealanders refer to as their O.E. –
their overseas experience. There was a "squat" – young people
from New Zealand and Australia in a house in Islington owned
by the Council but unoccupied and boarded up. There was a crow-
bar break-in and a new Yale lock put on the door. The house was
rewired for electricity, reconnected for water, and five or six
friends moved in – not legally, but the law on squatting was complicated, there were certain rights once you were in, and they were
not evicted. Work was not difficult to find if you were young and
flexible, passport regulations were not as strict as they had since
become, and for more than two years Sam lived and worked in
London, and travelled in Europe, as the young from the Common-
wealth did then, coming and going across the Channel in a dodgy
Bedford campervan bought cheap and shared with friends.

In London there were young women in his life, girlfriends,
some memorable and regretted when they left, others forgettable
– or forgetful (of Sam). The best remembered and most regretted
was Simone Sauze. Simone was French and engaged to a young
Parisian, Gustav Robert. She had come to London to improve her
English which she needed in her work. She and Sam became friends

and then, after a time of confusion and some conflict, they were lovers.

In those pre-A.I.D.S., or pre-A.I.D.S.-consciousness days, Sam assumed that every young woman willing to share his bed was on the pill; or that she would say if she was not, in which case he would take the necessary precautions. Most were. Either Simone was not, or she was erratic and forgetful in taking it. When she raced back to Paris to be with Gustav, Sam didn't know (and wouldn't for many years) that she was pregnant. It should have occurred to him but it didn't. Her departure and their farewells were full of arguments and reconciliations, pain and anger and tears, none of which he understood. She left him feeling bereft, that he'd been too casual, that he hadn't done enough, or soon enough, to keep her. It was a time he would always remember with regret. Once gone, Simone severed all contact. Twice he went to Paris in search of her, but had no success. She was gone from his life, it seemed for ever.

So his memories of Paris were destined to be as a place of defeat. But memory is selective, and in Sam Nola's case it tended to be upbeat. Even (and sometimes, he thought, especially) places of sadness were good ones to return to in memory. Because they were sad they were intense; and because they were not the present reality, they could be taken or left according to the mood and need of the moment.

Paris as he recalled it was a city of romance shrouded in a rather distinguished melancholy, with the fine sad tones of accordion music, *péniches* going by along the Seine, the smell of dust and scent of candles in the holy alcoves of the Sacré Coeur, café tables on pavements and under trees, and the Palais and Jardins de Luxembourg with gravelled tree-lined walks, handsome statuary, and the Medici Fountain. The Paris of his memory was sad because

Simone had left him and couldn't be found; it was beautiful because it was Paris, and because it was alive with the language she had murmured in his ear in those Islington nights.

He went in search of her without an address or telephone number; and seeing on a map the Jardins de Luxembourg a short walk from his hotel in the rue Madame, began his hunt there only because he remembered her saying once that as a young girl that was where she had gone to play tennis. For days he behaved like a tourist, wandering the streets hunting for her face, his eyes and ears absorbing so much more because they were not finding, and would never find, what they were looking for.

Often afterwards he told himself, or friends if they were listening and the moment was right, the story of walking at night in the rain from one café or restaurant to the next, reading the menus and the *prix fixes*, in the grip of an indecision that could be broken only by a sudden forced (and usually wrong) choice; and in the midst of all this melancholy rambling, somewhere in a warren of dark streets around the area of Saint-Sulpice, a moment when he and a stranger each went to pass between two parked cars and so confronted one another, and when he looked up he recognised the actor Marcello Mastroianni, star of Fellini's *La Dolce Vita* and 8½. Sam's instant recognition, and the pleasure it gave him, must have been obvious. He stood back, acknowledging the godlike presence, and gestured for Mastroianni to go first, which was accepted with a smile that unfroze the moment and the night. What made it special was that nothing was said. A tribute had been offered and accepted, and Paris had been for an instant bathed in a Fellini light.

But it was a light that couldn't be other than fleeting. It was only a day or so later, still wandering, that he met, on the steep narrow Metro stairway to the rue de Rennes, a group of children who danced about him, patting him on the arm, the shoulder, the back, all shouting, demanding money, one holding up a newspaper in front of his face as if there was something they wanted him to read. He gave them some coins and they were gone, leaving him wondering what all that had been about – until it occurred to him to check for his wallet and that was gone too.

In the dingy police station right on the place de Saint-Sulpice he reported his loss. "Les Yugoslavs" was the weary response. These were Gypsy children and this was the way they were set loose to operate from camps on the edge of the city, their parents, or handlers, knowing that French law in those days did not permit police to arrest minors.

By the time Sam had made his statement (necessary, he was told, not for the police, who knew the criminals and could do little to stop them, but for his insurance claim) and come out of the inner office, the waiting room had filled with people there to report the same offence. The little gang of dancing miniature thieves had swept through the *quartier* snapping up wallets, money, unconsidered trifles, and on into the hinterland of the Boule Miche. Sam's cash was gone and his driver's licence. It was more a nuisance than a disaster, because in his luggage he still had passport and traveller's cheques. But it had the effect of making him stop and ask himself what he was doing; and confront the fact that Simone was gone, that he wouldn't find her, would not see her again. Summer was ending and suddenly it seemed the "O.E." was over too: it was time to go home.

During those two years of freedom Sam had tried his hand at writing – in fact had written a whole novel, a thriller which he called *Damn Your Eyes*. It was, he supposed, an attempt to find something that might take him away from the law which had once seemed an attractive prospect, but which had begun to look restricted and unexciting. There were no "creative writing" courses in those days. People who wanted to write just bought paper and a portable typewriter and set about it. Sam had done that. His portable was a blue Olivetti, and he applied himself to it intermittently in Islington and while on the move in the camper-van. He was fond of *Damn Your Eyes*, not so much because he was sure it was good, but because he had memories of working at it in strange and often lovely settings – in an olive grove in southern France, under umbrella pines beside a rural railway station, in an Italian vineyard on a hillside in sight of the sea. However it might appear to others, to its author its pages evoked scenes and fragrances which had nothing to do with what was happening in the story, but sprang from the circumstances in which they were written.

One last thing during the autumn of those final months in London was to find an agent. He was a somewhat off-beat boozy character, new to the trade, who would, he said, take it on. Two days before Sam flew out from Heathrow for San Francisco en route for Auckland, a contract was drawn up and signed.

Back in New Zealand, half excited to be seeing home as a foreign territory, half horrified by its random rawness, Sam set about doing what you did then if you were young, qualified, and a New Zealander. In summary, he fell in love with a girl called Ngaio, married her, fathered their two sons, worked, saved money, bought a house . . .

It was all, step by slow step, quite conventional, middle-class, prosperous, proper. It was as things should be. It was right. His parents were pleased with him; his employer (he was in commercial law) favoured and promoted him. His discontents were quiet, his boredom average, or anyway not extreme. He remembered London and the latitudes of his youth as, he supposed, his father's generation remembered World War Two.

From time to time, with long intervals between, word came from his agent about the progress of *Damn Your Eyes* through a succession of publishers. One thought he should cut the whole of the Paris section; another thought the Paris section was full of promise and needed to be expanded. A third saw deeper elements that could convert *Damn Your Eyes* from thriller into literary fiction, but would require a complete rewrite. Some rejected it out of hand but never took less than six months (and prompting from the agent, prompted by Sam) to make the decision known. It was five years after his return to New Zealand that "feedback" (as it was beginning to be called) stopped altogether. Two or three years later again Sam enquired and was told his agent had been stung to death by bees on a visit to Central America. No-one in the agency knew what had become of the typescript. It was supposed to have been posted back to him but had never arrived. By that time Sam was a settled commercial lawyer, prospering in Auckland and thinking about buying a boat.

The ending of that life after two decades, the separation, the divorce, the guilt (yes, there was guilt), the signing over of the family home to Ngaio and the boys, leaving his safe job, coming back to London to look for a new one, sorting out passport formalities – that was a year of his life he would want to forget. Parts of it came back to him in moments of weakness, especially at 3.00 a.m. after too much alcohol. Sometimes, in company with his Oxford friends, Charles and Githa, he joked about it as his blue period – "like Picasso's, only darker". He tried to see it, when it had to be seen at all, as his time of liberation. Breaking the bonds couldn't have been other than painful, and they had to be broken – that's what he told the darkness of 3.00 a.m. He tried to be Edith Piaf and regret nothing; even sang it to himself in the half-light, waiting for the next car, the next ticking black cab at the curb-side, along Gloucester Terrace.

In all of this – the pain of transition, the separation from family and friends, the shock of finding himself "doing everything" (which meant shopping, cooking, cleaning, washing, ironing as well as going to work), there was a certain thin thread of exhilaration. There was another thread, equally thin, of hope – though for what, he was unsure.

The first three or four weeks back in London were a blindstorm of anxiety, self-recrimination and regret, from which, not knowing that better things were to come, he might well have given up and gone home. He had found temporary work on what was called "documentation" at New Zealand House in the Haymarket and was looking for the kind of legal work he was qualified to do when he saw advertised, and applied for, a job at the London branch of Interbank America. It was a lawyer they wanted, from his kind of commercial background, and the advertisement was full of the usual daunting imperatives disguised as friendly predictions: "You will work closely with prime brokerage and equities financing groups . . . You will negotiate trading agreements and liaise with regulators in different jurisdictions . . . You will form close working relationships with traders and management . . ."

There was a succession of interviews, none seeming to offer either clear hope of success nor promise of failure. Now he was being called back for another, the important one it seemed, with Reuben Leveson, the man who would be his boss if he got the job.

He left Gloucester Terrace with the sun shining and emerged up the long escalator out of the new Canary Wharf station (massive and beautiful, a modern equivalent of the ancient cathedrals) into the open air to find rain sheeting down out of a black sky. In the short time it took him to reach the Interbank America building he was sodden.

The boss, who looked ten years younger than Sam, reached out. "Reuben Leveson – Reuben," and they shook hands. "I'll call you Samuel if that's O.K."

"Sam."

"Sam? Even better. Do sit down."

He went out for a moment and returned with a towel. "Here. You look like a drowned duck."

Sam applied it briskly and scrabbled in his briefcase for papers.

"Don't worry about those. Coffee?"

They were in a kind of reception area with comfortable Scandinavian chairs and low tables, a small screen showing the markets and a larger one for teleconferencing, and one picture window looking out on the square. For a while they talked casually, about finding a flat in London, about how Sam came to be there – whether it was his first time and how he found it changed after two decades. He was being assessed, he supposed, not for what he was expert at doing, but for what he might be like to work with. Because he liked Reuben Leveson he felt at ease and hoped he might even be making a favourable impression.

"We're interested in you as a commercial lawyer," Leveson said. "A lot of your work would be with contracts. Your interviews have gone well."

"Have they?"

"You didn't think so?"

"I wasn't sure. That's good news."

"No, they were good." He glanced down at a sheaf of papers. "Your refs describe you as meticulous."

"I'm glad."

"Are they right?"

"Yes, I'm afraid so."

"Meaning . . . what?"

"Just a bad joke really. Meticulous is another word for boring. Can be."

"Are you prepared to be boring?"

"I am."

"Have you seen the trading floors?"

Sam had not and was shown them now – or rather, shown one, the Equities floor, where shares and derivatives were traded. The other two, he was told, Fixed Income, and Commodities, looked pretty much the same.

The floor was literally that – one level of the building, without partitions, as big as a football field and filled with row upon row of desks. At each a trader sat looking at Bloomberg screens, at least three, sometimes as many as five. Around the walls were time-zone clocks for New York, Tokyo, Hong Kong, Sydney – the world's markets. Sometimes there were flurries of activity on one or another part of the floor, two or three standing behind someone working, all watching the screen; at others the traders, who, most of them, appeared to Sam to be very young, were sitting back in their chairs chatting.

Sam was introduced to Tom Roland, the oldest by some years, a survivor of the days when the floor had been a vast room full of people calling numbers, waving signals and shouting into their phones.

"Tom's an oddball," Reuben explained as they moved on. "No-one should continue trading at his age. It's bad for the health. But he doesn't want to move and there's a kind of superstition about him. I suspect the management think if they moved him against his will the whole system might come down. Off the premises Tom's a poet – said to be quite good. Here, he's cautious but sound – never puts a foot wrong."

It was only when he was showing Sam to the lifts that Reuben asked, "When would you like to start?"

Two children were born during Simone's first marriage – Leticia (Letty), who was supposed to be Gustav's, and Marie who was Gustav's indeed. It was when the marriage foundered that Letty told her mother she had never felt she was Gustav's daughter. The answer was unexpected but not unwelcome. "You feel like that," Simone said, "because you're not his daughter. Your father is a man I fell in love with in London – a New Zealander."

Simone married again and had another child, Hélène, three daughters to three fathers. The new family lived just outside the town of Uzès, north of Nîmes and west of Avignon. Letty liked it there and liked her new step-father, Georges Clairmont, teacher at the village school of Saint-Maximin. But the idea had been planted that she would one day track down and meet her biological father, the New Zealander Sam Nola. Studying Medicine from the University of Paris she took graduate work at the Great Ormond Street Children's Hospital in London and became more focussed in her spare time on the pursuit of her (as London was teaching her to say) "real dad". With help from a service offered by the Salvation Army she tracked Sam's story from London back to Auckland and to London again. She believed now that they were fated to meet – as if its inevitability sprang not from her will but from the stars.

Letty located Sam's work-place, Interbank America at Canary Wharf, and learned a little about what he did there. She went to look at the building in that extraordinary precinct that had been thrown up in the Thatcher and post-Thatcher years, a fragment of Manhattan or Chicago picked up and transported en bloc, skyscrapers and all, to the London Docklands. She watched staff coming and going. Once she followed the man she believed was Sam Nola and stood near him on a crowded carriage on the Jubilee line. When they got to Baker Street she followed him through to a platform of the Circle line, watched him fight his way into another carriage, but didn't follow any further. She thought he looked nice. If that was indeed her father she would be glad to know him, and would like him to know her.

Christmas was approaching. Normally she would have gone home to have it with her family, but didn't object when her name appeared on a list of staff posted to stay on duty at the hospital. This would involve long night hours of being on call but with not much happening. During one of these nights she began drafting a letter to Sam Nola. She wrote carefully, and rewrote. It was important it should not frighten him away.

Christmas was a bad time for Sam, worse than he allowed himself to acknowledge. The days got shorter, the lights came on and the decorations went up along Regent Street. He told friends near and far how much he loved it, the English Christmas – the *real*

33

Christmas. It was true, half true; but he had to keep saying it to hold at bay his loneliness, and the consciousness of all he now lacked. Yes, Christmas here was real in a way it could never be in the southern hemisphere summer; but he was assailed by memories of the beaches of Northland, of December sun on sand, and pohutukawa leaning out over the water shedding red stamens into the shallows; or of green mangrove harbours with rickety jetties and two small boys fishing.

For Christmas Day that year, 2001, he had an invitation from Tom Roland, the man he had been introduced to on the trading floor. He knew it was a charitable gesture. He could imagine Tom's wife, Hermione, whom he had met at a staff party, saying, "You must ask that poor chap from Auckland for Christmas – away from his family. He'll be all alone."

Tom was civilised, unassertive in conversation, often quirkily funny. He seemed to know an enormous amount about many things beyond the world of banking, so when a conversation faltered for want of a word or a fact or a date, Tom was likely to supply it. He was diabetic, liked good wines and just occasionally drank too much and passed out. He wrote poems, and though shy about them, sometimes showed them to friends.

Once after a few drinks he explained to Sam how there were weeks and months when he couldn't write anything and at these times of "poet's block" he became depressed. Other times, the poems came in a rush, out of the blue, often in the middle of the night. He kept a pen, a torch and a notepad next to his bed because if he didn't write the idea down at once it would be gone in the morning. In his younger days he'd been persuaded by friends to publish a small collection at his own expense. It was called *Floating*, and he liked to say it sank without trace.

"It had beautiful blue covers," he told Sam, "with a Japanese ideogram on the title page done with a brush. I was told it meant 'floating' – or something close. Maybe 'boating'." He laughed. "I believed in those poems. Thought I was destined to be up there with – you know?"

"Larkin, Hughes . . ." Sam ran out names that would have been in the air then.

"Yes, well . . ." Tom looked away into the distance. "I don't suppose I thought I was in that league – even then, in my days of optimism. It was a modest little thing, but lovely to look at. Thirty-two pages. Hand-made paper. I had a couple of hundred printed, twenty-five signed and numbered. I gave copies away for years and didn't think about keeping some for myself. Suddenly they were gone. Haven't seen a copy for a long while."

He seemed willing to accept that his poems were probably "no good" but that didn't stop him writing them. Nothing could, except those unhappy times of writer's block. It was a kind of curse, as if the Muse had settled on the wrong person and wouldn't release him. There had been one or two early successes with magazine editors and then nothing. So Tom went on writing poems – "Art for art's sake," he said, with a reckless laugh, "and to hell with publishers and editors."

"I'm not just one of Shelley's 'unacknowledged legislators'," Tom said. "I'm an *unpublished*, unacknowledged legislator." When he showed a poem it was, Sam thought, with the dim hope that someone intelligent and sensitive would tell him that at last he'd done well. But praise came usually from boozy friends in effect paying for the drinks he went on buying them.

The Rolands lived in a large apartment that had once been a warehouse, looking out on the river at Bermondsey. The sitting room was wide and high, with ancient beams, polished wood floors and rugs, comfortable couches, framed prints and lithographs around plain white walls. The piano was a Bechstein baby grand. There was a Christmas tree, a big one with many coloured lights, shiny baubles, and presents ranged around it on the floor.

Sam was introduced to the family – daughter Bridget and husband Vaclav, both musicians; and son Claude, his wife Jane, and their new baby who was already receiving Christmas lunch from the breast. On television, with the sound off, someone was speaking outside number 10, where it appeared nothing at all was going on.

Presents were distributed, including a small one, a token, for Sam. He had brought nothing, not even wine. There should, he thought, have been something. Flowers for Hermione, or fancy Swiss chocolates. He tried to think what he might say to excuse this lapse and could think of nothing. Silence would be best.

The lunch was good-humoured. Crackers were pulled and jokes read out – the sillier the more enjoyed – and paper hats put on. There were amusing stories about friends and banking colleagues. Somehow the talk got around (as it mostly did in those weeks immediately after the event) to 9/11 – where they had first heard about it, seen the images; how it would be if such a thing happened in London. They imagined watching it across the Thames from this room. What would the targets be? But mostly the buildings weren't tall enough for anything like the same effect – the planes, first one, then the other, flying straight into them, like burning spears, penetrating to the heart; and later those sights on television of people falling from the upper floors, tiny bodies hurtling down . . . And then the buildings themselves collapsing, and the long shots that made it look as if Manhattan had come under nuclear attack and was burning . . .

While the conversation continued, Hermione left the table and returned from the kitchen with the pudding wrapped in blue brandy flame. They all applauded. Sam took this as a chance to get up and stretch and do a circuit of the room. Out there the tide, which an hour earlier had been pushing up against the flow of the river, had now turned, the two running seaward together, fast. Not far upriver was Tower Bridge, and beyond it, from this south bank, the City and St Paul's. Tom had followed him to the window. "Sweet Thames run softly till I end my song," he quoted.

Back at the table 9/11 was left behind. The subject was music now, Richard Strauss, one of whose piano trios Bridget and Vaclav were rehearsing. Hermione said Strauss had been "a naughty old Nazi who wrote music in the mornings and played cards in the afternoon".

"No," Bridget said. "That's not fair."

Tom said there was not another composer who wrote music that was so beautiful, so ravishing.

Well, Hermione said, you didn't have to be a good man to make beautiful things.

"What is beauty?" That was Vaclav, the Central European asking the big question.

"I'll tell you," Tom said. "Or at least I'll give you an example. It's a line from a poem." And he quoted – twice, the second time giving it full measure, "I am still / The black swan of trespass on alien waters."

"Your own?" Sam enquired.

"I wish," said Tom, shaking his head.

Hermione said it sounded like Shakespeare. "It does," Tom agreed, "or it could be, but it's not."

Sam was repeating it in his head, thinking these were alien

waters for him, and wondering was he the black swan of trespass?

"We give up," Bridget said.

But now Tom himself was momentarily stumped. The name was eluding him. He was standing at the head of the table, one finger in the air, eyes closed. "It's by that imaginary Australian."

"What do you mean *imaginary*?" Bridget said.

"Invented. Someone invented him, and passed him off as real. Ern . . ."

Of course. Sam had heard of this famous hoax. "Something like Smelly?"

"That's it," Tom said. "Malley. Ern Malley."

Still holding that finger aloft, like something that had to be saved, but tilting forward in quick short movements, each one taking his nose closer to the table, he seemed to fall asleep, or unconscious, and rolled sideways out of his chair and on to the floor. It was a graceful roll until the last moment when his head thumped against the polished floorboards.

Sam arrived back at Gloucester Terrace earlier than he'd expected but not before the last of the light had gone from the afternoon of that very short day, feeling half-relieved to be alone, and yet lonely – at a loss how he should occupy himself in the remaining empty hours of the compulsory festival. Who was it had called it "the festering season"? There was a sad truth in that sometimes, and not only for those who were compelled to spend it alone. His last Christmas with Ngaio and the boys had been a shocker, best forgotten.

On the table in the downstairs entrance, where mail was delivered by the postman who had a key, and sorted by Mrs Barton, his widowed landlady in the ground-floor flat, there was a letter for him. There was no stamp, so it must have been found among the commercial stuff that came through the slot and lay littering the floor. He didn't recognise the handwriting. He took it up to the first floor where Mrs Barton's cat Trinnie (short, he'd been told, for Trinidad), a regular visitor, was waiting at his door. He let her in and followed. Inside he dropped the letter on the table while he removed overcoat and jacket and put the kettle on. He put a small handful of cat biscuits in a saucer kept for her. He was not sure Mrs Barton would approve. Was he alienating her pet's affections?

He turned the television on and sat at the window with his tea. The cat sprang lightly into his lap, and he stroked her flanks and knuckled her head. She pushed against him, her front claws just emerging in a faintly felt kneading movement against his thighs.

There were moments now when it seemed that the front window and what could be seen from it was his prison, representing the limits of his new life. In the weeks since taking the flat he had become absorbed in watching and attempting to interpret the life of a man about his own age in the flat opposite, who lived, as he did, on the first floor; but he had his office downstairs at street level. There were no signs or notices in the office windows to attract customers off the street, so what went on there was part of the puzzle. Each day a young woman arrived on a motor-scooter and opened the office, while upstairs the man had breakfast and got himself ready for work. Sometimes, but not often, the young woman came up and seemed to share breakfast with him. He was always gone at the weekends. Sam assumed there was a home, probably a wife and family, somewhere out of London, and the flat above the office was kept so he wouldn't have to commute to work.

But today – and it would be the same right over the Christmas–New Year break – there would be nothing to watch. The office was closed, the flat unoccupied, curtains apart and only a single lamp in one corner of the sitting room beside a stainless-steel sculpture of a female figure that looked like something from the era of Art Deco. The small Christmas tree downstairs in the office had the look of a token for business customers, not a serious affair as there had been at the Rolands'.

Sam was watching the B.B.C. News with the sound turned right down as he opened the letter. A replay of the Queen's broadcast was just ending. A few moments later there were shots of the Pope, no longer able to stand, but blessing the Christmas crowds from his chair in the window.

A photograph fell to the floor. Sam moved to retrieve it and Trinnie, displeased, jumped down and went to the door.

He let her out; returned to the letter and the photograph. It was a young woman. The face seemed familiar. The letter was two sheets, handwritten and signed "Yours with sincere best wishes, Leticia Clairmont." It told him almost without preliminaries, that she had reason to believe she was his daughter . . .

He read it right through, skimming, and then a second time, very carefully.

He got up and walked twice around the room. It made him conscious how small the space was, how confining. He walked into the back bedroom, the one he slept in, away from the traffic noise.

And of course – that was why the face was familiar. It reminded him of long-ago Simone. The likeness was striking.

He returned to the letter and took in the details, one by one – Simone's assurance that Sam Nola was Leticia's father, her two marriages and three daughters. The letter ended telling him its author would be disappointed, but would understand and accept, if he didn't wish to meet, or even acknowledge her existence. She would respect that and not pursue it any further.

A walk, that was what Sam needed – outdoors, space, fresh air. He wondered whether he should be alarmed but could think of no reason why. He had thought often of Simone, especially since the collapse of his marriage.

He put on coat and scarf and went downstairs and out into the chilly street. He walked around Cleveland Square and down to Queensway, thinking that he should take his time, give this news a night's thought, sleep on it . . .

Even as he was thinking this, standing on the cold empty pavement outside Whiteleys, he was dialling her number.

2

NORTH OXFORD

CHRISTMAS WAS NICE, OF COURSE, BUT SAM HAD FORGOTTEN how long the winter that followed could seem (who was it had said March was "a cold bleak month, indistinguishable from eternity"?), how grey the London days, how you craved sun, brightness, the colour blue, a distant horizon line, far hills or a mountain standing out in bold outline. Sometimes (rarely that year) there were clear days with luminous blue skies; sometimes days of snow which, while it stayed white in the parks, cast its pale radiance upward over everything. But soon the streets turned to brown sludge, radiance vanished, the cold that hurt fingers and ears seemed to get into your bones and worse, into your brain. Depression threatened as buoyancy lapsed. At work people talked of summer holidays and planned their escapes so far ahead it seemed a kind of fantasy. "O for a beaker full of the warm South," yearned the travel brochures.

There was a poem by Philip Larkin had often come into Sam's mind since he left New Zealand. It was about hating home, and leaving it –

> Sometimes you hear fifth-hand
> As epitaph:

He chucked up everything
And just cleared off,
And always the voice will sound
Certain you approve
This audacious, purifying,
Elemental move.

It's the poem of a safe stay-at-home and about what a kick he gets out of sentences like "He walked out on the whole crowd". It had seemed amusing when Sam read it as a student – amusing and true; but only half-true. Because Larkin was really mocking those who had the courage he lacked to act on that impulse, to turn their backs on an old life and start a new one.

But now that Sam had himself "chucked up everything / And just cleared off" the poem's humour seemed much darker. Once you had made, had *really* made, the "audacious, purifying, / Elemental move" there was the feeling of an amputation. Two whole decades of his adult life had been lopped off: it was too much, and part of him wanted to go back and reclaim them.

At his worst, in those 3.00 a.m. moments, what had stopped him deciding to go back was not courage. It was pride. To come creeping home would be inglorious, ignominious. Would Ngaio have him back? Very unlikely. Would he find as good a job as the one he'd given up? Probably not. Would his old friends, the stay-at-homes, be laughing behind his back? Certainly.

No. If this was a mistake, for the moment he was going to have to live with it. *Courage, mon vieux!* (Why/how did French help? He didn't know, but it seemed to.) *Je ne regrette rien!*

And now things were beginning to improve. He had a daughter. And he had a job with what seemed good prospects –

some prospects, at any rate. The balance had swung in favour of staying, seeing it out.

There were also his friends in Oxford, Charles and Githa and their little bronze boy Martin. Sam Nola and Charles Goddard had been names that went together when they were young, both clever boys at Auckland Grammar. At university Sam had combined Law and Arts while Charles did Arts alone, languages and literature. In four years Sam completed B.A./L.L.B. and the following year was admitted to the bar; in the same four years Charles completed an M.A. with first-class honours and won a scholarship to Oxford. By now they were on separate paths.

So while in his O.E. years Sam lived the raffish life in the Islington squat, coming and going across the Channel in the dodgy Bedford, making love to girls, falling in love with Simone, and writing a thriller destined to be lost in the post, Charles embarked on an Oxford M.Litt., soon converted to D.Phil., and wrote a thesis on the sonnet as a form in the English language, from Shakespeare to Lowell with an appendix on James K. Baxter.

Charles had been briefly back in Auckland in 1981, the year of violent protest against the Springbok tour and in time to be best man at Sam's marriage, an occasion when they appeared together both wearing bruises earned during the battle of Marlborough Street outside Eden Park that had since passed into legend. But Charles was home only on a visit that year, anticipating the call back to Oxford where he would soon be appointed to a university lectureship, and later elected a fellow of his college.

Sam's boys were already five and eight before Charles was even married. Githa was born in Kenya of Indian parents who had been evicted from Uganda. In her teens she had been sent to a British boarding school and had come from there to Oxford on a scholarship where Charles had been her tutor. They had one child, Martin now aged nine, and lived in a tallish red-brick house in North Oxford, close to the Dragon School where Githa taught and Martin was a pupil.

Sam liked Martin and got on easily with Githa. There was a room for him in their house when he wanted to be out of London, and when they needed a child minder. At first he didn't crowd his luck, but soon saw that it was their luck as well. He was a dutiful and practised parent. So far from home and family he enjoyed the job and was entertained by Martin.

Oxford was an escape from the prison he sometimes felt London to be. He liked the river and the parkland, the bookshops and pubs, the feeling of the life of the university going on not quite untouched by the larger world, but shielded. To balance it out and put the fairness of the arrangement beyond doubt, there was the spare front bedroom in his flat in Gloucester Terrace. Sometimes they were in his house when he was in theirs.

Martin had his own Oxford which he was eager to share. It involved the river and the life of ducks and swans and waterfowl, fish and frogs. It included the Port Meadow with its roaming cattle, and the lock there allowing passage to barges and other river traffic. There were rowing crews, eights and fours, on the river and houseboats on the canal.

Martin was an only child, a lone ranger. "I'm a little emperor," he told Sam. It was something he had read about China – that a consequence of the one-child policy was that most Chinese children were onlies. They didn't learn to share, or to fight, with siblings, and grew up self-centred and demanding.

"Do you think you're like that?" Sam asked.

Martin shrugged. "I don't think so, but I'm not sure." He didn't seem greatly concerned. "Do you?"

Sam ruffled his hair. "You don't look like a Chinaman to me, Martie. Maybe you're a little raja."

As they watched four swans, cock, hen and two cygnets, the parents gliding watchful on the still backwater while the cygnets pulled at edible strands among the grasses at the edge, Martin told him that this was what his mum had wanted, "the perfect nuclear family". But it hadn't happened and she would have to hurry because of her "biological clock".

"Her biological clock." Sam repeated it. "You're very knowledgeable, Mart."

Being with a nine-year-old made him behave as he had with his own boys when they had been that age, and a moment later he was quoting – misquoting – declaiming in an imitation Irish accent, two lines by W. B. Yeats –

> "Upon the brimming water among the stones
> Were nine and fifty scones."

Martin looked at him hard, frowning.

"That's an Irish poet," Sam explained. "Fifty nine – that's a lot of swans isn't it?"

"You said scones," Martin said.

"It was a joke."

Martin laughed. It was a polite laugh. "You make a lot of jokes."

"Do I? Sorry."

"That's alright then," he said, "I like your jokes. They're cheerful."

"Thanks, Mart. You're very kind. I suppose I'm cheering myself up."

"Are you sad?"

"No. Well, everyone's sad sometimes."

"Mummy said you divorced your wife."

"I think we divorced one another."

"What was her name?"

"Her name was – and is – Ngaio."

"Ngaio. I've never heard that for a name. How do you spell it?"

Sam spelled it. "It's a Maori name."

"Is she a Maori?"

"No, she's Pakeha – like me and your dad."

"Didn't you like one another?"

"When we got married we did."

"And then what happened?"

"I'm not sure. We started having fights."

"Mummy and my dad have fights."

"Well, everybody does. All married couples."

"So that wasn't why."

"It was a symptom I suppose – a sign that something was wrong."

"What was it?"

"What was wrong? Oh God I don't know, Mart. Maybe we were bored." After a moment he said, "Possibly I made a mistake."

Easter 2002 came at the end of March. Letty was to spend it in Paris. By then, although it was only three months since that first, Christmas night meeting, Sam and Letty felt they knew one another, liked one another, had fun together. Her reason for going to Paris had to do with a young man: it seemed there were plenty of those in her life, but this one, Marcel Saint-Jacques, Corsican-born, Paris-trained, a surgeon, was "special".

Sam told her that on the Easter Saturday he would be there himself. He didn't tell her why. In fact there was no reason, and since she didn't ask he didn't need to invent one. He suggested they should meet at the café on the place de Saint-Sulpice. They would have coffee, perhaps a meal, go for a walk. If it was convenient, Sam might meet this Dr Saint-Jacques.

Sam had not been to Paris since the time of his unsuccessful attempts to find Simone. In those days, if you weren't flying you took the train down to Dover, then the ferry to Calais and on again by train. It took most of a day. Now, thanks to the tunnel, you got on at Waterloo and off less than three hours later at the Gare du Nord, from which it was only a short Metro journey to the place de Saint-Sulpice and the room he'd booked himself in the rue Madame.

It was exciting to be back after so long. The beauty, the elegance, the rich associations were everywhere and undeniable. He and Letty met at the café that looked out on the square and the fountain. It was spring and the chestnut trees were coming into new leaf.

They walked to the Luxembourg Gardens and followed the gravelled paths between the lines of trees, up past the tennis courts to the Palais, and then back towards the Medici Fountain. There were spring flowers everywhere, and the wintry branches were now lined with new green or, depending on the type of tree, offering green in bouquet-like clusters. The Medici pool, which at Sam's long-ago last visit had been showered and swamped by leaves from the plane trees overhead, was now clear, perfectly reflecting its flanking urns and, at its head, the statue of an outsize and hairy green-bronze god leaning down from his rock and seeming to catch in the act a much smaller pair of lovers in pale marble.

Autumn then, and now spring. Sam squeezed Letty's hand as they walked away and she returned the pressure. He didn't tell her that the fountain was the place where he had once shed tears for her mother.

Tom Roland sat in the dark watching lights on the water, hearing the river's rush against the piers below his window. On his lap there was a printout of his new poem. But it wasn't a poem – only half a poem. And it wasn't his. It was the Devil's. The Devil had come to him around midnight and dictated it. That was how it had seemed at the time. He had half woken and scribbled it down on the pad he kept beside his bed, and had gone back to sleep. Later he woke again and took it to the table where he was sitting now, looking out on the river. He had worked at it for more than an hour, sorting out line lengths and rhymes (the Devil was good at them – better than Tom himself), tidying and typing it up, reading and re-reading, always making changes, improvements.

So it was not simply the gift of his dream visitor. It was Tom's, too. But without the visit there would have been no poem. He was pleased with it; but not pleased that it stopped as it did, unfinished, and that he couldn't see where it should go next. He felt like Coleridge writing "Kubla Khan" and interrupted by the man from Porlock.

Not that it had been a real devil with horns and a tail; but Tom had known at once who it was. He'd felt this, without any doubt. The visitor hadn't seemed evil; not even frightening – more theatrical than sinister, Tom thought; or perhaps operatic. He might have burst into song, basso of course.

49

People made pacts with the Devil; sold their souls for promises of worldly favours. What had this devil wanted? There had been no requests; no talk of trade. But it was only half a poem. If he came again he might charge something for the second half.

Tom went over the lines. He couldn't quite read them in the dark but they were there in his head now, imprinted – he'd worked so hard at them. He read it as if seeing in the dark, seeing the run of it line by line on the page –

> Some Toms sing for their supper,
> One was a piper's son,
> Some grow old and howl on the heath –
> This is the story of one:
> Clever Tom who hatched in his head
> Ideas like chickens he sold for bread.

> *Bolt your window, bar your door,*
> *This I never told before;*
> *That wind against the house-wall hurled*
> *Cold with the coldness of the world*
> *Will shout a moral if it can.*

> This little chicken went to market,
> This one he kept in his head –
> Their welfare was Tom's precious care
> And his care, well-fed.

> Tom's neighbour's coop caught fire,
> He doused his own with water;
> Tom's neighbour's wife fell ill –

He fucked their daughter;
And gently, steadily over the scene
The rain fell down and kept it green.

It was that line "He fucked their daughter" that had shocked him fully awake and interrupted the flow. He had never used that word in a poem, yet it belonged in this one, proving somehow that its author was not Tom Roland but the Monsieur le Noir who had brought it to him in sleep. Tom was only the vehicle; the amanuensis.

He heard Hermione's bare feet padding towards him in the dark. The big ball of electric orange light from the far side of the river gave the room a peculiar glow.

"Darling, it's 3 o'clock."

"Sorry, love. Did I disturb you? Can't sleep."

She came close, sniffed his breath, patted his knee and squeezed his arm.

She didn't trust him, and she was right: he didn't trust himself. But now, all at once without any fuss or effort, he'd stopped drinking. And the Devil had rewarded him – but only with half a poem.

He told her, "I didn't do very well on the trading floor yesterday."

"Well, there have to be ups and downs, surely."

"I suppose."

She had an arm over his shoulder, leaning against him, both of them half asleep in the half-light. Dreamily he let out the thought that had been coming and going. "They always tell you that you can't drive as well after a few drinks. But I always drove better . . ."

"Up to a point."

"Up a point, of course. Beyond that I was pissed. But I was thinking just now, I danced better when I'd had a few . . ."

"Danced?" She laughed. "When did you dance?"

"Before I met you I used to go to dances. I was very good."

"Were you darling?"

"And French. After a few drinks . . ."

"French?"

"I could speak it."

She straightened up. "Darling, you're not talking yourself into . . ."

"No, no. It's just I was thinking about my losses on the floor today. While I was drinking I never put a foot wrong."

"But you never drank during the day – did you?"

"No that's true, I didn't."

"So what are you talking about, Tommy?"

"You're right. Cobblers." He took a deep breath. "I've written a poem."

"Yes, darling? That's good." He recognised her indulgent tone.

"It is good, as a matter of fact. But it needs finishing."

"Then you must finish it, Tommy."

"If I can, yes."

"Tomorrow. Now let's make ourselves a cup of tea, and try for a bit of sleep."

He listened again to the river. Listen to the river, he told himself, and the other half will come. "Sweet Thames run softly . . ."

He got off the window ledge and followed her to the kitchen. In his head the half-poem began again –

Some Toms sing for their supper,

One was a piper's son,
Some grow old and howl on the heath –
This is the story of one . . .

There was a dinner party at the North Oxford house which began with champagne in the garden at the back. The guests included the Latimers, Jake and Jan; a novelist, Ivan Pemberton, short-listed that year for the Booker Prize, and his latest wife Sophie; the Oxford Professor of Poetry Iain Feeney; and others whose names Sam didn't catch, or remember, including a very small, very witty literary editor from London, and a large and loud travel writer, recently returned from Sarawak. The conversation was full of book-talk and quotations, and eager disagreements on questions like whether Edward Lear had got his lines

On the Coast of Coromandel
Where the early pumpkins blow

from India or New Zealand.

Ivan Pemberton recounted how he'd once been on a book tour to Australia and New Zealand, and his laptop had been stolen from a hire-car at Pauanui – "on the Coast of Coromandel" – hence the question about Lear's poem. What surprised Ivan was that this theft had made New Zealand's national news – "ENGLISH WRITER'S LAPTOP STOLEN". The fact that it contained work on a new novel made it worse. New Zealand was ashamed; and even the thief must have been affected by the sense of a national disgrace, because the laptop reappeared, left on the steps of the Coromandel police station.

Politics came and went from the conversation, and already Sam could feel the divisions opening up on the question of Saddam Hussein's W.M.D.s. These were touched on and quickly abandoned like the hot potato they were; and then away the conversation went again on something literary, like whether "What's Become of Waring" was a poem by Browning or a novel by Anthony Powell (it was both, they decided) and whether it had anything or nothing to do with a poem by Paul Muldoon called "Why Brownlee Left" which began (according to the little editor who had it by heart) –

> "Why Brownlee left and where he went
> Is a mystery even now."

This was late in the evening and they had moved indoors. Across the corner of the table from Sam was a woman whose face was familiar but whose name he hadn't caught. She smiled at him, as the conversation rattled on with much inventive hilarity, around the question of what had become of Waring and why Brownlee had left. "It's the alumni wave," she said in the tone of a fellow outsider. "We've been swept aside."

"Should we have gone with it, d'you think?"

But no, she didn't think so. "I prefer watching from the bank."

He knew her as an actress, but it was an uncertain recognition. She was petite, quite beautiful, with a lot of auburn hair which she tossed about self-consciously. "I think you have a famous face," he said.

"Famous except that you can't put a name to it. That's what television does for one."

"I've come from New Zealand," he explained. "I live here now, but I'm rather out of touch. I know you're an actress."

"You sure?"

"Fairly sure. Aren't you?"

"Acting's what I do," she confirmed, and held out her hand. "Elvira Gamble."

"Of course. It's an honour . . . Sam Nola."

He asked where she was working now and when she said at Stratford in "the Scottish play" he asked her role and was told, "I'm Missus."

"Oh God of course you are." Because he was embarrassed that he hadn't assumed it, he said the first thing that came into his head. "You're quite small for the part."

She was amused. "Do you think of Lady Macbeth as large?"

"I suppose I must . . . Doesn't she say she'd pluck the baby from her own breast and dash its brains out?"

"*If* she'd resolved to. She's talking about resolution. And in any case, killing babies doesn't require size."

"No of course it doesn't." He was slightly daunted by the thought of an actress who could take such a part, and in such a famous place. "It must be difficult . . ."

"The role? There's a certain ferocity of course. 'Infirm of purpose, give me the daggers!' You have to sound as if you mean it, and as if you'd do it. It's all in the voice."

That night Elvira Gamble drove him back to London. On the way, as they cruised along the almost deserted M40, he told her about Letty. She thought that was exciting. "Your Perdita," she said, and he didn't tell her that Charles had said the same.

She told him about a house she planned to build on a piece of land, on the edge of a village in the Cotswolds, bought with money she made for her part in a movie. She had the radio on, very low, or perhaps it was a C.D., playing Chopin nocturnes. He felt mellow and they were at ease with one another.

Dropping him at Gloucester Terrace she turned on the interior light and handed him a small pad and a pencil. "Write me your e-mail address and I'll see you get a ticket."

"Would you? I would have come anyway, now that I've met you."

"We'll have a drink afterwards."

"Wonderful."

He thought of kissing her cheek but to avoid ambiguity in so small space he shook her hand. "Thank you, Elvira."

"El," she said. "As in *elle s'appelle . . .*"

"*Merci*, El."

"*De rien, Monsieur.*"

On the street he turned to wave, but Lady Macbeth was already accelerating away.

Sam worked on towards the late summer when he was to get three weeks' leave. Feeling better about himself, or at least less threatened by gloom and despondency, he worked at making the flat in Gloucester Terrace a little more like home. He improved his kitchen equipment and began to use the French version of a big illustrated cookbook Letty had bought him, *La Cuisine Italienne* by Carlo Capabalbo, which she said he could use for improving both his cooking and his French. "When you can't be bothered cooking or reading," she said, "you can look at the pictures." As adjuncts to this tome he bought smaller things like Lizzie Spender's *Pastability*, and Miranda Seymour's *A Brief History of Thyme and Other Herbs*.

He bought a comfortable armchair and a floor rug. The rug was a Bokhara. He had seen the word in Ivan Pemberton's shortlisted novel and enquired about it, and somehow the enquiry had led to buying one.

He went to the enormous Tag art sale in Pimlico and bought two lithographs by Dalì, done as illustrations to an edition of Dante that had never reached publication. They were not signed and were from the largest numbered edition, a bargain at £100 each. For the same price there was a little black-and-white wood engraving by Eric Gill, similarly unsigned, and he bought that too. It was called "The Doctor's Tale" and dated 1930. There was a large letter H, and four human figures in medieval dress. One man wielded an immense sword, and a woman, on her knees before him, appeared ready for beheading. A week or so later Sam read in the *Guardian* that Gill had been a sexual predator. But the lithograph was elegantly done; and as Hermione Roland had said, you didn't have to be a good man to make beautiful works of art.

He had bought books, some in Oxford, others browsing on Saturday afternoons in Charing Cross Road. In Notting Hill he found a set of shelves for them, brought it back to Gloucester Terrace in a taxi and set it up in the back bedroom.

Across the street he thought things might be getting warmer between the first floor *pied-à-terre* and the downstairs office. There was another breakfast with the secretary; she worked later and seemed in no hurry to leave. The wife (or the woman Sam had designated that role) came and went at odd hours, unpredictably. There was an air of something either about to happen, or recently happened and hidden; but whether it involved the bedroom was unclear. Everything (if there was anything) was, he decided, either incipient or impending.

He became more enterprising about theatre seats. At painful expense, but remembering his failure to bring them a token at Christmas, he secured three seats in the stalls at Covent Garden for Verdi's "Simon Boccanegra" and invited Tom and Hermione to be his guests. Tom announced, as they talked in the foyer about ordering a supper and drinks for the interval, that he had given up alcohol. He'd had enough of just cutting down – from now on he was dry; and perhaps he was, though Hermione cast Sam a sceptical glance. So it was over a San Pellegrino-only supper during the first interval that they sorted out the intricacies of the opera's plot: in particular that Fiesco's adopted daughter, Amelia, was really the natural daughter of Boccanegra and his great lost love, Maria.

More economically, he went with his young banking colleague, Maureen O'Donnell, to see a new movie called "Nine Queens". It was about a scam in Buenos Aires which ended with the scammers racing to the bank with a certified cheque worth hundreds of thousands of dollars, only to find the doors chained up and crowds in the street clamouring for their money.

They had both heard of the banking collapse in Argentina but knew next to nothing about it. "It couldn't happen here," Maureen said as they sat over a pizza and wine afterwards in Leicester Square. "The Government would step in."

"But in Argentina," Sam said, "didn't the Government step in there?"

"Did they?" She supposed they must have. "But Argentina . . . It's not Britain is it?"

That night he dreamed he was back on the vineyard west of Auckland where he had grown up. His alarm woke him at 6.30. He listened to a taxi ticking down in the street, and the accelerating whirr of the milkman's electric delivery cart.

He reached across to the bedside table and switched on the radio news. Drifting towards sleep again he seemed to hear, "Weapons of mass destruction" repeatedly. He shook himself awake and it was only John Humphries on Radio 4, talking to the winner of the Booker Prize. Sam didn't catch the name but it was not Ivan Pemberton.

3

SAINT-MAXIMIN

THE VILLAGE OF SAINT-MAXIMIN SITS ON A HILL ABOVE THE main road to Avignon, two or three kilometres east of the town of Uzès. Between the village and the town a back road, the Chemin de la Coste, which becomes the Chemin des Chênes Verts, runs through vineyards and fields until it veers off into a walking path down through woods, past a chateau and mill-house and over a stream, the Alzon. Here the walker can choose either to climb straight up into Uzès, or go on below the walls of the town, continuing through woods along the stream past another mill-house, and finally up a steep path that comes out at the cathedral and its *tour fenestrelle* – the famous windowed tower, said to be unique in France.

Along that back road, a kilometre or so from Saint-Maximin, Georges Clairmont, teacher at the village school and second husband of Letty's mother Simone, lived in a house on several hectares of land inherited from his grandparents. There was a small vineyard, a field of ancient olives, a field planted in sunflowers, and one of a grass that looked like a kind of wheat, this one always referred to as *le champ rouge* because in spring it blazed red, or red-orange, with poppies. Behind the house, beyond the olives and among cherry trees and *chêne* oaks, there was an old stone shepherd's cottage – one room downstairs, two up – that had been refurbished for visitors. It was there Sam stayed when he went with Letty for their late summer break in 2002. Simone and Georges were going away on holiday; the second daughter, Marie, was visiting her father, Gustav Robert, in Paris; and Letty and Sam would stay with the younger daughter, Hélène, looking after the house and feeding the two cats, André and Gide. Sam relished especially the morning view from up there, over the roof of the main house and all the way to the dark green hills beyond the valley of the Gardon, the whole scene with colours and skies like a painting by Van Gogh.

But before Georges and Simone left there were a couple of days when they were all together. Georges, always in his red trousers ("like an Italian on holiday," Letty said), reminded Sam of those male movie stars the French favour – Gérard Depardieu or Vincent Lindon: large and tousled; not smooth, but with a good voice, full of cracks. He had intelligent eyes and, though full of enthusiasms and keen to expound them, he was also capable of silences. He must have been seven or eight years younger than Simone, and Sam thought she was rather proud of that, pleased with herself for having escaped Gustav into the arms of this fine fellow. Whether she was likewise pleased to have escaped Sam, he had no idea. At least there were no signs of regret.

Simone had worn well. Sam remembered a story about Dickens meeting in middle life the woman he had been deeply in love with as a young man and had wanted to marry, and his feeling of relief as he recognised what a lucky escape it had been. There was no such feeling with Simone. The passing of the years had done her no harm. She was good-looking and smart, and still with something mysterious which took him back. Between them now there were no-go areas – wariness on both sides, questions that would remain unasked. But many memories could be safely shared, and information about the intervening years exchanged.

Georges' passion was the village, the region and its history right back to Roman times. He had grown up there, gone away to Paris for a decade or more and returned, bringing Simone, to take up the few hectares of family land and the teaching post in the village. He talked of his childhood in the 1970s when there were still donkeys to carry loads up and down the steep streets, and horses to harrow and plough the surrounding fields; when the village had a *boulangerie* and an *alimentation*, and two or three times a week a butcher's cart, a fish cart, a cheese cart visited, and what was now called Suzy's was the café where the locals met. Now Suzy's was for sale and would probably be turned into an up-market restaurant for "Parisians and foreigners" who were buying cottages in the region and doing them up as holiday homes. The supermarket down on the main road had put the small shopkeepers out of business, so you couldn't even buy your breakfast croissant in the village. It was all bad, Georges said with a wry smile; but the village still had a vibrancy which he felt in the kids he taught – and the region had its wines and its history. One had to make the best of the changes time brought; and it was obvious a very French kind of life still went on. On the board outside his school Sam noticed you could still read, from the last day of term, the proper French *carte* pinned up to tell the children their choices for lunch.

As for its history – Georges was currently reading letters by Jean Racine ("France's Shakespeare" he explained, in case Sam didn't know) who in 1661 had been sent to live with his uncle, a canon in the church at Uzès. The young Racine had been giving his two guardian aunts in Paris anxiety about the company he was keeping, and since he had a lot of talent and little or no money, it was hoped he might find a vocation in the church. For a time the poet had charmed his clerical uncle and impressed him with his grasp of the writings of the church fathers; but in reality the southern region's light, the flowers and fruits and vines, the clear starry nights, the heat of summer and even the violence of its storms all stirred in him a sense of the warm south as he had found it in the classics. They spoke to the poet in him. The local dialect he found almost unintelligible; but the beauty of the village women needed no translation. He wrote clever letters. He addressed a witty poem to the cicadas, asking them to turn down their racket and spare his ears. He described long walks, sometimes all the way to the (even then famous) Pont du Gard. He rode a mule from town, through the woods to Saint-Maximin, to supervise masons and labourers who were constructing, on his uncle's property, what was still the village's only chateau. But after six months his pretence at interest in a clerical future became too difficult. He was pining for Paris and the theatre, and would soon return there and make his name and his fortune.

Georges Clairmont in his red trousers expounded all this in a mixture of English and French. They spent two evenings all together, one mother, two fathers and two daughters, and on the morning of the third day Georges and Simone were, as Sam said to Letty, making her laugh, "released into the wild". That afternoon Letty took him to see *la source de l'Eure*, the spring the Romans had tapped to supply Nîmes, twenty kilometres away, with water which still flowed out of the ground, clean and clear, and was still tapped as a supply, but for Uzès now, no longer for Nîmes which a thousand years ago had discovered its own.

Letty was not the daughter of Georges, but she had the same tendency to believe knowledge was valuable (especially knowledge of France), and to impart it like a teacher. Sam had to know everything there was to know – or at least as much as she did – about the aqueduct by which the Romans conveyed this water from its source to the Pont du Gard, and so across the valley of the River Gardon and on, all the way down to their "camp" (in reality a city with an arena) at Nîmes. The immense structure, built of stone blocks each weighing six tonnes, was a triple set of arches (a second built on the first, a third on the second), the stone honey-coloured on the Avignon side in the morning light, on the Uzès side in the evening. Georges had spoken of camping under it as a child, and even walking, heart in his mouth, across the topmost arches; but you could do neither of those things any more. Now it was a U.N.-designated World Heritage Site, there to be admired and protected, floodlit at night and with a car park and an information centre.

But for a thousand years water which welled up out of the ground at the source below the walls of Uzès had taken the path of the aqueduct, lowering in altitude only a few centimetres in each kilometre of distance, reaching the river valley and crossing high over it along the top of the Pont du Gard, and then continued (not as the crow flies but rambling as the right contours for a steady descent were found) until it had emptied into the reservoir at Nîmes. It was a miracle of engineering and ingenuity, which invited you to admire not so much itself as the human race, and to shield out, or not quibble over, questions like who had given the orders and who had carried them out, how many had died in the process and how, if at all, justice or human rights had fared in that equation. Thousands had lived without justice, not one without water.

But Sam's holiday was not to be all instruction. Most mornings he and the two sisters walked along the back road that smelled of fennel (the plants studded with white snails, like bright buttons on a green coat) and on through pine-scented woods into the town, to have coffee in the place aux herbes and return with supplies. The olive trees were laden and the oaks dropped their small acorns, the cups grey and the acorn pale green. There was a rocky track up from the first of the mill-houses, and here some of the white stones were covered with thick green moss. On days when the sky was clear and the sun shone through the trees, the colour was ordinary, even dull; but on a day after rain, when the moss was wet and the light dim, Sam saw it as if in another life, a different planet. Green greener greenest; green absolute. There were small blue flowers along the paths, and yellow late summer crocuses, their colours of an almost equal intensity.

In the afternoon, after the siesta hour, they went swimming in the River Gardon, the one that flows under the Pont du Gard, but further upriver at the village of Collias, where schoolboys jumped from great heights into the deepest parts, and large fish could be seen cruising against the flow.

It was September already but the swallows still swarmed over the village morning and evening, hurtling and diving in their imitation of the Battle of Britain. What were they doing up there? High over the rooftops there had to be invisible life – flying things to be caught and eaten on the wing. The village doves kept up their repetitive exchanges. Sometimes in the evening in Uzès the starlings suddenly rushed the darkening sky in an inexplicable clattering panic, and it took them many minutes to return to the places they'd fought over and now had to fight for again. After nightfall, when the swallows were tucked away and the bats had taken over the night watch, there was sometimes a pale silent owl that swooped in a great arc from the church tower to the far side of the village.

The clock in Saint-Maximin chimed (twice each hour – the first right on time, the second a minute late) from 7 a.m. to 10 p.m. and then fell into the deep silence of a night in provincial France. The church bell, mechanised and automated, boomed for matins just after seven in the morning, again at noon for sext, and at 7 p.m. for vespers. But there was no priest and the doors were locked. What sort of church was it, Sam asked, that called the faithful to worship three times a day and locked them out?

"Our sort of course," Letty said. "The French sort."

She and Hélène were alike in appearance, young replicas of the Simone he had fallen in love with two decades and more before. They could wear one another's clothes, had similar walks and hand movements, and their voices were so alike he could not tell which was speaking when his back was turned. Yet one was his daughter, the other no relation. He noticed they were competitors in everything, even for his attention. Hélène mocked her sister as the *professeur* and told her she was being a bore when she talked about the Roman aqueduct. Letty pretended indifference to this, as if her prior claim on his attention was beyond dispute.

One day on their walk into town they climbed the path from the second mill, the Gisfort, and came out on the belvedere beyond the cathedral. While Sam took photographs of the *tour fenestrelle* and of a plaque commemorating Racine's sojourn in the south, the sisters drifted inside. He followed and was faintly surprised to see Letty genuflect and cross herself. He sat in a pew, Hélène beside him, and together they watched while Letty went over to a side chapel and stood in silent contemplation of a figure of the Virgin. After a moment she came over and asked him for two euros. They heard the coins clank into the receptacle.

"An audible purchase," Sam said.

"So you can't cheat," Hélène said.

"You could use small change."

"The magic wouldn't work."

"The Virgin would know?"

"Of course. And so would you."

Letty had chosen a squat red candle which she lit at the Virgin's feet. "There must be something she wants," Hélène said.

Outside again, standing in the bright sun, he asked Letty, "Were you brought up Catholic?"

"Of course," she said. "We're not Zulus." When he frowned at this, she added, "Or British."

"You too?" he asked Hélène.

Hélène shrugged. "I was christened of course. I can take it or leave it."

Letty was laughing at him now. "You mean you should have been consulted?"

"I'm surprised, that's all." But he knew he should not be. He remembered Simone's little acts of compliance when they had visited churches all those years ago. "Your great-grandfather Nola was Catholic," he said. "But he married a New Zealand Protestant and lapsed. What do you pray for? I suppose one doesn't ask."

"No, one doesn't ask. I might be praying for you, Papa."

"To the Virgin?"

"Why not? One can ask her for anything. She may not oblige, but she will listen."

"It must be great to be so sure you're heard."

"No I'm not sure, *Monsieur*. But hope springs eternal, doesn't it."

"Ah yes, 'ope," he mimicked. "That's what it does. Springs like an onion."

One afternoon, instead of swimming, he walked a second time into town. The late summer heat was persisting. The grapes along the road were ripening. He picked a bunch and ate them to quench his thirst. Soon it would be harvest time. The tall vine-straddling machines were coming out of their barns and being tuned up, trailer vats hosed out in readiness. A small brown viper, so still he thought it dead, slithered away when he touched it with the toe of his shoe. He walked on, watching his own shadow accompanying him, black and sharp-edged on the red-yellow stone and beaten clay, bending slightly forward like a man with the weight of the sun on his back. It put into his mind a painting by Van Gogh; and at the same time it threw him back sharply to that earlier life, when he'd walked along a similar road, with the same scents of pine and eucalypt, thyme, fennel and rosemary.

Those moments of recollection made him want to go further south, to see the Mediterranean again. He had good memories of eating seafood – paella or bouillabaisse, or simply spaghetti marinara; of sleeping on the beach; or parking the campervan under umbrella pines beside a small coastal railway station and writing his thriller. It had been a time when each new day mixed the excitements of writing with those of discovering the Côte d'Azur, that magical name blending and becoming one with its own realities of sun on terracotta walls and orange roof-tiles, of mimosa, vines and olives, of the *grande* and *moyenne corniches* with their steep drops and hairpin bends, the hillsides crowding in and looming over little rocky bays and inlets, and a sea clear at close quarters and at a distance incomparably blue.

So he and Letty took off south to spend a few days in Bandol, leaving Hélène to mind the house and feed the cats. They swam, ate well, talked late into the night and drank good wine. He told her the story of his thriller, which at first he found hard to remember but which came back gradually, piece by piece. She told him it was good, he should resurrect it, and he knew it was not, and that he should forget it – but even that story, with its fragments out of his own life, and its passages of sheer improbable invention, had its own piquancy and its own nostalgia.

They were on the road again heading back towards Uzès when the rain began – intermittent at first, then steady, finally heavy, with black skies full of detonations. The lightning seemed to burn inside the blanket of the cloud, and then to break out of it in jagged piercings. Their pace slowed while the sky behaved as if an important crucifixion was happening, and the roads turned to rivers. Reaching Saint-Maximin late in the day they skidded and stalled and swerved up Georges' clay drive, coming to a stop in the parking space behind the house. Letty opened the door as if to get out, then shut it again, groaning, and put her hands to her face.

"What is it?"

"*Voilà.*" She waved at it. There was a powerful motorbike parked at the back door, black and shiny and wet with rain. "Jean-Claude," she said.

In Bandol she had told him about the unsatisfactory boyfriend from Dijon, the dope-smoking computer wizard, the brilliant, mad, occasionally violent and deeply-in-love-with-her, or anyway unwilling-to-give-her-up Jean-Claude.

"That's his bike?"

"It is."

"You sure?"

She was sure.

They got out into the pelting storm and made a dash for the door. Just inside were a motorbiker's leathers, helmet and boots, shed like the skin of an insect or a mollusc. A wet oilskin lay beside them.

Through another door and there he was in jeans, T-shirt and socks, playing cards at a table with Hélène under an overhead light. She was absorbed and hardly looked up.

"Jean-Claude," Letty asked, "what are you doing here?"

She spoke in English and he answered in French. He said he was visiting old friends. That's what they were, weren't they, old friends? And wasn't that what you did? You visited and they welcomed you.

She said in general, perhaps, yes, but he was not welcome.

He said Hélène had welcomed him. Look, they were playing cards. She had made him coffee. She had invited him to stay for a meal.

Letty turned away, angry and impatient.

"Who is your friend?" he asked, still in French, but nodding at Sam.

"*Il est mon père,*" she said.

"*Ton père!*" He seemed to find this amusing, but held out a hand for Sam to shake.

Letty said Jean-Claude should leave.

"*Dans l'orage?*" He appeared to be more amused by this than by the idea that Sam was her father.

"No," Hélène said. "Don't be unreasonable, Letty. Listen to it."

70

All four together listened. The storm was raging. And then, in just that moment, a flash of lightning followed by a huge immediately overhead clap of thunder cut the light. Hélène checked in the kitchen and reported the power was gone. "Where's the fuse box?" Sam asked, but neither of the sisters knew.

"*La cave,*" Jean-Claude said. And then in English for Sam: "The cellar." He asked Letty whether they had a torch.

Hélène found one and he vanished down the stairs. They could hear him singing down there. After a minute or two the lights came on.

"*Bravo,*" said Hélène. "*Bien fait,* Jean-Claude."

The luggage was brought in from the car and the rain continued, with its accompaniment of bangs and flashes and deeper reverberations. The gods were not pleased and neither was Letty Clairmont.

Hélène turned on the television for news and they saw the President, Jacques Chirac, insisting that the U.N. weapons inspectors should be given time to do their work in Iraq. Military intervention was unnecessary and would be opposed by France.

"That's good," Letty said. "France has a veto in the Security Council. That means there will be no war."

"*La guerre arrive,*" Jean-Claude said, flatly, emphatically. When he spoke French it was as if in defiance of the visitor. America and "*les Anglais*" would tell the Security Council to fuck itself. "There will be war," he said again. The bastards had made up their minds and nothing would stop them.

While they watched the news it was agreed in undertones between the sisters, and then aloud, that the unwelcome one could not be turned out into the storm. He could stay one night. Sam would not retreat up to his stone cottage but would share bedroom space with the visitor. Letty's anger appeared to abate a little, enough for the general mood to improve. Hélène lit candles and laid the table with orange paper napkins and a little arrangement of flowers at the centre picked from boxes on a sheltered veranda. Over the meal, a fish stew she had been preparing during the afternoon, the sisters taught Sam songs of the region and sang them together with Jean-Claude, who sang with head down and mobile phone in hand, as if the words were coming to him as text messages. Sam knew already the one about dancing on the Avignon bridge, but there were others. One was about a shepherdess who guards her sheep and makes cheese of their milk –

> *Était une bergère,*
> *Et ron ron ron, petit patapon,*
> *Était une bergère*
> *Qui gardait ses moutons, ron ron*
> *Qui gardait ses moutons.*

By candlelight they sang and ate while the storm rumbled and cracked overhead, beat on the roof, flashed through the shutters and swirled past the sides of the house.

In the morning after breakfast they ventured forth in oilskins and rubber boots. Floodwaters were racing off the upper slopes above the Chemin de la Coste and down through the lower vineyards. The grapes on either side of the road were taking a pounding. In the woods, paths had become streams. They walked only far enough to hear the Alzon roaring among the trees below, taking with it green metal fences from around the chateau. Through trees they could just make out the first mill-house with water around the windows of the upper floor.

That afternoon Sam and Letty set off in the car for supplies but the Alzon was now up and over the road and they had to turn back. Hélène, however, had raided larder and fridge and put together eggs for an omelette, pasta, cheese and tomatoes for another course, lettuce and onions for a salad; and then, at the last minute, at the back of the fridge had found a sealed plastic bag of *soupe de poisson* with a separate little container of *rouille*. They were not going to go hungry.

For a second day the storm raged, and the news was of cars swept away and tankers overturned, crops destroyed and vineyards buried in silt. Whole houses along the Gardon had been destroyed. The top section of the Pont Saint-Nicolas had been washed away and the road to Nîmes was closed. There had been drownings, people killed by lightning strikes and falling trees. When they drove into Uzès they found bread queues and a water truck.

But by the third morning the storm was over. Jean-Claude climbed back into his leathers and boots and made ready to leave. The helmet was resumed and his face disappeared behind a visor. Hélène kissed the visor on both cheeks. Sam, who had begun to like him, shook a leather glove, and Letty dismissed him with a wave of the hand. With a returning wave and a roar from the bike's engine, Jean-Claude wheeled, skidded and slid down the drive on his side. Brown with mud, he climbed on again and rode away. Letty wept.

By the time Georges and Simone returned the worst of the rain was over and the waters were receding. Sam, Letty and Hélène drove to check on the Pont du Gard. Branches and whole trees clung to its flanks, and the waters, though dropping now, still roared under it, around and through its massive arches, up and over the banks on either side. But the structure itself was unimpressed. It had seen it all before, many times. The Romans had built to last.

There was now a shortage of flights out of the region but Letty had secured them AirEire bookings from Nice and Simone insisted she would take them there. They set off in good time. There was that diversion to Daudet's mill and through the town of Tarascon also in honour of the writer Letty had nominated as her new father's French text for study. The weather getting better every moment, the sun shining and the roads, fields and woods steaming, they were somewhere between Mausanne-les-Alpilles and Aix-en-Provence when a motorbike ranged up alongside Simone's Mégane. Letty groaned. "*C'est lui*?" Simone asked.

It wasn't possible to be sure because the rider never looked at them. He should have been covered with mud, but there were still quite heavy rain showers so it could have washed off. No-one had taken note of his number-plate – but Letty was sure.

"*C'est lui*," she said.

The bike kept level with them for just a few hundred metres, the helmet and visor looking permanently ahead, as if unaware of, or indifferent to, the car, and then accelerated away, easy and fast into the distance.

Now every motorbike was of interest but there was no further sign of this one until they were down on the coast road getting close to Nice. Once again he came from behind, ranged alongside, held his place there for less than a minute, and raced away.

"Clever trick," Letty said wearily.

When they reached the airport he was waiting in his leathers, helmet and visor in place so that still they couldn't be sure it was

Jean-Claude; but nobody doubted now. They ignored him, checked in, had a coffee with Simone, and were saying their farewells, still watched by the leatherman, when Letty relented and went over to bid him a cold farewell and deliver her harangue about getting on with his life and letting her get on with hers.

Back in London and back at work after the AirEire flight, the bus "hijack" by the swarthy malcontent, and the Polish Club supper in which Jake Latimer laid to waste the name of Tony Blair, Sam received the promised e-mail from Elvira Gamble inviting him to see her in *Macbeth* at Stratford. They exchanged warm messages and agreed on a night. She said there would be a ticket waiting for him at the box office.

Over drinks afterwards he told her that her performance had been brilliant, powerful, terrifying and beautiful.

She listened, head slightly bowed – and then, slyly, "I wasn't too small, then?"

He laughed. "Oh God, what a stupid remark that was. You were the size of your performance. You were massive."

As before, they talked easily. She asked about his Perdita, and about his work at the bank. He told her what he'd been doing in France, described the storm and the floods.

"Global warming," she said. "Welcome to the new millennium."

He was struck by how totally Lady Macbeth had been left in the dressing room. Here, touching knees with him, laughing when he joked, meeting his eye when he was silent, Elvira Gamble was all charm and sophistication, softness and poetry.

He asked about her plan for a house in the Cotswolds and she told him it had gone no further. Really, she said, it was such stuff as dreams are made on, something to talk about driving late at night with a friend, and to think about when she couldn't sleep.

"Such stuff as dreams are made on." As he repeated the floaty quotation, to which that practised voice had given such magic, he thought, "Your move, Sam," and didn't make it.

Again they parted on good terms, with promises of future meetings, and with a faint sense of deflation. He reproached himself. But there was also a feeling of relief that he hadn't embarrassed himself, or her, and that he was, after all, still more or less in charge of his own ship.

War and banking

4

THE GRAND HOTEL, STOCKHOLM

THE CHRISTMAS OF 2002 WAS STILL SOME WAY OFF BUT approaching when Sam received an e-mail message from his older son Petar (named after grandfather Nola). E-mails had gone back and forth, small pieces of, or requests for, information, and awkward, faintly embarrassed greetings for birthdays and Christmas. But this was close to a communication, or was meant to be – the kind of thing that would once have been a letter, taken an hour to write and a week to reach him. It told him that Mum wanted Pete to pass on the fact that she was "seeing" Kevin Davenport.

Sam winced at the euphemism. It meant they were fucking, didn't it? Or maybe not. Since leaving home Sam had felt guilty at the thought of Ngaio alone; now he felt jealous at the thought of her with company. He had never disliked Kevin Davenport but he did now. Possibly he'd never liked him either, even when they were friends. That was a new thought and it amused him, made him laugh.

There was other news. Pete was doing well at his courses in the Business School; and Geoff (who seemed to have taken the marital break-up harder than his equable older brother) was intending to enrol next year for Arts and Law, the double degree Sam himself had done. They were "all a box of birds etc" – and there was news of how the All Blacks were doing in the Tri Nations.

Sam was glad to hear from his son; but his thoughts kept returning to Ngaio and Kevin Davenport. "He's a nice enough guy," Pete wrote, "but not as nice as you, Dad." And there was the suggestion that Mum was "probably wanting someone for her old age etc".

The Nolas and the Davenports had been friends for close on fifteen years; and then, at a time when others among their contemporaries were parting or parted, the Davenports had caught the contagion and announced they were having a trial separation. Sam wondered whether a successful trial would mean divorce or reconciliation, but hadn't asked.

Something, the couple insisted, had been wrong from the start. It was "a chemistry thing" Kevin said. Sharon had always been hard to live with. For example, she had never learned to squeeze the toothpaste up from the bottom of the tube. He had, it now seemed, lived many silent uncomplaining years with toothpaste tubes squeezed in the middle. Another deficiency was her driving – always in the lower gears. "She won't change up," he said. "Even on the open road she won't use fifth."

Sam had suggested an automatic which would do the changes for her, but Kevin said he preferred "the stick shift" (an Americanism picked up on his travels) and didn't see why he should change cars just because his wife wouldn't learn to use "the whole octave".

Sam liked that – "the whole octave" – and stored it away. This was a time when he still had no awareness that his own marriage might be precarious, and so, while sorry for his foolish friends, had felt free to find secret entertainment in the slow-motion collapse of their house of cards.

In a tirade of brutal frankness Sharon had told Ngaio that Kevin was a golfaholic who cared more about his putter than his prick. He was stubborn, conservative, and no good at the little things. What the little things were wasn't clear, but Ngaio thought she'd been talking about presents. Kevin had gone on a business trip to Australia and come back with nothing except an"Abo" memento for his mother.

And then, when the lawyers were already drawing up divorce papers or a separation agreement, Sharon had been killed driving slowly to Hamilton. A teenage car thief pursued by police had crossed the centre line (police pursuits, together with "adventure tourism" accounted for a high percentage of deaths in New Zealand). Sharon died two days later without regaining consciousness. "So much for being a fanatic about the speed limit," Kevin said bitterly, as if it had been her lack of speed that had killed her.

So there was a kind of inevitability that the two, Ngaio and Kevin, friends of many years and now both alone, should be "seeing one another". Why, Sam wondered, had he not expected it? It was as well the message hadn't come direct from Ngaio or he might have shot one back advising her to be sure always to squeeze the toothpaste up from the bottom, and change up to fifth on the open road. "Use the whole octave, darling; the complete fucking spectrum."

But he settled himself in earnest to do his reply to Pete. It went through a number of drafts and was copied to Geoff and to Ngaio. It began by saying how glad he was to have news from home, especially that his two boys were doing well academically, and how he looked forward to the time when he would fly out to see them both graduate. Of the news about Ngaio and Kev he said if she was happy he would be pleased for her. In the meantime he had some pretty surprising news of his own; and he related how he had discovered – or rather she had discovered him – a French daughter from a long-ago adventure.

He set it all out – dates, circumstances past and present, a description of Letty, and even something about his recent holiday in France and the floods. The message ended:

> I hope you and Geoff won't feel you've been displaced by
> this new daughter. No-one, you know, could do that to my
> two champions. Even though I'm so far away I think of you
> both every day, worry about you and love you as much as
> ever.
>
> Do keep me posted with your news – and Ngaio's plans too
> since it seems she prefers not to tell me herself. Enough from
> me for now, old chap, but with love and best wishes à toute
> l'équipe, as we who aspire, not to master, but not to be
> mastered by, la langue française, are learning to say.
>
> from your dad
> Sam-I-am.

This had no sooner been sent than he began to feel uneasy about it, not as a message to Petar but as one copied to Ngaio – so there had to be another, this time just to her. While he was drafting it, stopping and starting, deleting and beginning again, his laptop signalled an incoming message. It was Petar again:

> Wow Dad, amazing!!! A sister! Or half a sister and all French –

> I like it! Glad she's nice and cheers you up. We all worry
> about you out there in the world. Love from Pete.

Sam replied at once:

> Working late? So glad you're pleased, Pete. And keep in
> touch, won't you? Big hugs for you and Geoff from your
> Old Mansambo.

Now he went back to drafting his message to Ngaio. He had made several beginnings and now gave up indirection and told her, straight out, that his first reaction to the news about Kevin had been jealousy. As he wrote he found himself slipping into a tone of affection. He stopped to think about this. Was he trying to charm her away from Kev? Had he been keeping her in the deep freeze of his consciousness just in case this "running away" experiment should fail? He concluded:

> I'm struggling with this, Ngaio, but it's probably enough if I
> say I'm always thinking of you and the boys and hoping
> you're happy. Please send me your news direct rather than
> via Pete. You know I will always respond [he wrote "respond
> with love" but deleted it]. Ever, Sam.

He pressed "send" and read it over. It wasn't good – but how did you respond properly to the news that your ex was "seeing" someone new? With joy, if you had any sense, he supposed; and with quiet approval if you wanted to appear cool and the master of the situation. He could manage neither joy nor cool, and so appeared simply rattled.

Two days went by before she replied:

Dear Sam,

I'm sorry you felt jealous when you heard that Kevin and I
have become close, but you know of course you have no
right. It's what divorce is all about, isn't it? Kev and I go back
a long way and enjoy one another's company, but we are
both busy people so there's not as much time together as
we'd like, and none for looking back I'm afraid.

A new daughter, and French! If I said Bonnes félicitations!
would that be bad form or bad French – or both? I'm glad
she gives you pleasure but I hope she won't distract you
from your responsibilities to Petar and Geoffrey, who need
you even though you've removed yourself such a great
distance from them.

I hope your work is going well and that you haven't caused
yourself too much of a drop down the ladder by this middle-
aged adventure.

Widowed love

Ngaio

Sam read, the lines and between the lines. They were full, not
quite of thorns, but of prickles. She and Kev "go back a long
way" – what was she hoping he would make of that? "Widowed
love" was a nice touch, snappish and clever. Fuck you, bitch! It took
him back to the time of their final days together in the bunker,
the Berlin of their marriage in ruins and the Russians closing.

As the days went by and October began to hoist its colours among the trees in Kensington Gardens and Hyde Park, Sam spent a lot of his leisure time at Gloucester Terrace with Mrs Barton's cat. He didn't need to entice her in, she came and went by her own choice, scratching at the door to have it opened. He fed her, let her occupy his lap and sometimes his bed. Something in Pete's message had stuck in his mind – that Ngaio was "probably wanting someone for her old age etc". It made him laugh – especially the "etc". Age, he explained to Trinnie, was relative. She, for example, Mrs Barton had told him was five cat-years old. That made her 35 in human terms – twelve years Sam's junior. Next year she would be 42 to his 48, and the year after they would hit 49 together. "After that," he told her, running fingers through her fur, "it will appear to you that I'm getting younger. It probably doesn't seem fair, but it has to do with the theory of relativity."

Trinnie rolled on her back and signalled indifference.

He walked a lot in the park, going through the Marlborough Gate, past the Italian garden along a path beside the Serpentine. Across the water ran a row of posts, each occupied by a single bird – gull or cormorant – holding on to possession against challenges, while on the water swans swanned and ducks dabbled. He passed the figure of Peter Pan and turned right, up to an enormous statue done (a bronze plaque recorded) by G.F. Watts in the first years of the twentieth century – a naked horseman leaning back, staring up, one hand shading his eyes. It was said to represent the "restless aspiration towards achievement in the world of material things" but to Sam it seemed the figure was staring precisely through a hole in the trees at the bit of sky through which passed, at intervals of one minute, or one minute twenty seconds, the jetliners drifting in westwards to a landing at Heathrow. A few hundred yards on came a peculiar obelisk inscribed:

IN MEMORY OF

SPEKE

VICTORIA NYANZA

AND THE NILE

1864

Sam remembered Speke only as a name associated with an argument about the source of the Nile. In any case he supposed these places represented outposts of empire on which Speke had set his British mark. The name, without forename or rank, seemed to go together with the naked horseman, and Peter Pan and attendant fairies, as indicators of the human mind in its imperial mode – childish, courageous, grandiose and not quite sane.

Sometimes he went on past the Serpentine Gallery all the way to the Albert Memorial – enormous German Albert in gold on his consort's chair under a cathedral-like canopy, surrounded by figures representing the work and wisdom of the ages and the greatness of empire, his broad back to the park and his eyes on the vast hall built to commemorate him. Size mattered. It represented not so much his importance to the world as his importance to a widowed queen and empress.

Sam did floor exercises, press-ups, sit-ups, until they hurt, and thought of taking up jogging, even of working up to the London half-marathon that was being promoted at the office. Under instruction from Letty, who was busy at the hospital, but called him two or three times a week and had lunch or supper with him usually on Thursdays, Sam read Daudet's *Tartarin de Tarascon*, a school edition with glossary, looking up words as necessary and reckoning that his speed and comprehension were improving.

He saw little of Mrs Barton, except at the fortnightly handing over of the rent, but he often heard her singing echoing up the stairs. She did Ella Fitzgerald songs in a good imitation of the voice. His conversations with her were typically British, being mainly about the cat and the rain that was falling, or would be soon, and the sun that was promised later. Mrs B. had been brought to England from Trinidad by her parents before she had reached school age so her accent was pretty much pure London, but with a just detectable Caribbean flavour. Her late husband, she told Sam, had been ten years her senior, born just before World War Two, and had come with the first wave of immigrants from Jamaica in the 1950s to work on London's buses.

"There used to be terrible fogs in those days," Mrs Barton said. "He always said they destroyed his lungs but really it was smoking. That's what killed him."

Sam knew her first name was Betty and was invited to use it, responding in kind that she must call him Sam; but somehow they always returned to being Mrs Barton and Mr Nola. As for the paying of rent, it passed fortnightly in a discreet envelope from his white to her black hand, always a moment of obscure but quite palpable embarrassment. Sam told friends Mrs B. was his landlady, but he was never sure whether she owned his flat as well as her own, or (more likely) acted for some invisible owner of the whole building. All he knew for certain was how much he was to pay, and that applications for repairs and maintenance went first to her.

He kept watch on the little business across the street, convinced something had changed there but unable to identify what it was. It was like skim-reading a page of *Tartarin* – he felt he knew what was going on but needed the glossary for particular words. And then one day the secretary, sitting at her screen, stopped typing and said something to the boss who was standing, his back to her, shuffling papers in the open drawer of a filing cabinet. He came across and stood behind her. She pointed at the screen. He read and commented. She made a reply, laughing and half turning. He leaned forward, reaching down and putting a hand over each of her breasts (which were not insignificant, Sam had noticed). She leaned back and her head touched, pressed against, rolled slowly over, his crotch. There was no suddenness, no surprise. Their actions, first his, then hers, were those of established lovers.

At that moment the phone must have rung. She picked it up and he returned to the filing cabinet. The sexual moment was gone and it had become the office again.

Across the road the unseen watcher punched the air, like a tennis player who has just hit a winner. "*Yes!*" – Sam Nola impersonating Tim Henman. It was a cheer not so much for the hunter male who had scored, as for himself as accurate observer. For the two in the office, and others of course, it meant no end of trouble – but not *his* trouble. There was much to be said for the role of neutral witness, non-combatant observer.

No such role for Britain's leader, its latterday Churchill or wannabe Winston. Both versions of Tony Blair were now being touted. It was late September when he released his dossier on Iraq, full of weapons of mass destruction and the means to deliver them. Saddam Hussein had rockets that could reach Britain in forty-five minutes. Or was it could be readied for firing in forty-five? And was it Britain they could reach, or British territory? The details didn't seem to matter. Sam bought the *Guardian* for the fine print, but saw the popular dailies on news-stands with their little words in big letters filling the front pages:

FORTY-FIVE MINUTES TO HELL
and
SADDAM'S DEADLY ROCKET THREAT

The nation was divided between the big-print brains who accepted the P.M.'s word, and the small-print brains who didn't; but there were exceptions – people who wrote and read small but were big for Blair. Christopher Hitchens, notably, was one; and Sam's old friend Charles Goddard was another. Since Githa believed the case for war was being cooked, and had begun to be angry about it, it meant the North Oxford household was divided.

Sam discovered this rift when he went to look after the little raja while the Goddards went to an opera at Garsington. They left quite early in the afternoon and Sam took Martin to the Phoenix cinema in Jericho to see "The Two Towers", the just-released second of *The Lord of the Rings* trilogy. Afterwards he and the boy wandered along the canal looking at houseboats and then, on the way home, bought fish and chips from the fast-food wagon parked outside the Radcliffe Infirmary.

Sam stayed overnight and it was next morning over coffee, when the talk turned to Blair's dossier, that the gulf between Charles and Githa showed itself. She'd had, she said, such high hopes for Blair, but he was a disappointment.

When Charles didn't respond she added, "Worse than a disappointment – more like grief. He's a disaster."

Sam said that he and Letty had heard President Chirac on the news in France saying that the weapons inspectors should be allowed to finish their work, and that France would not support military intervention.

"And France," Githa said, "has a veto in the Security Council."

"The French are such hypocrites," Charles said. When this was met with silence he said, "You can't expect a country that's a world power to take a hit like 9/11 and do nothing."

Githa pointed out that the 9/11 hijackers had been Saudis, not Iraqis.

Sam began to say something about Jake Latimer but Charles cut across him: "I can't talk to Jake any more. He's a ranter."

"High-class rant," Sam said.

"He's indignant," Githa said. "And he's right to be. So am I."

Charles left the room.

As she drove Sam to Gloucester Green to catch his bus back to London Githa apologised for Charles.

"Nothing to apologise for," Sam said. He had felt this was a subject it might be prudent to avoid, or at least to remain neutral about; but it crept over you. It was in the air, unavoidable, and demanding you take sides.

She said Charles was influenced by Ivan Pemberton. "And Oxford's a creepy place. After a while you can feel the lichen and moss growing over you. I think we should go to New Zealand or Australia – we'd both find jobs there."

"Of course you would."

"But he won't." And then, as if she was feeling a twinge of guilt at her own disloyalty: "I suppose he's right about 9/11. I mean, it has to come into the equation somehow."

"I guess so, Githa darling," Sam said, kissing her lovely bronze cheek and hurrying to get out of the car. He didn't know where that darling came from. It was a sudden rush of affection of a kind he was prone to, living alone.

That Christmas Sam received his first bonus – £50,000. "Is that a mistake?" he asked.

Reuben Leveson, head of the Credit Products section and his boss, looked over his shoulder at the number on the printout, and smiled his enigmatic smile. "Not enough?"

"No, no, I . . ."

"Too much?"

"I was wondering what I did to deserve it?"

"Don't ask or we might review it. Happy Christmas, Sam."

He resolved to take trouble, as he'd neglected to do the previous year, to buy nice presents, not just grabbed up at the last minute, but things that would in some way match the receiver. It was a good sincere resolve and he had some successes. Best came when he was browsing in a second-hand bookshop in Cecil Court just off Charing Cross Road. There among hundreds of dusty slim volumes on the poetry shelves was a copy of Tom Roland's first and only book. It was in good condition, still with its blue cover and Japanese ideogram, and its title, *Floating*. It was number seventeen of twenty-five signed and numbered copies and cost him £3.50. He would post it to Tom; and (this was his other resolve) he would say thanks but no thanks to any invitation (there had been one already) for Christmas Day. As an experiment, even a test, he would spend the day alone.

For himself he bought new trainers, running shorts and vest. That week he began pre-breakfast runs, down Gloucester Terrace and around the park. His muscles ached, his heart thumped and his lungs hurt in the frosty air, but he was glad of the old sensations, the pain and the peculiar sense of growing taller as he ran, riding high within himself.

On a whim, but influenced by a conversation with his work colleague Maureen about her boyfriend Stig's home city and how much she loved it, he took himself to Stockholm for four of the Christmas days. At a little over £300 per night he put himself up in the best hotel, the Grand, overlooking the harbour and close to the royal palace and the old town. He ate large breakfasts and spent a lot of time walking the handsome, frozen streets in gloves, overcoat, warm hat and woolly scarf.

There was snow, floating, hesitating down out of mysterious skies, drifting and heaping up in parks and gardens and melting into the waterways that hurried down from lake to harbour. The tall blonde young Swedish women were creatures out of mythology, snow queens; and there were still all the signs and symbols of the festival of St Lucia – the saint both of light and of the shortest day. Even the tailor's dummies in the shops were Lucias, with candles in their hair or fixed in their crowns. Everywhere in the city, as the sun which seemed only just to have come up began to go down again, there were not only the usual Christmas firs decorated and shining in all the windows, but also candles, or candlelights, in pyramid frames. There were glimpses of wonderful interiors, opulent and yet so orderly it was almost a kind of austerity. It was as if the further north you went the more real Christmas became; as if it hadn't been designed at all for the southern hemisphere, or for any time or place where the sun was more than a distant spectator.

On Christmas Eve he talked to a woman in the bar at his hotel – also tall, blonde and blue-eyed, but Russian, and speaking English with lovely vowels and rolling consonants. Her name, she said, was Nastasya, and she called him Myshkin, which he liked because she made it sound affectionate. She was charming, and willing. When she suggested he come with her to the cathedral for Christmas evensong he said, "But I thought . . ."

"Yes, Myshkin," she said, laughing. "But why not to church first? Don't you like to sing?"

He did, and they sang together, he in English, she in Russian, the choir and congregation mostly in Swedish. As they walked back to the hotel, hugging together, the snow coming down now heavier and faster, she told him that three years ago she had brought her mother and her daughter, now ten years old, from Russia. Living in Stockholm was not cheap, and this – entertaining civilised foreign gentlemen – was how she kept her little family afloat. The deal was all clearly laid out, and he was pleased. It was a transaction without obligation, without before or after; a paid-for love affair, with a beginning, a middle, an end.

He liked her very much, too much, and thought, "I could marry this woman" and for just a moment felt alarmed at himself.

He slept well, didn't hear her leave, and woke to the dusky light of a Stockholm Christmas morning. In his bathroom she'd written in lipstick on the mirror

SPASIBO MYSHKIN!

S RAZHDESTVOM – HAPPY CHRISTMAS

DASVIDANIYA

NASTASYA FILIPPOVNA

After breakfast he sat at the table in his room looking out at the frosty harbour, and then down at a sheet of the elegant hotel notepaper, asking himself what he should write in the letter he owed his parents who did not use e-mails. He had airmailed a Christmas card and token presents, but that wouldn't be enough – they would be wanting news. He amused himself imagining a letter that began, "Dear Mum and Dad, I'm in Stockholm and just spent the night with a very nice Russian call girl, with the wonderful name of Nastasya Filippovna. We went to church first – to the cathedral, which is pink. How are things with you?"

He thought of Nastasya's account of herself, the little family – ten-year-old daughter and elderly mother. Maybe in real life she had a big vodka-drinking Russian pimp at home; or a smooth Swedish businessman-crook. Even the names she'd given them, Nastasya Filippovna and Prince Myshkin, came from a novel. But these reflections didn't spoil his feeling of fondness for her, and even gratitude. She was nice, and she was welcome to her story, which would become part of his, and might even be true.

Sam's father, now closing on eighty and always hard to predict, might enjoy the joke; his mother almost certainly not. "By the time your children are in their forties," his father had written recently, "it's time to ship out. You know the Irish song, 'Swim out O'Grady, for you're not wanted here!'? But O'Grady's still wanted around the house (dishes, vacuum cleaner, lawns). So he totters into the sea and totters out again, but he knows it's there – the sea's there if needed."

They were living now in a beach house at Papamoa not far from Tauranga, and Sam allowed his mind to linger briefly on the image of blue ocean, a line of white wooden baches and bungalows low to the ground but elevated on the dunes, staring out at waves rolling in and breaking in white lines . . . and began writing:

Dear Mum and Dad,

I received a rather large bonus from Interbank America this Christmas and by way of (undeserved) reward I'm giving myself a taste of luxury in Stockholm, a beautiful city, austere in the Swedish way, though when I say that I think of the colour pink as somehow predominant, and that's hardly austere. A nice Russian woman I met here last night told me the Nobel laureates stay in this hotel, or did when the ceremony was held earlier this month. She'd got to know one of the two who shared the prize for economics. Apparently they'd both (quite separately I think) done experimental work on the psychology of banking – what makes us take risks, or not take them, and how irrational our decisions are – stuff like that. I wonder what we could all learn from that. Probably not very much. Meanwhile U.S. troops are massing in the Gulf and the world seems to be drifting into a war, but we all carry on, don't we, as if it won't happen or doesn't matter. Last month the British government sent notices of call-up to 10,000 reservists, so there's no doubt they mean to be in boots and all, and the stuff about what Saddam must do to save his country from invasion is just so much hot air. Whatever he does, it's coming.

But this letter is really to tell you I have some surprising news . . .

And he told them the story of Letty. Years ago this news might have upset them. Now that they'd adjusted to his divorce, and appeared to accept that he was (as his father said) "of a different generation, who do things differently" he thought they would find it at the very least interesting, and might even be excited – pleased to learn that their count of grandchildren had now gone up to six.

5

CANADA SQUARE

THERE WAS NO ESCAPE FROM IRAQ, OR NOT FOR LONG.
by February 2003, when Sam was invited to lunch with Reuben
Leveson, all the talk was of United States Secretary of State Colin
Powell's appearance before the U.N. General Assembly. It was a
speech long in delivery and (some believed) short on credibility.
What Secretary Powell wanted the General Assembly, and the
world, to understand was that Saddam Hussein not only had
W.M.D.s and the means to deliver them. He also had mobile
factories, like mobile homes but smaller, more like Mr Whippy
vans, scuttling about the desert manufacturing toxic sub-
stances: "Ricin, for example, Ladies and Gentlemen. Less than a
pinch – imagine a pinch of salt – will cause shock and respiratory
failure. Death comes within twenty-four hours and there is no
antidote."

And he held up for all to see a phial of a white powder: Death
in a bottle, between thumb and forefinger.

He also offered satellite photographs which only experts could
interpret, but which he assured his audience proved there were
missiles ready, hidden among palm trees in remote desert loca-
tions. He played tapes of conversations in Arabic which the U.S.
had bugged, and which revealed Saddam's scientists warning

one another that the UN weapons inspectors were coming, and discussing ways they might be evaded or deceived.

He cited British intelligence that Saddam was still attempting to acquire materials, yellow cake and aluminium tubes, for the manufacture of an atomic bomb. "These are not assertions, Ladies and Gentlemen, they are facts."

Once again British papers, the big-print ones, carried the Secretary's work forward in headlines:

SADDAM'S MOBILE DEATH FACTORIES
and
IRAQ'S KILLER BUGS READY TO GO
and again
COLIN POWELL'S REVELATIONS
"THESE ARE THE FACTS"

"It's bullshit," Reuben Leveson said.

Sam supposed it was. "But how many people know that?"

"Well you know it, Sam. And I know it. We don't have to worry about the world, do we?"

When Sam didn't reply he said, "It's called pretext. To go to war these days you have to have one."

"Unless..." Sam said.

"Unless?"

"Well... unless you're the one attacked."

"Saddam won't need one, that's true."

The place was an Italian restaurant, Amerigo Vespucci, right there in Canada Square on Canary Wharf among the big banks, where the waiters in their red and black aprons knew the boss as "Mr Reuben" and treated him with eager, jovial disrespect which he seemed to like, or at least did nothing to discourage. He called them by their first names, Luigi, Marco, Tonio, and referred to them as his "three Musketeers". He was a regular and had asked already, as they were sitting down, for "that Chianti Putto I liked so much last week."

"These three come from Naples," he told Sam. "Undernourished little guys who grew up poor. Do you know the region?"

Sam said he'd been there, long ago and briefly. "Had all my stuff stolen." For just a moment, as he said it, the feel of the place came back to him, smoky green and silver olive trees, a pale chapel among dark cypresses high on a hillside . . . "From a campervan."

Reuben Leveson nodded and pulled a face that acknowledged, with a mix of amusement and regret, that theft was what tended to happen there. "See Naples and sigh," he said. "I go through it on the way to Maiori sul Mare. My sister and her husband have a house and a yacht on the Amalfi coast – it's a favourite of ours." He said he thought D. H. Lawrence had written something there. "Wagner too, I think – something in the *Liebestod* line."

There had been no hint of why they were having lunch. Sam's first thought had been that it might be to tell him they were "downsizing" and on the principle of "last on, first off" he would have to go. His second was that he was not important enough to need a lunch if sacking was to happen. In any case there had been the Christmas bonus, which hardly suggested dissatisfaction. All the signs for Interbank America at present were of health and high spirits. Maybe the boss just liked to get to know his staff.

The wine came, they gave their orders, including what Reuben called "*acqua con fizzy*". One of the three Musketeers laughed as at a well-worn joke.

Reuben said, "I have your papers from the passport office, by the way."

"That's good," Sam said. He hoped it was good. "Everything in order?"

"Just a few details needed about your employment here – and my signature."

"Thanks, Reuben. Sorry to give you the chore."

"My pleasure." He swirled the wine in his glass. "You're a *Gastarbeiter*. You know the term? It has an honourable history. I come from a long line of them – all the way back to Moses."

Their dishes arrived, brought with a good deal of panache, and with the usual interruptions – wine glasses topped up. Pepper? Cheese? Did they want salad? The *acqua con fizzy* was uncapped and poured, with a repetition of the joke.

As the Musketeers withdrew, Reuben raised his glass over his *braciole in salsa rossa*. "Here's to Croatia."

"Croatia?" They touched glasses and Sam sipped. "How odd."

"The wine?"

"No. Wine's fine. I meant the toast."

"Well, they've just had a war. And they won, didn't they?"

"They did, that's true."

"And you're Croatian – aren't you?"

"Oh I see. Well, yes . . . No. How do I answer that?"

Reuben sat back, smiling. "You decide."

"I have a Croatian grandfather and my older son, Petar – spelled p-e-t-a-r – is named after him."

"That's a start," Reuben said. "And you've visited."

"Yes."

"Recently, I believe."

"If six or seven years ago is recent."

How did the boss know this? He asked: "How do you know this?"

Reuben's smile suggested what was being said was not to be taken too seriously. "A good employer takes an interest in his staff."

"How scary."

"Don't be scared. I want to do you a favour."

While they ate, observing the minute's silence that comes (the ice broken, the drinks poured, hunger aroused), Sam was reviewing what he knew of this man: only that he was easy to work for, seemed clever, and always faintly amused as if remembering a joke that he didn't intend to repeat. He was said to have bought a big house in Notting Hill and spent a lot of money rebuilding and redecorating it.

"Tell me about yourself," Reuben said.

Sam was disconcerted by the directness. "What do you need to know?"

"Anything."

Sam shook his head and held his hands open signalling something like helplessness, incomprehension.

"O.K., for example, do you miss your sons?"

"Of course."

Reuben sat back and laughed. "Well, we won't waterboard you."

Sam said, "I'll tell you about my daughter."

"Daughter? Didn't know there was a daughter. That's good. Fire away."

Sam explained. Reuben listened, was interested. Sam let the story take its course, which led finally away from Letty and to the floods in France.

"Attachments," Reuben said. "My sister tells me I'm 'commitment-averse'. She'd like me to have a wife and kids. But this Letty of yours seems ideal. Someone else does the work and pays the bills and you get a grown-up daughter."

"You should try it."

Reuben thought about that. "I think you have to be a Prince of Monaco . . . And then it's not ideal, is it? Not like yours. It's something done to you rather than something you do. An accident. An oversight. No, you just got lucky, Sam."

"I believe I did."

A moment later they were talking about schools – Sam's, Auckland Grammar, Reuben's, the City of London School. "Yes, a private school. There wasn't much family money, but I competed for a place and got one."

He took his mobile out of his jacket, checked it, snapped it shut and put it away. "I want to talk to you about Croatia. There's a banking conference coming. It lasts about a week and I can't spare that much time. I plan to come for the last couple of days. I thought it might interest you to stand in for me until I get there. Sound interesting?"

Sam said of course, yes it did.

"You have relations there. And the language."

"Three words," Sam said. "Or ten."

"If you have ten, learn ten more – and then another ten. Isn't that how it goes?"

"I guess my Croatian . . ." Sam began, but Reuben waved it away. He didn't need, or want, the detail.

"One thing you discover," he said, "is the importance of the local culture. Croatia just got itself independence. They're proud of that and they make a lot of fuss about the language – like to pretend it's different from Serbian. It's not, of course. They use Roman script and the Serbs use Cyrillic. Apart from that it's about as different as English English from Scots English. But you know how it is – a few words and a symbol or two mean a lot, especially if some blood has been spilled. Think of the Irish – Bloomsday and Bloody Sunday. Or the Scots."

"Yes, it's important," Sam confirmed.

'You're the only one in Credit Products with a Balkan connection. And you've got a brain – and I think the capacity for discretion, am I right?"

Was he right? And what was there to be discreet about? "I'm forty-seven," Sam said, as if that was an affirmation.

"During World War Two," Reuben said, "the Croatians had their equivalent of Auschwitz, did you know that? Jasenovac. Bad place. They killed Jews, Gypsies, and so on – gays probably – the usual. But mostly Serbs – the ethnic enemy. They didn't have gas chambers or crematoria. It was done by hand. The bodies were thrown in the Sava. The S.S. were appalled – sent memos to Berlin saying "These people are barbarians."'

Sam remembered the Sava, a wide placid river with stop-banks that ambled through the lowlands of Zagreb. He wondered what this was meant to convey to him. That the Balkans was a dangerous region? That no-one's hands were clean? He said, "My people were out of there much earlier."

Reuben nodded. "But the loyalties stick, don't they?"

"Some things stick. Traditions, habits, talents – and when there's trouble the loyalties are revived." He thought of saying that it was Croatians who had started the wine industry in New Zealand but said only, "I grew up on a vineyard."

"You know your wines then."

"I can pretend." And then, "I might be pretending at this banking conference mightn't I? What happens? What will I need to do – or to know?"

"Not a lot," Reuben said. "People give papers, get to know one another, talk about current banking issues, and have a nice time – that's about it. A lot of it is confidence-building – and showing the flag for your bank and your country. Croatia wants to make it into the E.U. They have Germany's backing, but a way to go yet. They're wanting to impress. You just look and listen, take a few notes . . ."

"And be impressed?"

"And be impressed – exactly. A little flattery goes a long way."

So the matter was settled. Sam would go to Zagreb. The conversation drifted elsewhere, then returned.

"There'll be a colleague – André Kraznahorkai. Here . . ." He wrote the name on a small pad and handed it across the table. "Hard name to remember. I think of him as Hawkeye from Hungary. Makes it easier. He's Hungarian but works from Prague. He's a good guy – very bright. He and I have worked together a lot. He's doing something for me now. You should look out for him. I'll tell him you're coming."

Sam watched for signs that the boss was in a hurry to be done with him but there were none and they lingered over the meal. Reuben talked about fast cars and the Grand Prix circuit, about his sister, her twin daughters, her three step-sons, her husband, Sir Frank Vogel, knighted "for services to sport and the Jewish community" which had meant in reality, he said, "for a fat cheque to the Tories". The sport was tennis. He'd been very good in his day, and then a senior administrator, but now was confined to a wheelchair.

Later, when Reuben had paid the bill, they headed back

across the square to Interbank America. As they passed the Reuters Building Reuben stopped to check the market numbers that ran around its walls.

"And don't worry about your passport," he said. "I'll have that sorted for you this afternoon."

This was a time of people marching in the streets, protesting as the momentum towards war built up. February 15 was the big one. In London the day was grey and chilly.

Attempts to stop the march by edict, and then a trumped-up security scare at Heathrow, had failed to make any difference. Disbelief was in the air. Everywhere the P.M.'s name was being re-spelled BLiar. Despite the bitter cold the marches were huge – in London alone said to be more than a million.

Letty marched with a group from her hospital, and persuaded Sam to join them. They met in Gower Street and were marooned there for two hours, eating sandwiches Letty had brought, drinking bottled water and shouting slogans. By the time their part of the march reached Hyde Park the speeches were over but the excitement continued. It was like a party.

Tom and Hermione Roland marched. Along the Embankment Tom accepted and shouldered a *Daily Mirror* placard that said STOP THE WAR. "It's poetry," he told Hermione when she laughed. "Brevity is the soul of wit."

In Oxford, after a quarrel, Githa joined a silent vigil in St Giles while Charles sulked in his room working on his book, but sneaking downstairs at intervals to see how things were going in London. Given a choice, the little raja went with mummy. He had read that Saddam Hussein had given free refrigerators to illiterate

Kurds if they learned to read, and he said it would be wrong to drop bombs on him.

Ivan Pemberton was also watching it on television, and writing an opinion piece in which he asked why, if they were serious about it, did the protesters look so cheerful? Why couldn't they at least *look* serious? And why would anyone British want to be seen to be linked under the banner of the British Association of Muslims who had forced Salman Rushdie into hiding for years and who promoted death for apostates?

At the end of that day Sam and Letty dined together with her colleagues. Letty asked how could a war possibly go ahead in the face of so vast a display of international indignation? Sam wondered how at this late stage it could be stopped. An enormous engine had been set in motion. What swirled around it now was only words.

On March 20 George Bush's Operation Free Iraq was launched with what the Pentagon and America's generals had given a name to: "Shock and Awe" – night-long bombardments, mainly of Baghdad, but also of other Iraqi cities, on a Cecil B. DeMille scale. In the biggest hotels war correspondents were already in position, and so, minute by minute, hour by hour, T.V. cameras rolled and the world was shown the sights and sounds of the destruction as it happened: incoming missiles whining through the night and crumping home, bombs raining down, shells flashing and exploding, targets disintegrating, whole buildings collapsing. Nothing like it had ever happened before and been seen happening in such raw detail. The whole world sat at home and watched a war.

After several nights of bombardment came the invasion. It was not quite a pushover, but very nearly. Within three weeks Baghdad was occupied, the oil fires had been mostly brought under control;

the big men of Saddam's regime had abandoned their palaces and slipped away into the nation's mysterious hinterland. The people had not everywhere, as Vice-President Cheney had promised they would, flooded into the streets to welcome their liberators. Some few did and, coached by Marines who mined and dislodged an enormous statue of Saddam in Firdos Square, manned ropes and pulled it down while the cameras rolled. Most stayed out of sight and waited; or prepared for resistance, or to take revenge on those in their society they hated most – the other kind of Muslim, Sunni or Shia; the Christian or Kurd – or just the bastard who wrecked your business or stole your wife. Chaos was about to come again, but the war was won, or the claim that it was could briefly, plausibly be made.

MISSION ACCOMPLISHED was the banner that swathed the aircraft carrier George Bush was flown out to off the coast of California, from the upper deck of which, wearing an airman's battle gear, he told his fellow Americans that combat operations in Iraq had ended and the fight for liberty and peace had been won.

Three days before Sam was to fly to Zagreb he was in a meeting when Maureen O'Donnell came to tell him there was a young woman in Reception wanting to see him. "Not now," he said. "Tell her I'm in a meeting."

"I told her that," Maureen said. There was a faint smile. "She's weeping."

Sam looked up from his papers. "She's what?"

"Weeping, Sam. Says she's your daughter." Clearly this was not believed – just a story.

"Oh shit." He rushed from the room and took Letty to his office.

It was Jean-Claude again. He had turned up at Great Ormond Street and was threatening to kill Sam. "He wants to know where you live so he can kill you."

Letty had long ago told Jean-Claude that Georges Clairmont, whose name she had taken when Simone married him, was not her father. In Saint-Maximin he had been introduced to Sam as the real one. He had now done some detective work and discovered that her father's name was Gustav Robert. Therefore Sam, the Anglais, was in fact her lover – the older man in her life, the cause of his own failure with her, an obstacle he now intended to remove from the planet.

"Is he serious? I mean the threat . . ."

"I don't know. I don't suppose he would kill you – not really. But he scares me, Papa. He's what people here call a mad bugger – *tu sais*? He might do anything."

"Where is he now – precisely?"

"Precisely – *sais pas*. Somewhere in London."

"You told him the facts – that Simone and I . . ."

"Yes of course, I explained all that but he won't listen. He wants to see the evidence – D.N.A. Documents. I told him there were no documents. Legally I'm the daughter of Gustav Robert. That's what the documents will show."

"Does he know where you live?"

"I don't think so. I certainly haven't told him."

"Well don't panic, Letty. He's probably just bullshitting, but we'd better tell the police. He won't hurt *you*, and I'll keep an eye out for him. If he gets in touch with you again, tell him the police are looking for him. Tell him about extraordinary rendition, and that they'll beat him up and send him to Egypt for interrogation and torture."

She managed a smile. "Yes, he would believe that."

In the course of Sam's lunch break they made their statement to the police, who were mildly interested, somewhat helpful, said the immigration authorities would be notified and the police at Paddington alerted. For the moment they should both remain vigilant, and report any sightings. They were given a number to call – or, of course, in an emergency 999.

In those few days before Zagreb, Sam became aware of motor-bikes as never before. They were everywhere, and all in one way or another threatening. In Gloucester Terrace sudden accelerations, and, equally, quiet idlings, sounded the alarm. Even the secretary's machine across the street caught his attention and caused him, so to speak, to identify it and check it off. But Jean-Claude, having issued his threat and planted fear, disappeared.

While Sam was waiting at Heathrow for his flight he had a call from Letty. A handsome young cop had stopped by at her flat to assure her that Jean-Claude had returned to France.

6

ŠUBIĆEVA

Sam had not been entirely frank with Reuben Leveson about the extent of his experience of Croatia. What had taken him there had been news that the death of a relative made his Dalmatian-born grandfather, Petar Nola, and the grandfather's younger sister Rosa in Zagreb, inheritors of a small property. It was a few hectares of land, with two small houses and a barn, on an island a ferry-ride from the coastal town of Šibenik. Grandpa Nola, in an Auckland retirement village, full of nostalgia for the land of his birth and for the favourite playground of his childhood, somehow grasping at it on the brink of extinction and too unwell to travel himself, asked Sam to go for him, to secure his part of it, to bring back photographs and relevant documents – and a handful of the sacred soil, if New Zealand bio-security would permit; or if not, then maybe just a small stone.

It was the war following the break-up of the old Yugoslavia that had caused the death of the previous (and childless) owner, and it was the war that delayed Sam's visit. Cities were shelled, atrocities committed, piles of corpses concealed and uncovered, villages destroyed and refugees created; but by the time Sam was ready to go it was losing momentum, concentrated in just a few areas. Croatia had won an independence soon to be recognised by the U.N. Commercial flights were resuming; life in the new independent Croatia was moving back towards something that eventually might be called normal.

The grandfather's co-inheritor, Sam's Great-Aunt Rosa, would look after him in Zagreb, or at least house him there; and a distant cousin several times removed, Maja, who lodged with the old lady, would drive him down to the coast as soon as the roads were open again and safe. That was the plan. So when Sam arrived in Zagreb after a 26-hour flight from Auckland by way of Singapore and Munich, weary but pleased to be out of New Zealand for the first time in so many years, it was Maja who met him at the airport.

She presented him with a small bouquet, embraced him in a manner he thought of as Russian, and made a short speech in English from which definite and indefinite articles were largely absent. It was because of this welcome that he first thought of her as Comrade Maja.

"Welcome home," she concluded.

She was small, neat, nicely shaped, and with the face of a pretty and intelligent animal, a cat perhaps, with something of the cat's potential for independence, aloofness and charm. He did not recognise all of this at once, but he was instantly attracted, and felt that to show it with easy compliments would not be welcome.

He made a speech in return, similar but with articles in place; thanked her and said he was indeed happy to be home. This was diplomatic but untruthful. What was exciting about the moment was that he felt not at home but far from it.

"I have car," she said.

"Good," he replied. "Car is good," – and noted that he would have to be careful not to slip into imitation of her accent.

Maja, he soon discovered, was a product of the old socialist state – intellectual, well-read, serious, even idealistic, and still somewhat disapproving of the West and of capitalism. As a child, a member of the Young Pioneers, she had worn the red bandanna, camped in the woods, learned to distinguish wholesome from poisonous mushrooms and equally to listen out for political traitors and report them. She had been a member of Zagreb's Communist Youth Choir, had sung rousing anthems and marched in May Day parades saluting their hero and liberator, Marshal Tito. "Always ready" had been their motto. She was a teenager, about to earn an important next-stage medal in the Pioneers, when the whole thing had fallen apart. The Berlin Wall came down and, stage by stage, socialism's Eastern European house of cards had collapsed. Maja's memory was of deep teenage disappointment – even anger: she had really wanted that medal.

Now she was a half-hearted nationalist, a slightly sceptical supporter of Croatia's new independence. She worked as a distance stenographer, receiving court documents and verbatim transcripts by e-mail and typing them up for filing and for next-day circulation among the parties. This made her hours irregular and her place of work moveable, so she was able to spend time with Sam while they waited for news from the south. Zagreb had a Viennese charm, one outcome of its history as part of the Austro-Hungarian Empire. But mixed in with that was the mark Tito's brand of socialism had left: heavyweight memorials to workers and partisans, and state apartment blocks, ugly and often falling into disrepair. It was in one of these, up four flights of marble stairs, that Maja lodged with widowed Great-Aunt Rosa who greeted him warmly as the grandson of her brother and seemed surprised, even shocked, that he spoke no Croatian apart from yes, no, hullo, goodbye and thank-you.

Maja told Sam she had lost her boyfriend in the war – killed by a sniper in the streets of Sarajevo. When Sam showed signs of commiserating and wanting to give her a chance to tell him more, she changed the subject. She was grim-faced at that moment and he felt she didn't want to be seen to weep.

Suffering jet lag, he lay awake in the nights listening to the late trams clanging in the street below, the intermittent sounds of domestic war and peace echoing up the interior light-well, the basso rumbling of Aunt Rosa's large refrigerator which dated from the days of Tito. The war had made Maja a fitful sleeper and she liked to pass the midnight hours watching videos and movies. Soon Sam was joining her. They sat on cushions and beanbags on the floor of her room, covering themselves with sleeping bags or quilts against the cold. Sometimes he was asleep before the movie finished, his head on her shoulder, or resting on her thigh while she stroked his head. They were held in suspension waiting for news from the south, where one troublesome area of Serb resistance, the Krajina, remained between Zagreb and the object of Sam's visit.

They talked easily together about things outside their own lives – about the world at large – and silences were seldom awkward or embarrassing. Sometimes they played chess, the silent game; and sometimes Maja put on records or C.D.s, Italian or Dalmatian songs that were now and then cheerful but more often full of a sadness that was so etched into the melody you didn't need the words to understand. It was during this hiatus period that they became lovers. It was strange because they said so little about their feelings for one another. Simply, it happened in those dark hours after midnight – easy and natural, as if it was just another way of keeping warm. They were physically attuned. It was something Sam looked back on later as a sort of ideal state – wordless and self-sustaining.

Once or twice it happened while they were watching a movie. It was not intended and little or nothing was said. Sam would have said there was love between them now, but the word wasn't uttered.

Great-Aunt Rosa cooked for them and they ate their main meal with her in the middle of the day. Sam supposed the old lady knew what was going on and didn't disapprove. She appeared to think that he was good for Maja, and perhaps equally that Maja was good for him. She spoke no English and he no Croatian so their exchanges, few and sparse, were in French, of which he had a small amount from his younger days, and she only a little more.

His time away from New Zealand was limited and as soon as the news suggested there was a chance of getting through to the coast they set off south in Maja's noisy East German Trabant with a dashboard gearstick and a tendency to complain and refuse. It was, Maja said, a mule of a car but capable of heavy loads. She was attached to it, and to get parts for it she had once crossed over the border into Hungary.

There was little traffic on the road and soon they were seeing first signs of the war – burned-out farmhouses, abandoned crops and animals, villages undamaged but sinisterly empty ("ethnically cleansed" he supposed), or blasted and burned but still occupied. The landscape changed, sometimes green and golden, other times charred black. They had been warned to be cautious when stopping because in some places the roadsides were still mined, and in others there might be a Serb, angry, displaced and with nothing to lose, who would take a shot at them.

As they drove, not looking at one another but ahead up the long empty roads, he asked about the one she had called her boyfriend.

"He was like you," she said. "He had wife." She pronounced it "vife", of course. He asked were there children.

"Like you," she said again. "Two."

"Boys?"

"Girls. Two little girls."

"Did the wife know?"

"That we were lovers? No." And then: "Next time for me, if there is next time – everything will be . . ." She hesitated, feeling for the word.

"Visible?"

"Not hidden. Yes, visible."

They had gone up and over what had seemed like a range of mountains and were coming down on the other side, when she suggested a stop for lunch at a restaurant overlooking the plain. It had once been a favourite of hers. Now there was a hole blasted in one wall and part of the roof had come down. They were the only customers. "You will like this place," she said. "Ships is speciality."

"Sheep," he corrected.

"Sheep?"

"That's plural or singular. One sheep, two sheep. Same as fish. One fish, two fish – although of course you can say two fishes if you want. But you can't say two sheeps."

She looked at him and began to laugh. "This is joke?"

"Not joke," he said. "English."

There was no menu, just the chef's *plat du jour* which she translated as rack of lamb. The lambs had lied about their age but the cooking was good and the servings generous. Along with the meat

115

went a mint-flavoured sauce, green beans and a purée of mashed potatoes and mushrooms. Somehow the meal, the hole in the wall and bigger hole in the roof, and the explanation about ships and sheep put him, put them, in a happy mood. They were confident now that they would get through to the coast.

But as they were nearing their goal they began to run into obstacles – police warning signs, roadblocks, military checkpoints. At first Maja was full of determination, the Young Pioneer captain looking for alternative routes. But finally there was an encounter on a back road with two Croatian soldiers, one of medium build the other exceptionally tall, both probably still in their teens and carrying automatic weapons. Up ahead, a tank blocked the narrow road while the two came down to ask where Maja and her friend thought they were going.

She gave her story, that Sam was a journalist from New Zealand and she his driver and translator. The soldiers were unimpressed. Sam could not understand exactly what was being said, but tone and body language were clear enough. Something was going on down the road beyond the tank and they were saying in effect, "You don't want to see it." The tone was boastful, full of iron-faced swagger.

"They're telling us to go," Maja said.

While the tall one clicked on and off what might have been the safety catch on his weapon, the other wandered around the car, kicked the tyres, opened a rear door and helped himself to food from a box on the back seat. Sam and Maja kept their eyes ahead, not feeling it would be safe to challenge or complain.

The soldiers were both munching sandwiches now. "Nice," one told her in English. And to Sam, holding it up for him to see: "Nice."

The other had taken the keys from the dash and was opening the boot. Maja's laptop was discovered and taken to the side of the road. After a brief consultation the tall one came to say they were impounding it.

She pleaded, told him it contained work for the courts which could not be replaced. "He wants money," she said. Sam scrabbled for his wallet and offered some notes which he thought afterwards might have been 200 kuna. It might have been more – more than the machine was worth, but the money was accepted and the machine returned to the boot which was slammed shut. Handing back the keys, the tall youth delivered Maja what sounded like another stern warning.

As she reversed and found a place wide enough for a turn, two menacing shots were fired overhead. At Sam's last sight of them the soldiers were sharing the money.

What Maja had been told was that there were still Serb military in the area. She and Sam were unlikely to get through, and if they did they might be treated as spies, or even Croatian fighters. "I am sorry, Sam."

He patted her arm. "No, I'm the one to say sorry. I got you into this."

So they set off back the way they had come, leaving danger behind. Somewhere on that return journey, off the main road and in an area of extraordinary clear streams and waterfalls, they stopped and took their cardboard box into the woods and had a picnic of what the scavenging warriors had left. Sam remembered it nostalgically, he eating slices of Great-Aunt Rosa's bread with cheese while Maja only nibbled and smoked.

He asked again about the dead friend. What was his job; his profession?

He was a jazz musician, she said. He had a band, and he wrote about music in the magazines.

"He could make a living?"

"Of course. He was famous. Yugoslavia was big. He played in Zagreb, but in Belgrade too – and Novi Sad – all over."

"So he didn't care about independence for Croatia."

She shrugged. "Not to die for. And wife is Serb. She has gone back there, to Novi Sad with daughters."

Aunt Rosa welcomed them home. She was sorry they hadn't got through – it was her inheritance too – but she said peace would come, and then . . .

Three days later he and Maja were at the airport saying good-bye. This time there were no speeches. She tried not to weep, wept, hugged him, and said very little. Feeling his throat tighten, his eyes prickle, he told her she was lovely, that he would miss her, that he would always remember her.

They had gone a great distance in a short time, and now there was nowhere to go but their separate ways.

So Sam returned to New Zealand without a certificate of title, photographs, or even that handful of the sacred soil Grandpa Nola had wanted, though there was for the old man a small white stone taken from the stream where they'd picnicked. But Sam came back with what felt like a larger stone – the weight of feeling that he had been out of the cage of home and family and was now back in it, the key turned, his future determined, laid out for him like an iron map.

Restless, he talked too much about the visit, about Maja especially, and then admitted, when pressed by Ngaio, that they had been lovers. Now he knew well enough what had only been a blur at the time, that if the beginning of the end of his marriage had to be located somewhere it would be there, in Great-Aunt Rosa's worker-state apartment on a street in Zagreb that was called Šubićeva.

All of which was much more present in Sam's mind as he flew in to Zagreb than any thought of the banking conference he was to attend. In the years since that first visit Grandpa Nola had died, Great-Aunt Rosa remained in her apartment on Šubićeva, and Maja had gone to America "to discover" (as she'd explained to Sam in one of her very occasional e-mails) "whatever the reality proved to be behind a man called Bob I've got to know on-line". After that there had been a long silence, and then a message to say she was married and living in Chicago. "Bob's not lovely," she wrote, "but he's employed and articulate. As you know, darling Sam, I need someone to talk to in the daytime and watch movies with in the nights. Bob can talk and he can watch, and he says he loves me, so he will have to do." She said she was working as a translator and that it didn't pay well, but life in America was pretty good, and "it's nice not to have to hate anybody". Like all her messages this one ended "Hug hug – Maja". He wondered if those hugs might contain a secret signal, but knew that in truth they were no more than a sign of long-ago affection.

Flying in over woodland alternating with crops and pasture, Sam recognised the orange-roofed houses, often with three floors, spaced out along country roads. He recalled long stretches where houses like these had been burned but left standing – not bombed but quickly set alight by a passing military force, one side or the other, Serb or Croat, eager to destroy and move on. No sign of that now, or none from the air; and no sign of the military at Zagreb's unremarkable airport.

Along with several others from the flight who turned out to be banking reps, he was welcomed – once again with a small speech and a bouquet of flowers – and taken by car to the Esplanade, Zagreb's most elegant hotel, where the conference theme was displayed on a large banner, dark blue and gold, in the foyer, and repeated on handouts and gifts prepared in a shiny package for each delegate:

2002–3 HAS BEEN A GOOD YEAR FOR BANKING
LET'S MAKE 2003–4 EVEN BETTER

There were flowers and fresh fruit in his room, a fancy chocolate on each pillow, two white towelling robes, his and hers, hanging in the bathroom, oils and unguents for bath and shower, and a view looking down over a square he remembered well, with a grand equestrian statue of Tomislav, the first Croatian king. To the right was the main railway station, a handsome neo-classical building with a fountain in front; and just beyond, a central stop where blue trams came and went, loading and unloading. In the open area between were many stalls scarlet with strawberries.

Sam's excitement, as at the recovery of something essential and neglected in his life, was intense, and he was propelled out into the city to explore and rediscover. He had a feeling of knowing where he was, and found his way to another square with another equestrian statue at its centre, a man mounted in uniform with sword raised as if leading a charge. Under it were the words BAN JELAČIĆ. "Ban", he remembered, meant something like prince or viceroy. It was the figure of a great Croatian leader of the nineteenth century, a monument which, Maja told him, the Communist government had removed from this central position and dismantled because they considered it compromised the sovereignty of the Yugoslav Federation. Now, to assert its independence, the new Croatia had put it back.

He bought himself coffee and a cake and watched the people coming and going, wondering whether it was his mood, or the post-war reality, that made them look so predominantly handsome – healthy and in good spirits. As he sat, the noon cannon boomed out from its tower and the pigeons did their daily wing-clapping scatter. On an outdoor stage a solemn-faced group, dressed in knee breeches, bright socks and Tyrolean hats, danced to the rhythmic cracking of their own stock whips.

Sam took out the conference programme and tried to focus on what were to be the offerings for the three Zagreb days. The list read:

Euro versus Dollar?

Goldilocks and Dot Com

Risk Management Systems – their purpose, do they
    have one?

Mezzanine Loans

Green Retrofitting your Premises: how to do it
    and make a profit

C.D.S.s and C.D.O.s: welcome to the maze!

Lessons from Argentina

How Big a Cushion is Enough?

I.M.F. and World Bank Healing: good science or
    alternative medicines?

Credit Rating Agencies: could three become one
    and do the job?

Green Business, Mean Business!

Swiss Banks and U.S. Tax Evaders
Statistical Arbitrage – algo-sniffing v algo-spoofing

He put a ring around a few of the topics. They were running in tandem so choices had to be made. He needed to know more about mezzanine loans so that was circled. Credit default swaps and collateral debt obligations were a maze indeed. He should listen to that one, but would he be enlightened, or put to sleep? Swiss Banks and the motions the U.S. Congress was making towards having them identify tax evaders was an interesting subject. How many members of Congress were serious about this, and how many were only going through the motions while in fact obstructing?

That afternoon he chose the session on mezzanine loans. At the end of an hour, during which he stared through a clerestory window at a flotation of clouds and tried hard to concentrate, he came away with just four notes on a notepad decorated with what might have been a Zagreb coat of arms:

secured by stock and/or other ownership stakes
real estate boom continues – "no end in sight"
high returns to investors with middle-tier security
ample secondary finance to borrowers

– these plus a note asking himself whether it was sleight of hand to call what was really the ground floor the mezzanine. This was hardly a day's work, but who was checking?

That evening there was to be a dinner hosted by the mayor of Zagreb; but first came drinks in a large room with French windows opening on to a terrace. There was no-one he knew and he floated on the edge of conversations in various languages. He eavesdropped on the ones in English – American and British – listening for differences. The Americans sounded pompous, batting very large numbers about, always in dollars; the English were trivial, about schools and clubs, and the numbers were mostly cricket scores. He assumed none of them were saying what they meant, or anything they considered important – not yet, not here in open concourse. The serious talk would go on in pairs, or small groups of friends and associates, in what used to be called (when that's what they were) smoke-filled rooms.

He drifted out to the terrace where some few were indeed smoking, though with the furtive look, apologetic or defiant, of the lower orders, the dying breed. There was a faint waft of flowers and scented shrubs from the gardens.

A stranger approached him, right hand extended. "You are Mr Nola, I think. I am Kraznahorkai. André Kraznahorkai."

So this was Reuben Leveson's Hawkeye from Hungary. Tall, lean, with a trimmed whitish beard and hair long at the back, combed down over the collar, he didn't quite fit the mould of the banker. Sam shook the hand. "Sam Nola. Very pleased to meet you."

They spoke about "Mr Leveson" whom André Kraznahorkai said he greatly admired. "I understand you are deputy."

"Deputy?"

"For Mr Leveson, yes?"

"Filling in for, might be more accurate. He should be here himself by the end of the week."

"By when we shall have moved to coast."

"I'm looking forward to it. I hope to swim."

Mr K. pretended a small shudder.

"Reuben assured me it won't be cold," Sam said. "Fresh, maybe, but not cold."

"One man's fresh is another man's cold." Like most people who manage to make a joke in a language other than their own, Kraznahorkai was pleased with this one and repeated it.

Sam smiled an applauding smile.

"And you are Englishman."

Sam thought of various words, like "interim" "probationary" and "on appro". "New Zealander," he said.

"Ah, New Zealand." There followed the usual exchange – a beautiful place but Mr K. had not been there. Climate. Population. Ethnic mix. *The Lord of the Flies* . . .

"Of the Rings," Sam corrected.

"Of the Rings, of course."

Sam asked Mr K. where *he* came from, amusing himself with the thought that the answer might be Transylvania, though knowing the real one. "I am from Hungary but I live now in Prague."

"The Paris of Eastern Europe," Sam volunteered, a phrase long ago tucked away for future use and now at last finding its moment.

"So it is said, and I think is true – a beautiful city which somehow many bad things have failed to spoil. You have been there of course."

Sam had not. "Like you and New Zealand," he said.

"But New Zealand is so far."

Sam said, "It depends where you start."

Hawkeye stared at him. "I start from Prague, of course."

"Of course."

Mr K. fell silent, aware there was something he had missed.

Sam said, "I don't think Reuben told me which bank you represent."

"I am businessman," Hawkeye explained. "Many things perhaps but yes, businessman – that describes my modest doings."

Sam liked the accent (many thinks . . . my modest doinks . . . and the absence of "a" and "the") which reminded him of Maja. He said, "I thought you might be a diplomat."

"Diplomat? But why?"

"You have the look."

But he didn't understand this expression. "Sophisticated," Sam said. "Smooth . . ."

André Kraznahorkai laughed. "Not I but you, Mr Nola, are diplomat. And your bank – Interbank America, it is . . ."

But he was interrupted by the call to dinner.

The places were named and Sam and Hawkeye were to be several tables apart. "We will talk in coming days," Mr K. said with a just-perceptible East European bow. "And with our friend Reuben Leveson when he arrives."

"I look forward to it," Sam said, tilting in response.

The dinner was punctuated with speeches – first in Croatian, then in English, German, French . . . The speakers were all enthusiasts and made free use of metaphor. Croatia was rising like a phoenix from the ashes, and Zagreb was the jewel in her crown. Capitalism was coming down the open road. The economics of the socialist state and the five-year plan were gone out the window and the free market had come in the door. Western banks were seizing the nettle. These were exciting times – a new millennium! As Wordsworth had said, it was a good time to be young, and even to be old was pretty good. (Ha! Ha! – big laugh here from the old boys.) Croatia was not yet part of the E.U. but with Deutschland's über-help it wouldn't be all that long. The World Bank beckoned, the I.M.F., the G20. The world was smaller now and you could conquer it with just your laptop and a bank account. No need for tanks and armaments (though there were times and places for those as well – tanks and banks, Ho! Ho!). But One World was where we were heading, bound together by the internet, e-mail, broadband, fibre-optics, satellite coms and the World Wide Web. Arachne was the goddess of the modern. (They drank to that. "Arachne! Goddess of the modern!" clink clink.) They were taking a last look over the shoulder, a last fast look at the old days of airmail letters, and telephones that had to be attached to the wall by a wire. Snail-mail and landlines! How had we managed? How did we make the world go round and our money systems work at that pace? Thank God and Bill Gates for the technology even though we sometimes cursed it and felt we were its slaves. On the contrary, we were free men, freer than ever . . .

"And free women." (A shout from the floor.)

And free women, of course – a raucous toast to that. ("Free women!" clink clink.)

The speeches were running on rather and there were signs of restlessness in the ranks. But all at once the next course arrived, the waiters pouring in through the swing doors bearing new dishes on trays at shoulder height.

Next morning Sam made time to find his way to Šubićeva and Great-Aunt Rosa's apartment block. Against a blank wall in the street outside there was a stencilled (or perhaps done freehand by a clever graffiti artist) silhouette of a Russian tank, its flag bearing the old Soviet hammer and sickle, and under it the slogan in English: THE REVOLUTION DEVOURS ITS CHILDREN.

He climbed the four flights with their teenage graffiti and

football slogans, their smells of cooking and whatever chemical was used each morning to swab them down. It was one of those moments when a former time, another life, re-enters by way of the nostrils – as though he had not been back to Zagreb until this very moment, when the whole previous visit, its darks and lights, rushed at him. At the familiar door he paused a long moment before knocking. There were sounds in there but some seconds passed before it opened, slowly. The old lady looked out at him, at first suspicious, not remembering or not recognising. And then all at once she let out an ambiguous whoop that might have been a yelp of pain which echoed up and down the stairway. She reached out as if to grab his hand, the other hand at her face, lurching sideways so her shoulder propped her against the wall just inside the door.

"Rosa – *comment ça va?*" he asked in what had been the only language they shared.

"Sam!" Come in, she signalled. "*Allez-y.*"

He took his great-aunt by the elbow and helped her indoors, where they hugged one another. "*Dobro došli,*" she said. And then, "*Bienvenu.*"

"Maja," she began, but then couldn't go on. It seemed she had to prepare herself for what there was to tell him. She found a chair and sat. "*Attendez,*" she said. "*Il faut penser.*"

What was it she had to think about? Something difficult to remember? A tram rumbled by in the street below. Sam went to the window and looked down at it, watching the forked top of its pole skimming along under the wire. He was trying not to guess what he was going to hear.

The old woman regained her composure and began to talk to him. There was something she had to tell him. Maja had gone to America – he knew that?

Yes, he knew.

And had married an American.

Yes, that too.

"So . . ." she said, using one of her few English words. And then, with sudden, dramatic emphasis: "*Elle est morte.*" It was like a line in a play, the mute e at the end of *morte* was given full measure, like a separate word.

"Maja?"

"*Oui.*"

"*Vous êtes sûre?*" But that was a silly question. Of course she was sure. You didn't say someone was dead if you weren't sure. But he repeated "*Morte?*" just to be sure himself.

"*Oui.*"

He met her staring eyes. They seemed full of things which, lacking a common language, he and she couldn't say to one another. It was as if the news made her uncomfortable rather than grief-stricken, and she was watching him, observing his reaction. Perhaps she and Maja had never been very close. Perhaps a quarrel had caused Maja to leave for America, and now Rosa felt guilty. Something was missing.

These thoughts were at the forefront of his mind while at some deeper level he was absorbing the blow, feeling what his aunt must be feeling – wounded and in pain.

She was telling him something in her own language, saying (he thought) that America was a very bad place, that Maja had been unhappy there, that the man she married was bad – perhaps a drunk.

But how did she die? "*Mais comment*, Rosa?"

Rosa made a gun of her hand and shot herself.

It might as well have gone off, audibly. In the silence that followed he absorbed the horror of it. Maja, with a hole in her head. Maja dead; her lovely body now just a – body.

"*Suicidée?*"

"*Oui.*"

He thought of the words they use in America for an undertaker's premises – funeral home. Had there been a burial? Cremation? Were there ashes to be scattered, and if so where – there or here? There were so many questions that would have to remain unanswered because they couldn't be asked.

He heard a child crying on the stairs, and the sound, echoing faintly up the inner light-well, of someone singing.

Rosa took his hand in a grip that was surprisingly strong and led him to the tiny kitchen. Over strong coffee she showed him – spread them out on the brightly patterned oil-cloth that covered the table – Maja's last letters. She had two, one to her in Croatian, and one to Sam, in English. His read

> Sam, dear friend
>
> My death is not meant to hurt anybody or to make a point. I have just had enough of my life and I am making early exit.
>
> A woman wishes to feel there are surprises to come. It is not to do with age. I think to do with personality. You live in the world, Sam, so surprises, including good ones, have a chance of finding you. With me it is like the old joke about the Jew praying that he win lotto, for months and months, until God finally says to him: "Go buy a ticket!"

Did I tell you I thought of having a facelift? I was beginning to dislike my reflection in the mirror. And I thought if I didn't like the result, good, I would jump out the window with a face worth three thousand dollars. Just another silly idea.

Remember "Sea of Love"? Ellen Barkin's crooked smile and beautiful backside? Seemed like a new beginning. I think I must have been dreaming. You never said you loved me – did you? Or maybe I was not listening.

Be well – I insist.

Maja xxx

Great-Aunt Rosa looked at him for recognition. Could he make sense of it?

Yes and no. Perhaps, when he'd had time to think about it, the answer would be yes and yes. "Sea of Love" was one of those movies they had watched in the night. It was about a cop, played by Al Pacino, trying to catch a serial killer and falling in love with a young woman (Ellen Barkin) who was a suspect – though he knew, or thought he knew, she couldn't be the killer because he was in love with her. So it combined sex and terror, with some great love scenes – one anyway; and a happy end, the mystery solved and the two walking together along a Manhattan street, anger turning to jokes and laughter.

Sam remembered it well, not just the movie but the heat it had generated. Aunt Rosa looked into his eyes and said she was sorry.

Later, at the door, he told her he would be back when the conference was over. He was almost sure this wasn't true. There was a small mysterious parcel out of his past which Maja had taken with her to wherever it is the dead go. He would never be sure quite what it was. Perhaps his great-aunt, too, knew that he wouldn't be back. It made it simpler saying goodbye.

He did not at once return to the conference – couldn't face it, or even think about it. He walked a long time, up into the old town and beyond, thinking about that message. A new beginning, she said. It had been a time when he'd needed one but was refusing to acknowledge it, even to himself. He thought of the final scene of that movie, the two walking down what must have been Fifth Avenue, joking, in love.

There had been good jokes with Maja too. It shouldn't have ended like this. His sense of loss when the news had come that she was married had been acute; now he had lost her twice over.

Something else came back to him as he walked. It was a story by a Croatian writer which Maja had told when they were having their picnic in the woods. They talked about it on the drive back and she'd more or less told it all over again, so it stayed with him.

It was about a none-too-scrupulous door-to-door salesman of worthless educational and how-to books. He comes to a war-wrecked village, mostly abandoned, just a few old or wounded people remaining. He knocks at a door and is called inside by an old man, half-blind, slumped in a chair who thinks he's the doctor. The old man's wife is ill and he has asked the only person in the village with a working phone to call for help. Greeted as the doctor, the salesman plays the part. He goes to the bed in the corner of the room and finds the wife dead. He tells the old man she's doing fine. Soon she'll be up and ready to dance with him. He asks if there's anything to drink. There is – a flagon of home-brew, strong stuff, and the traveller suggests they share it. When the old man says he's been told he mustn't touch it, it will kill him, the salesman says, "Hey, who's the doctor here?" and pours bumpers for both. When the old man is drunk, which happens quite fast, the salesman gets him to sign up for a set of books. The old man signs, downs another glass and soon slumps into a stupor. Now the salesman goes through the dead woman's clothes and dresses up in them, putting on lipstick, face powder and dabs of scent. He shakes the old man awake and says, "Come on darling. Dance with me." The old man, drunkenly enchanted by his wife's recovery, dances on and on until he collapses and dies. The salesman picks him up and lays him on the bed beside his dead wife. He takes from the woman's apron the money to pay for the books her husband has subscribed to, writes a receipt, changes back into his own clothes, washes the lipstick from his face, and leaves.

It had seemed like a parable of Croatia and its war – one that created its own reality, its own peculiar truth, and had stayed with him, like Grandpa Nola's white stone. Now there was Maja's farewell message to keep alongside it. "You live in the world, Sam, so surprises, including good ones, have a chance of finding you."

7

ZADAR

FOR THE NEXT DAYS, THE ZAGREB DAYS BEFORE THE
conference moved to the coast, Sam tried to look forward rather
than back. He was haunted by Maja's final message, but determined to keep it in its place.

He wanted to understand more about the intricacies of C.D.S.s
and C.D.O.s and though they would not keep the thought of his
dead distant cousin at bay in the nights, in the daytime they would
occupy his mind. Everyone in investment banks and hedge funds
(the big money) now had a finger in the sub-prime mortgage
market pie – the parcels of loans that the major banks and lending
institutions were exchanging in what might have been a game of
pass the parcel. Sam understood the principle – that since most
mortgage loans were safe and only a few at any one time failed,
it was, or should be, statistically close to certain that any bundle
of them could be treated as collectively safe. But if the whole
process was so profitable that more and more money was being
lent with less and less concern about security, didn't it become
important to know a great deal more about what was in the bags
before you traded them?

This was a question he tried to frame at the end of a seminar,
but he was tentative and it was swept aside. So much money was

being made so fast, no-one wanted to listen to questions about how long the good times were going to last. Didn't he like his bonus? Wasn't he looking forward to a bigger one next year? Those things were not said, but they hung in the air over anyone who expressed a doubt. And in the end, if the clusterfuck happened and the whole system failed, blew up, crashed, it was O.P.M. wasn't it – "other people's money" – so why fret?

Sam also kept an eye on the news from Iraq. Everybody did; and yet it was hardly talked about. He had an impression of people stopping on the way to something more significant, watching a television set but already half-turning away making clear this was just a quick glance. No-one wanted to be seen settling in front of a screen that wasn't a Bloomberg. It was as if the war was a public embarrassment. Sam would sometimes ask someone fluent in Croatian to translate this or that item. Mostly he just guessed, or caught a few minutes of C.N.N.

The pictures were clear enough and told their own story. There were many kidnappings in Baghdad and a day or so later the kidnapped were found dead, often headless with marks of torture. The commonest images were of explosions – car-bombs, roadside improvised devices, mines, mortars – and the wreckage they created. Sirens, ambulances, people running, crunching over glass, shouting, waving the crowd aside, carrying stretchers; American soldiers breaking into houses, bursting through doors, going after snipers who had fired at them from rooftops; Humvees and tanks graunching over, and crashing through, wrecked streets. Museums were being looted, public buildings desecrated, public utilities destroyed. America's new Iraq was emerging, taking shapeless shape out of the demolition of the country that had been Saddam's wicked but orderly fiefdom.

The hunt for weapons of mass destruction went on. No success so far, but confidence was expressed that they would soon be found. How could they not be? They were the reason for all this – for the little boy with both his arms blown off, for the wounded little girl wandering the streets with no mother or father or anyone at all to take her in. And in this war, which the President had declared over before it had really begun, Americans soldiers were still dying every day.

After three working days in the capital the conference moved to the coast, first to the city of Rijeka. There was another mayor, a new welcome, gifts and mementoes in shiny packages, a civic cocktail party with speeches. But the sense of serious intent was slipping away. Rijeka had an air of purposeful commerce, but it was positioned on the Adriatic, with warm sunshine, waters blue in the distance and translucent up close, a western horizon that burned bright orange as the sun went down, and skies that turned to velvet after it had gone. There were nice little towns on either side of the city, and delegates went to them on excursions, swimming and eating where the rich of the Austro-Hungarian Empire, and the Italian invaders of World War Two (who called Rijeka Fiume), and even the masters of the Communist era, had gone to enjoy their leisure.

On the second day they were driven up into hills behind the town to have lunch at a homely establishment that made its own spirits and fortified wines. There was cut firewood beautifully stacked in piles behind the house, ready for winter; a wine press, farm implements, some ancient mill-wheels propping terraces on which the vines were in leaf and grapes just forming – all this and a distant view all the way down sheer slopes to the sea. The lunch went on through many courses, cooked *à la campagne* with gaps and *grappa* in between, and lasted well into the afternoon.

When they got back to the hotel Sam was summoned to the desk. There had been urgent calls and numbers left for him. Mr Bukowski from the bank had been trying to get in touch with him to tell him something important about Mr Leveson. There was a message from Letty too, complaining that what she called his "self" was switched off. André Kraznahorkai who had vanished from the conference but would return, sent "shocked sympathy and sadness" and looked forward to the meeting they were to have in Zadar. "There are matters to be concluded," he said.

Reuben Leveson had been killed riding his motorbike. Sam had known about the fast cars, had seen the Ferrari, and heard about the dream, or fantasy, of owning a Lamborghini, but about a motorbike, nothing. No doubt this too had been powerful – another dream machine.

Sam rang Willard Bukowski. After due, though routine, expressions of "sadness at this great loss" Willard asked did Sam know, had Reuben been coming for anything particular, or just to show the flag?

Sam said a meeting with André Kraznahorkai had been scheduled for Zadar. There was nothing else that he knew of.

Kraznahorkai? Willard had never heard of him. "Do whatever needs to be done," he said. And then, "You should be back here in time for the funeral. He's Jewish, but they're not kosher or observant or whatever you call it – not rushing him into the ground. Cremation, in fact – Golders Green. His sister wants to take a little time . . ."

"Whatever needs to be done" – Sam hoped what was needed would be obvious, or better still that there would be nothing at all.

"This is a king-hit for Credit Products," Willard said. "We'll talk about in-house rearrangements when you're back. There will have to be some. I hope you're ready for that. Reuben shouldered a load." And he wished Sam goodnight.

Sam relished these Willardisms, but the humour, the pleasure they gave him, quickly faded and he went to bed struggling with what he knew were banal reflections. Maja, dead; Reuben Leveson, dead. They engaged different levels of feeling, but the metaphysical puzzle was the same. Gone, finished, terminated – but they stayed with you, in your head, part of your reality. The life expired, yes – but slowly.

He drifted towards sleep, thinking about one, then the other; but it was Maja who came to him in a dream. She took him by surprise and he woke to the dark and the silence feeling he was at the bottom of a pit.

Next day they were into their coaches and on the road again, early – nomad bankers striking camp and moving on. A very few latecomers had been added to their number; more had departed and there were empty seats. They drove through pretty towns and fertile countryside. Then for a time the landscape turned barren and rock-strewn. To the right across a narrow estuary an island seemed to go on and on beside them like a runner that kept pace, refusing to give up. It was uniformly yellow-brown with not the merest shading of green. But for the motion of the coach, you might have thought you were going nowhere.

Sam read for an hour or more and then fell asleep. When he woke the barrenness had been left behind. They were in Zadar, coming into the forecourt of a big white hotel that looked straight out to a very blue sea. The lime trees were in bloom and there were streets lined with them, their flowers, tiny yellow faces, seeming to look down. There were beds of lavender and rosemary. The whole town was fragrant. Olives were in flower in the gardens, figs were in good green leaf with the beginnings of fruit, and grapes were forming on the vines. There was bougainvillea and hibiscus in flower. In the market stalls cherries had replaced strawberries.

Sam wandered about taking it in, breathing the scent of the limes. The recent war had been through this town. Some of the buildings were pock-marked with what must have been machine-gun and heavier fire. There had been shelling from the hills and whole buildings brought down; but the worst of the damage was repaired now and mostly it looked spruce and prosperous.

After lunch Sam swam out from a little beach directly below the hotel. There were people playing chess under trees, and a café under an awning that looked out over the water. He dried himself, dressed, returned to watch some of the games of chess, then had coffee and read a day-old English newspaper.

That evening he followed directions André Kraznahorkai had left for him at the hotel. He went on foot, lost his way more than once, but eventually found himself where he was meant to be, on a handsome wide stone promenade that ran for two or three kilometres along the waterfront, with shops and small hotels, gardens and trees, and the sound of the sea lapping and slopping. There was a square with a church and bell-tower, and an open space littered with Roman remains – broken columns, carved stone plinths and fascias, broken statues, found and uncovered, or perhaps wrecked by recent bombardments. There were cafés and restaurants too, and at one of these, with the name Stomorica, he and André Kraznahorkai were to meet.

He was ahead of time, and while he loitered on the *riva*, a legless young man arrived in a wheelchair, levered himself out of it, stripped neatly to his shorts, crawled to the edge of the quay and, hand over hand, lowered himself down an iron ladder into the sea. In the water, with strong arms and shoulders and a thick head of hair he looked young and healthy. When he returned to the iron ladder and climbed back to the quay, he became something different, not quite human. Sam turned away while this hardly more than half-a-man sat on the pier drying and dressing himself, and then once more hauled and hoisted himself into his chair and wheeled back the way he had come.

The sun was going down. Only a few yards offshore a dinghy ran out a net in a wide arc, the oarsman pulling it slowly around full circle and back to the fishing boat where it started. As the crew winched it in, narrowing the space, there were silver flashes of fish jumping to escape. The net closed, closed further, until the boat began to tilt with the weight. The winch was stopped and the crew of three men hurried to dip hand-nets into the sea, pulling the catch on board, tipping the fish flapping into big steel vats. As the weight of the vats increased the ketch began to right itself. The engine was started and the vessel chugged slowly towards the docks, dragging what remained in the net.

Sam checked the restaurant again. André Kraznahorkai was waiting, watching him. He walked over and they shook hands. "Croatian fishermen," André said in a tone of admiration. "Boat is registered in Split. They will have tracked fish from there. This is spawning time so fish come in close."

He had a table ready, outside under an awning, looking out

to the sea. "This place is favourite," he said. "My father was Party official in Hungary. We had holidays here. It hasn't changed – still modest. Sea food is good. This waiter – I think I remember him from those days."

They sat and Hawkeye from Hungary poured the wine that was already open. For a moment he remained, head down. When he looked up again and held a hand out across the table to be shaken, Sam saw his face was full of sadness. "About Reuben Leveson," he said. "I am so sorry for you and sorry for self. He was great banker and nice guy – they are not always same person, you understand?"

"I didn't get to know him well," Sam said. "But yes, he was nice, you're right. Colourful. Unusual."

As they raised their glasses the waiter broke in on their moment of commemoration. He was a noisy presence and offered jokes, one in Croatian which Mr K. explained, another in a brand of almost-English.

"How many languages do you speak?" Sam asked when the clown had gone.

"Three, as you say, flu . . ."

"Fluently."

"Fluently, thank you. And three more, like English, not so good."

"Your English is good," Sam said. "And six languages – to me that's a mystery."

"You listen," Hawkeye said, "and you imitate. That is all. Like learning tunes. I have theory . . ." He stopped himself, and then asked, "Should I bore you with theory?"

"Please do, yes."

"Theory is that in history of human evolution song must come before speech. I think we sing to one another before words . . ."

He hesitated, looking to see whether he was being understood. "I think grammar and syntax of sound was first."

"Before vocabulary?"

"Before, yes."

"Like birds," Sam said. "Life would be an opera."

André laughed. "What Mr Chomsky would say I don't know, but I think it has to be so."

The meals came. It was time, Mr K. said, to talk of business. "Reuben Leveson's business, you understand?" He met Sam's eye across the table, "You knew payment was due?"

Sam's role had been described as "to deputise" but since his boss had expected to be there himself, that was only a courtesy and meant little. "I think he did mention it," Sam said. This was not true, but he felt it would be better, and he might learn more, if he didn't appear entirely ignorant. "I don't think he told me how much."

"Not a large amount." When Sam waited, "Three million," André said. "Three, and some odds and ends."

Sam nodded. "That's in . . . ?"

"Dollars. We work always in dollars."

Three. It seemed a lot of dollars to Sam. Mr K., on the other hand, spoke of it in a tone so relaxed it might have been a trifle. "Our problem," he said, "is that we are ready to pay."

To *pay*. That made a difference. Sam fiddled with his fork.

"I have been in talk with my people today. Money is in Switzerland. It was sent last week."

Of course it was. Where else? A numbered account.

Mr K. continued. "Mr Leveson sent us details we needed to establish identity and open account. Access is only to number and by codes. Only he can close it – or his heirs in event of death."

"I see." Sam was not sure what he saw, except that if identity had to be established the money was being paid to Leveson, not to Interbank America. Something was beginning to emerge.

André said, "We knew how much he valued discretion – as we do ourselves." And then, "He had no wife or child. Sister of course – Ruth. He spoke of her – very fond I think."

He took an envelope from his pocket. "Everything is here. Account number, access codes. Please see they go to right person. Sister, if you think so. Perhaps lawyer or accountant."

Sam wondered whether a receipt was wanted and then intuited nothing was wanted – just to be rid of an obligation, and the money. Nonetheless he allowed himself to say, "I'm not quite sure what I do next."

"You are deputy," Hawkeye said. "Do what our friend would have done."

"Indeed." And Sam put the envelope away in the pocket of his jacket.

For a while they ate in silence, looking out to sea, watching the last light of the sun die beyond the clouds on the horizon and the stars come out. "You know," André said, "Reuben and I we are both Jews. It brings closeness sometimes, but not to depend on. Different backgrounds. His family are German, but before he is born they are in Hampstead."

"And yours?"

"It is said my mother as baby was smuggled out of Munkács ghetto in basket of fruit. The rest of her family . . ." He pulled a sad face. "No survivors. My father's family escape into Russia and live out war in Siberia. Then return to Hungary."

"Also Jewish?"

"Also yes. Dedicated communists because Marx was Jew

and communism was supposed to include us. I had very boring childhood. At first we think we are safe inside Party. No-one is safe, not really, but we think so . . ." He spread his hands wide. "And then Uncle, also Party official like Father, goes out the window – dead."

"He jumped?"

"That is official story. They say, Uncle drank too much. Uncle had nihilistic tendencies . . . He was sober serious man. So we learn to live with fear and behave ourselves." He smiled. "Life goes on . . ."

He explained that he had married young and had one child. He had been manager of the Red Star swimming pool in Budapest. It was a former Turkish baths complex left over from the time of the Ottoman occupation, converted after World War Two into a modern heated swimming pool under the original glass dome, with a huge red star suspended at one end and a picture of Comrade Stalin at the other. You did your lengths between Star and Stalin. In winter you could look up from the water and watch snow falling on the glass dome.

"It was very nice," he said. "School parties come. Hungarian Olympic swimmers train there – especially water polo team."

His wife had been a Party official, and their boy a member of the Young Pioneers. Mr. K. had been, he said, "politically compliant" but he had developed a secret ambition – to escape to the West and get involved in finance. "I was devoted to big idea – you could say rebellion against Marxism, but not really. It was just dream. I tell no-one, not even wife. I think if wife knows she divorce me – maybe denounce me."

In his spare time (and his time, he said, was mostly spare) he studied western capitalism. You could do that, starting with *Das*

Kapital, and go on to modern books which analysed the system from a Marxist perspective to show it was designed to make the rich richer and the poor poorer. He accepted this analysis and no-one in his family or circle had any idea he wanted to become one of the rich getting always richer.

"I had plan, but I could not find way to escape – nothing is safe. And then no need – down comes Berlin Wall and soon I am free. I go to Germany, I go to London – that is where I meet Mr Leveson. We buy and sell together, make profit, invest. He is London agent for me. I put everything I have learned into practice. Prague is home now. Small office in Berlin also."

"And your wife?"

"Still in Budapest. She has pastry shop which I have financed. It makes loss so far, but she does not know and I do not say. She thinks she is big capitalist. My son is computer boffin . . ." He sounded less happy about the son.

"That's good, isn't it?"

"Good and bad. He is computer boffin and marijuana smoker." He shrugged and smiled. "You have wife? Children?"

Sam began with half answers – the kind you give when you're not sure the person asking the questions is really interested. Then, prompted by a man who appeared relaxed, not in a hurry, and keen to listen, he told his own story. But it was a new story now, as if he was revising it in the telling. Some years ago on a visit to Zagreb he had fallen in love with a distant cousin and this had set in motion the slow disintegration of his marriage. At first he hadn't faced up to what had happened, and was happening, to him. She was his cousin, after all; they lived half a world apart; he was married with teenage sons.

Meanwhile the cousin had gone to America and married. Now

– only two days ago in fact – he had heard that she was dead.

Hawkeye was sympathetic, as if something in the telling had touched a chord. But sympathy was not entirely welcome. Sam felt his throat tighten, and tears. Until this moment he had only wept only in his sleep.

"I'm sorry," he said, half laughing. "This is ridiculous. A grown man weeping under the stars."

"Not ridiculous." Mr K. lifted his shoulders and spread his hands. "You loved her, she dies, you are sad."

Was that how it was? Sam supposed it was. He was grateful for the kindness, but he would have preferred not to have exposed a weakness. He sat up straight and took a breath. The air off the sea was salty and refreshing. "Tell me," he said, "and please excuse me for changing the subject so abruptly; but doesn't the present state of the bond market frighten you?"

Mr K. smiled and shook his head. "Certainly it is going to crash."

"That doesn't worry you?"

"It is where exists opportunity. Biggest risk is biggest opportunity." When Sam's face showed doubt he went on, "Shorting, you understand?"

"You gamble on a failure of the market. Yes, but how do you know..."

"Instinct," Hawkeye said. "Right moment has to be chosen. Not moment when nerve fails. That is part I enjoy – risk. Reuben too. Too much sometimes. I am like him, but different. He has instinct but maybe not caution."

"As with the motorbike."

He nodded gravely and they were silent again until his phone rang in his pocket. He opened it, looked at its little screen and answered, "*Molim?*" then excused himself and walked away, down toward the now dark, lapping water, talking in a growl that might have been any one of the languages he was fluent in, or equally one of the other three in which, as in English, he could just "get by".

8

GOLDERS GREEN

Sam came back from Croatia bearing an envelope which he believed held the number of a Swiss bank account containing three million American dollars (and "some odds and ends"), and the code by which it could be accessed. It felt as if he was carrying a film noir suitcase full of banknotes. It wasn't quite the same, but he was unsure how different it was apart from the fact that this was a suitcase which fitted easily in the pocket and was therefore not in much danger of theft or interception at the border. Was all that money sitting there waiting to be tapped? The account would remain in Reuben's name. But what was to stop someone who had the code from opening a London account and emptying the Swiss one, perhaps slowly, bit by bit, into it? André Kraznahorkai had been glad to be rid of it – that much was clear. His obligation to his late friend had been acknowledged, his debt paid. Nothing had been said about where the money came from; and there was no clarity about where it should go.

It came back to Sam that he had once heard Reuben Leveson speak of Croatia as a place where there was – or had been – big money to be made out of armaments. As the Russians had withdrawn eastward after the fall of the Berlin Wall whole arsenals were left. Dealers in East Germany, Hungary, Czechoslovakia bought them up, or simply took possession of them and on-sold – and there had been a time when Croatia, building an army to free itself from the Yugoslav Federation, had been a willing buyer. Sam remembered Reuben rubbing thumb and forefinger together and saying how much money had been made that way. This was connected in Sam's mind with the much talked about refurbishment of a house in Notting Hill. Could arms sales have paid for that?

But the source was less what occupied his mind than what he should do next with the suitcase. To be in possession of it made him nervous; yet he was reluctant simply to be rid of it, especially because Hawkeye seemed, when Sam thought about him, such an unusual person, unconventional and rather appealing, and his instructions had been so unclear.

Reuben Leveson's funeral service was held in the largest of the three red-brick chapels of the Golders Green crematorium with its solemn cloisters studded with memorial plaques and its spacious green garden sloping gently up a lawn-covered area bordered by trees bright with new leaf. Some of the men wore yarmulkes, others were bare-headed. Two young women, perhaps eighteen or nineteen years old and obviously twins, handed out a little printed booklet at the door. Sam stood outside in the cloisters, flicking through its pages and waiting to recognise someone from the bank. There was a brief biography and pictures with explanatory captions – a very small Reuben with his sister on a stony beach "Near Whitstable" with the sea at their backs; a bar mitzvah studio photograph; the senior schoolboy in grey flannel bags and blazer with City of London School pocket; the Oxford undergraduate outside Blackwell's with wild hair and a very long scarf; the sailor on a yacht in the harbour at Monaco; the banker "At home with Percy" a fox terrier. On the last page there was a Hebrew text under the symbol of a green branch, broken.

Sam was greeted by Tom and Hermione Roland. He wondered whether Tom might have written a poem, an elegy, "Oh weep for Adonais he is dead" kind of thing, but didn't ask. As he followed them in he exchanged silent nods and signals of recognition with Willard Bukowski, and Mrs Mary Manoly from Commodities.

They all stood aside to let a wheelchair pass. That, Hermione murmured, was Sir Frank Vogel, pushed by his wife, Reuben's sister Ruth.

"So she's Lady Vogel," Sam said when she'd vanished indoors.

"She could be, but she calls herself Ruth Leveson. There's a previous wife who calls herself Lady Vogel. The twins at the door are Ruth's with Sir Frank."

Sam saw Maureen O'Donnell now, with her whatever he was – her Swede, squeeze, fiancé, whatever. His name was Stig Ardelius and he was tall, blond and very presentable – almost as good as the name. Maureen gave Sam a slight wave, not sombre exactly, but proper to the occasion, a small turn of the wrist and waggle of the fingers; and then, like a second thought and behind Stig's broad back as they moved indoors, a thumbs-up.

There were copious flowers on either side of what could have been an altar if that was what the service required, and a small pulpit to the left. The coffin, "plain but not cheap" Sam thought you would have to say, was already in place, slightly elevated and visible at the front to the left, pointed towards a small square hatch. The door to eternity, and Sam wondered whether you went straight through into the flames, or on to a trolley for transport somewhere beyond. Certainly the furnace couldn't be very far off, since this building was itself the crematorium. He asked himself whether he would prefer burial or cremation and decided – since mistakes were sometimes made – it would be better (though unpleasant) to burn quickly than to die slowly underground. He wondered whether someone had checked that the boss was really dead. He'd heard or read often enough of people declared dead and discovered at the last moment to be alive. Maybe one should ask to be put into one's coffin with a torch and a mobile phone. But then supposing you were really dead and someone, not knowing, called you. What would happen if a phone went off inside a coffin during the service? Should it be answered ("Sorry love, he's dead") or ignored?

When they were all settled and silent a rabbi wearing a yarmulke and prayer shawl greeted them from the pulpit, and read from (as he said) "the immortal words of John Donne":

> No man is an island entire of itself; every man is a
> piece of the continent, a part of the main; if a clod
> be washed away by the sea, Europe is the less, as well
> as if a promontory were, as well as if a manor of thy
> friends or of thine own were; any man's death dimin-
> ishes me, because I am involved in mankind. And
> therefore never send to know for whom the bell
> tolls; it tolls for thee.

He closed one text in a kind of slow motion, slowly opened another, and read:

> What ails you, sea, that you retreat,
> And river of Jordan, that you hesitate,
> And you, great mountains, that you skip like rams,

And you, small hills, leaping like lambs in spring?
Tremble, O Earth, at the presence of the Lord,
At the nearness of the God of Jacob,
Who turned the rock into a clear pool,
And the flint into a fountain
Of crystal light.

He spoke briefly and warmly now of Reuben Leveson as an admired and sometimes playfully wayward son of Zion. "We are here to celebrate," he said. "To lament our loss, but to celebrate the life of the man we loved." And he invited those named on the order of service to offer memories of their departed friend.

There were brief tributes from former school mates, with stories about cricket, fives, theatrical performances, a school trip to Paris and one to Zurich. The twin nieces, tearful but quite lucid and self-possessed, remembered a kind uncle who made good jokes. Willard Bukowski spoke for the bank, in stainless-steel sentences that sounded as if they were straight out of the reference file, ready should Leveson have needed one for his next job or a promotion. This was his reference for the afterlife, and a good one.

Finally came a eulogy from Reuben's sister. Ruth Leveson was tall with rather superior good looks, a fine nose and cheek bones, sensitive, expressive mouth and large brown eyes like her brother's. She was slim and elegant but nicely rounded. The voice was silky. The accent, like Reuben's, was middle-class London with what Sam thought (though he wasn't sure) was a slight but detectable Jewish thickening of certain vowels and consonants.

She spoke of her brother as a force of nature, a lovely headlong fellow who couldn't ever be stopped except, alas, by an accident.

That had always been on the cards. He'd had one or two minor ones. She had lived in fear of it and now the worst had come.

But recklessness, she said, if that was the right word, had been a style, almost a way of life, and whether it was to kill him or take him to the top was always going to be a matter of luck – good or bad. Well, now the luck had turned against him, but not before he had done great things, and it was those she wanted everyone to remember and acknowledge. There was the lovely house in Ladbroke Road, the cars, the yacht racing, the tennis at Campden Hill and the rounds of golf at Queenwood. Reuben was a winner. "Some of you have played croquet with him at Courteen Hall and you'll know what I mean when I say even croquet became a blood sport. Reuben played to win – in everything."

A lot of people here today, she went on, were bankers and accountants and would have heard it said they were the ones who knew the cost of everything and the value of nothing. It had been said of Reuben, too – and it was true enough he knew the cost of everything. But he knew value too. He had natural good taste. He was also the most un-miserly person she had ever known, and hadn't flinched from the fact that good things – wines, cars, clothes – were expensive. But when cost and value didn't match he had never hesitated to say so – out loud often, and in public. It could be embarrassing, but it meant he was not a snob – not ever, and not about anything. And knowing that difference between cost and value had been one of the foundations of his success in business.

She spoke feelingly but was in command. She concluded, "Reuben was my little brother. He was always affectionate and kind. He was funny, he was great company, he was clever, he was loyal to his employers and good to his staff. To us, his only family, he was unfailingly generous and we're going to miss him. His absence in my life will be huge."

She stopped there, overcome for a moment; and then, simply, "Thank you so much, all of you, for being here to remember him."

Now the rabbi took charge, reading:

By Babylon's waters we remembered Zion, and wept.
Our captors demanded music. They mocked us.
  "Give us the songs of your homeland."
But we hung our instruments in the branches of
  the poplars.
How could we sing the Lord's song to alien ears?
Jerusalem, if I forget you may my right hand freeze
  on the strings.
May my tongue fall silent if I fail to exalt you above
  all the places of my heart.

This was followed by a Hebrew prayer which the order of service indicated was Kaddish. After a silence all the more silent because the tones had been so ringing and rabbinical, there was another, El Malei Rachamim.

Silence again, which lasted some seconds – and then a voice Sam recognised as Leonard Cohen singing "Who by Fire".

Now the coffin began to move, very slowly, on rollers towards and through the hatch which had opened to receive it. The mechanism could be heard just faintly behind Cohen's slow build towards the big question. Someone was calling, but who was it? There was something about the cumulative effect of the song, Cohen's deep voice, the serious intensity he gave to lines which, like the ancient wisdoms already intoned, might mean next to nothing, or nothing quite lucid and connected to the world of the twenty-first century

– as if Cohen himself had become the rabbi. Who was calling? Who else but Death, or the Lord of Israel?

The last of the coffin disappeared and the small doors closed. There was no flicker of fire, no tongue of flame. It occurred to Sam that after all a burial was more satisfying for those left behind. They could drop things, flowers, clods of earth, even poems, onto the coffin lid. They could stare down at it, snug in steep-sided clay. He imagined dropping Hawkeye's envelope with the Swiss codes into the grave. Final payment! Such a great solution to the problem – and such an answer, too, to have ready if he should ever be asked what had happened to the money. "I dropped it into his grave."

Outside in the sunshine he looked for Maureen but found, or was found by, Tom and Hermione, who suggested coffee. They bought it at the very plain Fountain Tearoom and took their tray out of doors, away from the dark-green linoleum-covered floor, to sit at a table among beds of roses, each bush with its bronze plaque a memorial planting.

"It'd be interesting to go backstage," Sam said.

Backstage? They were puzzled.

"I was wondering whether you go straight into the furnace." He told them his thoughts about being alive in the coffin.

"Oh Sam, please," Hermione said.

Tom said, "I once knew a man who did the burning. That was his job. Shaved head . . ." He brushed a hand over his own greying skull. "Always wore T-shirts. He had a very innocent face, rather fine-boned and beautiful. He loved his work – liked to talk about it. I used to think of him as the angel of death."

Hermione looked sceptical. "When was this? You're making it up."

"Not at all. He was a drinking companion at the Spread Eagle when we lived in Camden. He told me you couldn't be buried alive, or put into the furnace alive, if you were embalmed – and apparently most people are. It's because the embalmer cuts the carotid artery . . ."

Hermione shuddered; so did Sam.

That evening Sam was to take Letty to the Indian restaurant, Spices, in Paddington, where they'd had their first outing together just after Christmas 2001 – except that it was no longer Indian, it was Thai, and the name was changed to Thai River. "*Plus ça change, plus c'est la même chose,*" Letty said. It was the location they wanted to celebrate, the place where they had found one another, father and daughter, and found they liked one another.

The talk at first was about what each had done since their last meeting. He told her about Croatia, about Zadar anyway, the lime blossom scenting the air, the huge fishing catch almost too heavy for the boat, the former communist swimming pool manager now a capitalist in Prague and Berlin.

She told him about her work at Great Ormond Street, and about a trip she and Marcel planned to make to Corsica so she could meet his parents.

While the conversation rattled on some part of Sam's mind was taking him towards telling her about Maja, and at the same time avoiding it. It would mean telling her about what the relationship had been, but that wouldn't have mattered. It was something else that stood in the way – something about Aunt Rosa, and the way she had conveyed the deadly news. Something was missing, and he felt he couldn't tell Letty until he had worked out what it was. He had to find a way of coming to terms with it in his own head – with the idea of Maja shooting herself – and as he thought this he recognised that he still thought of her as living. If Maja was dead, in his imagination she was alive.

There was for him this undertone, or undertow, to the conversation, a kind of monitor allowing him to articulate, or not, the thoughts that were stirring below the surface. It prevented him going in some directions, but it was perhaps careless about others. So in a moment he was telling her about Reuben's funeral and about the idea of dropping Mr K.'s envelope into a grave.

Envelope? She wanted to know what envelope – and now he had to tell her, though if he hadn't been thinking about Maja he would probably have avoided this subject too. The beans (if they were beans) had to be spilled. He was no good at keeping secrets, even his own.

She listened. Three million!

But Letty was French. She couldn't laugh about money – not for long. Soon she took on the look of an inquisitor, or (he thought) a tax official. Or was it the shadowy figure of the priest in the confessional, murmuring questions through a small slide-back grille? This was the other daughter, the part that was Simone's rather than his. Had he opened the envelope? she wanted to know. Had he told anyone in the bank? Did he know what Mr Leveson had done to earn it? Had he thought of crime, drugs? This Hungarian, Kraznahorkai, was he a crook?

He should leave it sealed, she said, and give it to someone at the bank. She was insistent about this.

The French, Sam reflected, were very careful and correct about money. Honesty had to be conspicuous, because it was socially necessary, and no-one believed in honesty by nature, or for pref-erence. It was to do with Original Sin and the Social Contract. Original Sin meant you wanted to keep it; the Social Contract meant you must not.

"Enough of money matters," he said at last, falsely jolly and brisk; and he gave her an account of Willard Bukowski's funeral eulogy – and went on from that to tell her about Tom Roland's drinking friend from the Spread Eagle, the one Tom had thought of as the angel of death, who had said no-one survived the embalming process.

When they had finished their meal he walked with her down to Bayswater Road where she would catch a bus. They were in good spirits; but she had not forgotten the money, and brought him back to it. "Three million," she said. "That's a lot of dollars, Sam-pa. You'll tell someone at the bank about it – won't you?"

"I will," he said, feeling at that moment that, though he didn't want to, he probably had no choice.

Next morning, still with a feeling of reluctance, he went to Willard Bukowski's office. Willard listened while Sam explained. His expression was at first neutral, then pained. He winced when André Kraznahorkai was named. "No need for names," he murmured. When Sam had finished he said, "This has nothing to do with Interbank America. We have no dealings with this man. This is one of Reuben Leveson's extracurricular adventures."

"But I got involved."

"Not our problem, Sam."

"I was there at the conference for the bank."

"You were there for the bank, but this was not the bank's business."

Sam stared at him across the desk. He had not been invited to sit and now Willard was standing too. Sam said, "I wish you'd just tell me what to do with this money."

"It's an envelope isn't it, which you say you haven't opened. You don't know what's in there. I suggest you burn it and forget about it. Or – I don't know – 'Return to sender' kind of thing, if you have an address. Pretend it never happened. You were in Croatia for us, not for Leveson – who, as his sister acknowledged in her eulogy, was a bit of speedster and liked to cut corners."

Had she said that? It seemed clear Willard had not liked Reuben, or at least that he hadn't approved of his way of doing things.

"Now, can we just agree that these matters have not been discussed between us and this meeting never happened?" He held out his hand.

Sam shook it.

Willard came around the desk and put the same hand on Sam's upper arm as he steered him towards the door. "Good man," he said.

That night the good man dreamed he was in Moscow, a city he had never visited. It was announced that everyone must be out of the underground by midnight or they would die, because the trains couldn't be stopped after that and anyone remaining would be run down and killed. Some failed to escape and died. Waking, it took him some time to recognise that there was no reason why anyone who stayed on the platform of an underground should be in danger, but his sense of these deadly trains running on and on through the night killing people was stronger than logic.

Lying awake in the early hours he found himself imagining what he would do with the money if in fact it was his. He thought mostly of gifts – to his boys, to Ngaio, to Letty, and so on through his family and friends. But there were things he wanted for himself; and the more detailed the thoughts became, the more money was needed. The "odds and ends" had to be multiplied and became another million. Before long four wasn't enough. He shook himself properly awake, took a shower and had breakfast with Trinnie, watching from time to time the office across the street for signs of life and wickedness.

He was invited to Oxford for a meal with Charles and Githa. Jake and Jan were there. They asked about Croatia, there was wine, his tongue was loosened. He meant to avoid telling them anything about André Kraznahorkai, but then remembered his theory of language, that singing of some kind, a language of music, might have preceded individual words. Charles thought the idea ridiculous.

Jan said as theories went, it was "elegant" and Githa agreed.

Jake was inclined to treat it with respect, and it was Jake who wanted to hear more about this Kraznahorkai. Sam told them about the Red Star Pool and Mr K.'s secret capitalist ambitions – it felt like a good story in the telling, and when he came to the envelope he didn't stop. That too was told.

"Three million U.S. dollars?"

"Yes. Not an exact figure. More, in fact."

Charles thought he should do as Bukowski suggested and burn it.

Jan said, "Give the money to a charity – Oxfam, or Save the Children. Greenpeace – what about them? Save a whale."

Sam hadn't thought of a charity.

Charles said, "I don't think you can play Robin Hood with the money if it's not yours."

Githa thought he should give it to Reuben's sister. "It belongs to her, surely."

"She's said to be very rich," Sam said, as if that excused his hesitation though he knew it didn't.

Jake picked up the bottle and began refilling around the table. "*Nothing* is what you should do. If it's not your money it's not your responsibility. Sit tight. Put it away in a drawer. Lose it. When you come on it again in a year or two – or even three – try the code, and if it works, start spending. If you need any help, call me." He raised his glass in wordless toast to that day.

After another uneasy night in Moscow, followed by early morning fantasies of boundless generosity, Sam rang the sister, Ruth, and asked whether they could meet. She seemed glad of his call. She had heard nothing from the bank since the funeral – not that there was any reason why she should, she said. But it was plain that she felt neglected. "Suddenly someone in your life's not there, and it's difficult to adjust. It leaves a hole."

She said she was going each day to her brother's house in Ladbroke Road to work her way through his things. Would it be convenient to call there? "Come on Saturday and we can have lunch."

He took roses and then, when admitted to the house, saw that the garden at the back was full of flower beds.

"Oh, but Reuben's garden has no roses," she said, filling a vase with water and spreading the blooms. "Not like these anyway. These are lovely. Thank you."

She told him her brother had only recently finished the rebuilding and decorating. "Come and look," and she took him around the rooms. There was a lot of space, fine furniture, works of art ancient and modern. "I think he must have had an adviser.

Reuben had good taste, but this . . ." She hesitated. "So perfect – all of a piece – you know?"

Reuben's housekeeper, Mrs Teagle, put out lunch for them on a table under an awning in the garden. There were breads and cheeses, a salade niçoise, bottled water and a Riesling.

"Reuben lived alone," Ruth said, "and Mrs Teagle came in on a daily basis. Cleaned, did his laundry, cooked, walked the dog. He had girlfriends, but they never lasted. And he tended to keep them off the premises."

"He told me you described him as commitment-averse."

She laughed. "It's true – and he was. I wanted him to have a wife and kids."

So they had lunch and talked about Reuben. Sam told her about the conference, the friend her brother called Hawkeye from Hungary, finally about the envelope, which he now, with a feeling of relief, handed her across the table.

"Three million. Do they know about this at the bank?"

Sam remembered that his conversation with Willard Bukowski was supposed not to have happened. He said, "I did tell someone there – a senior person. I was told it was nothing to do with them, and our conversation hadn't happened."

She nodded, unsurprised. "Reuben was unorthodox. That troubled them sometimes. He worked at the bank and for the bank, but he worked at home for himself."

Sam explained that André Kraznahorkai had described himself as a businessman, not a banker.

"He didn't give you a card?"

"No. It's odd isn't it, but I didn't think of it at the time. We had our meeting, he gave me the envelope, and next morning he was gone."

She picked it up. "He told you to give it to the right person."

"To the right person, yes."

"Didn't you think of keeping it yourself?" There was a challenge in this, not unpleasant, perhaps even amused.

His voice was quite steady as he said, "I think I thought of most things."

She wasn't displeased with that. "You look like a man who would think of most things."

"A friend suggested I should give it to charity."

"But you weren't sure it was yours to give."

"Or that I wanted to."

"You wanted the money?"

"Anyone can be tempted."

"Can they?"

As if combating that intelligent smile he asked, "What would Reuben have done – I mean if the circumstances had been the same?"

She laughed. "Good question. He would certainly have given it careful thought."

"I think just about the last thing André Kraznahorkai said to me was, 'Do what Reuben would have done.'"

"What Reuben would have done." She repeated it, smiling. "I begin to like this Hawkeye from Hungary. Such a mysterious instruction."

Sam said, "I got tired of thinking up ways to spend it. As soon as you begin to divide up three or four million you realise it's not very much. It's soon gone."

"So probity got you in the end."

"Probity – or scruples."

"Aren't they the same?"

"Yes . . . But no, not quite."

She appeared to reflect on that, and what he might mean by it. "You think the money's in some way discreditable? To do with the war there?"

"Your brother did tell me there was money to be made . . ."

"Yes, he told me that too. But then . . . Is the arms dealer responsible for what's done with the weapons?"

Sam remembered the legless soldier scrambling down the ladder into the sea on the Zadar waterfront. "Hard to know where the blame lies," he said. "If there is blame."

A little fox terrier came out into the garden. She reached down, patted him and fed him a scrap from her plate. "Percy," Sam said, recognising him from the memorial booklet.

"Percy's mine now . . ." She waved around. "As all of this is, probably – or will be, most of it. It seems Reuben didn't leave a will. We're hunting in all the obvious places, but no luck. His lawyer isn't aware of one. His friends say he intended to live for ever."

The sun was shining on the garden, and being caught in the circle of fountain water falling lightly over a small marble figure in the middle of a pond. It was as if the marble girl held over her head an umbrella of rain.

"You say it's Reuben's money," Ruth said. "But suppose I said it's not – or I didn't want it to be. You see what I mean?"

"That I can't make you accept it? Yes, I see that."

"What would you do?"

"Oh God, I'm not sure." He stood up holding his glass and took a short walk to the edge of a pool. There were orange and red fish cruising among green waterweed. He remembered Jake's idea that he should put the envelope away and lose it for a while. "I think at first I'd do nothing. I'd just make a note of the fact that you and I had this conversation . . ."

"And that for the moment I declined to accept it."

"Yes."

"Everything on hold." She smiled as if they had reached some kind of agreement. "Why don't you do that, Sam – may I call you Sam? And I'll do the same. Make the same note. It will give both of us time to reflect. If nothing has happened in six months or a year we should talk again – even if it's just to choose our charity."

He liked it that she said "our". Meanwhile, he thought (and it was almost as if he had said it aloud, and she had agreed), you and I might see more of one another.

9

LAMB'S CONDUIT STREET

During most of the summer months after the Croatia conference Sam was rostered to be at the office. The weather got hotter and by July, and on into August when he was almost the sole member of the Credit Products team still at his desk, temperatures went up into the thirties. He was not so much working as batting away enquiries and assuring clients that their concerns would be addressed when the office was back to full strength. So he read the papers and sat in the parks under trees, watching Londoners baring themselves to the sun and turning pink, and even flame-red, in the space of a lunch hour.

In Gloucester Terrace the afternoon sun beat in directly, the handsome north-east facades shone white in their long line, each once a house with servants, now divided and re-divided into flats and studios. The copious hanging baskets of flowers under the lamp standards had to be watered more often and more gener-ously. Sam walked to the Gate cinema in Notting Hill for movies, often on a Tuesday when it was half price, not because he needed to save money, but from an old bargain-hunting habit. On the other side of Bayswater Road the park's dense green seemed to absorb the main-road racket and somehow absolve it – the eye making amends for what the ear had to tolerate.

His feline friend Trinnie came and went, was secretly fed, grew fatter and more attached to him. Across the street the little downstairs office opened again after a summer break and the affair between the boss and the secretary grew more overt. She was upstairs more often for breakfast and for whatever else went on there. And then everything changed. The wife (if she was the wife) put in appearances. Sam thought there was a new chill between boss and secretary – no more hands on breasts; no more fondling pauses in the brush-past between desk and filing cabinet. He read a story, stories, in all of this, while acknowledging to himself that they might all, or mostly, be no more than wishful misreadings of the visible but limited facts of the case.

Sam exchanged three-way e-mails with Pete and Geoff, and they developed a new grown-up manner with one another – man-manner, bantering, common ground as chaps in a world where chaps were somewhat frowned upon (even by chaps), and where a slightly shamefaced camaraderie was in order so long as it didn't take itself too seriously or grow resentful that the world was as it was.

He took Letty, his "Perdita" up to Oxford to see a summer Shakespeare of *The Winter's Tale* in the gardens of St John's in which Martin had a small part as the boy prince, Mamillius, with just a few lines to speak. They met Charles and Githa afterwards and congratulated Martin, whose excitement hadn't quite abated, despite his having had to die early in the play and wait until its end to take his bow.

"You're a star in the making," Sam said. "Next time – a bigger part."

"Pity I had to perish off-stage," Martin said.

"Perish" Sam repeated. "Excellent word!'

Iraq was in the air but it wasn't mentioned. It was Charles' and Githa's elephant.

Letty took him to see an all-male cast doing *Richard II* at the Globe. They read it beforehand because she'd found the language of *The Winter's Tale* difficult. In the final act when imprisoned Richard, soon to be murdered, hears music, the actor, as if impromptu, did a few steps of an Elizabethan dance, a pavane or gavotte. At the end, when the cast came out to take their bows, the musicians struck up the same melody and the players reformed to do the same dance. It went on and on, becoming more vigorous, the audience clapping in unison.

As Sam and Letty emerged, both misty-eyed, "Why are we weeping?" Sam asked, laughing.

"Well, it was sad, wasn't it?" she said.

But Sam knew it wasn't the story, it was the dance had had this effect.

It was mid-July when Tony Blair flew to Washington to give a speech to a joint session of Senate and Congress and received seventeen or nineteen (reports varied) standing ovations. He had backed America at war. It was not going well but that meant they loved him all the more. He was the new Churchill, the iron Brit. America could depend upon.

This was in the air when Sam ran into Jake Latimer in the hot summer street coming from the B.B.C. where he had behaved, he said, with restraint "at great cost to my health, physical and mental". Sam had left work early and was heading for the bookshops of Charing Cross Road. Their exchange was brief – Blair, Washington, those standing ovations . . . Exactly as the war was turning uglier it was becoming clearer that almost everything said to justify it had been untrue. Jake grasped Sam's wrist and squeezed. "The bastards," he hissed. "The fucking arseholes. They have no scruples and no honour." And he rushed on.

For more than six months, during which Sam and Ruth became friends, and more than friends, the three million in the Swiss account was scarcely mentioned. Ruth came and went to her brother's house in Notting Hill, often bringing Percy and giving him a run in the park. Sam came there at weekends, and occasionally in the evenings, to help as she worked her way through Reuben's things. He was offered ties, socks, handkerchiefs, shirts. Now and then, when it was something he was especially tempted by and she insisted, he accepted. Sometimes they were purposeful, going through cupboards and drawers, making decisions about what could be thrown out and what might go to charity or be found another home. Other times they just sat and talked and drank coffee or wine together. Mrs Teagle still came for a few hours each week. A gardener spent the mornings of Monday and Thursday keeping the grounds in order. As the year moved on to autumn there were leaves to be swept and burned, fruit trees pruned and something mysterious dug in around the roots of winter perennials.

Still no will had been found, and probate would take time. There were a few surprises – a very large bundle of U.S. banknotes under shirts in one drawer; one of euros, smaller but not insignificant, under socks and handkerchiefs in another; and what appeared to be randomly stashed bundles of sterling notes among papers in Reuben's desk. The desk itself was, as Ruth said, "orderly but unconventional". There were detailed notes from Reuben's reading of biographies of men famous in the world of finance, and with no apparent political preference, right or left – Milton Friedman, John Kenneth Galbraith, Warren Buffett,

Maynard Keynes, J. P. Morgan. The notebook was headed by two quotations, but which pundit or biography they came from, or whether they were Reuben's own observations, neither Ruth nor Sam could guess. One said, "The market always underestimates the likelihood of change." The other: "When options are cheap, invest in the risk."

Ruth was trying to get an understanding of Reuben's dealings on the bond market, but not, she said, making much progress. "He seems to have kept what he did at home separate from what he did at work."

Sam didn't disagree. "But I think he must have used his role at the bank to give himself credibility outside it."

It was a Saturday afternoon. They were just about to give up and take Percy for a walk in Holland Park, and Ruth was packing papers back into their drawers and a filing cabinet.

"He was creating mortgage bonds at work," she said, "and shorting them at home . . . Wasn't he?"

"It's obvious he didn't set much store by the rating agencies. The banks rely on them, so what he did on his own behalf was going to be different."

"It's like betting against yourself."

"In a way."

"He was a gambler."

"I suppose so." He laughed. "It's called investing, isn't it?"

"And if I'm his principal heir – supposing we find a will . . ."

"Or even if you don't . . ."

"I may inherit his losses."

"I guess it's possible. But the premiums wouldn't have been large, because the bond market was supposed to be safe. I don't think you'd be badly damaged." As he said this he was taking into account that her husband was said to be very rich.

"I might have to make use of the Swiss three million."

"You might."

"So we'll leave it where it is, just in case, shall we?"

Again he liked it that she said "we" and pretended to put it as a question which required his consent.

Later, as they strolled down the wide walkway past Kensington Palace, and Percy raced away over the grass after a squirrel, she asked did he still think the Swiss money had come from arms sales.

"I don't know, Ruth. Maybe not. I've begun to wonder whether Kraznahorkai could have been his hedge-fund manager."

"From Prague?"

"It's not impossible."

She had another thought. "The Swiss account might be empty – have you thought of that?"

"It has crossed my mind."

"Hawkeye might have kept a copy of the codes . . ."

"And drained it. It's possible." After a moment he said, "Unlikely though."

"Why? It seems very likely to me."

"But you didn't meet and talk to him. If he'd wanted the money, why would he have bothered to hand over the numbers at all? And the amount's too small."

"Three million is too small?"

"That's my hunch. Mr K. would have dealt in bigger numbers." When she stared at him, unconvinced, he said, "Very big numbers."

And still the envelope remained sealed. For Sam at least – and perhaps for Ruth too – it was no longer a secret hoard waiting to be raided and spent. It was the seal which, if broken, might take away their excuse for being together.

On the afternoon of July 17 the heat was intense. Dr David Kelly, in his Oxfordshire kitchen swallowed, one by one and with difficulty, twenty-nine co-proxamol painkiller tablets. That done, he set off for his usual walk over meadows and into the woods. There at the place he had long ago settled upon, he lay on his left side in the grass and, with a pruning knife, using his right hand, severed the ulnar artery in his left wrist and watched the blood flow. Now he lowered himself right down and, on his back, stared straight up, watching the movement of green leaves against blue sky. David Kelly had been a U.N. weapons inspector in Iraq and had more than once told officials there that if Iraq complied with what the U.N., and now the U.S. and U.K. governments, were requiring, there would be no military attack. He had thought the reports of the weapons inspectors were going to be heeded and would determine peace or war. Now it was clear the reports had only been searched for excuses, justifications for an invasion which it had been decided would happen in any case. Angry and disillusioned, Kelly had agreed to meet a B.B.C. reporter, Andrew Gilligan. In a secret interview he told Gilligan Tony Blair's famous Iraq dossier was a falsehood "sexed up" to justify the war.

Somehow his identity as the source of this interview had been exposed, and yesterday, after a grilling from his employers in the Ministry of Defence, he had been brought before a Select Committee of Parliament and questioned about his actions. His voice had been faint and the air-con was turned off so his answers could be heard. The questioning had been abrasive, hurtful, accusatory, its intent to discredit him, and the reporter, and the B.B.C. – all three together. Today the reporter, Andrew Gilligan, would be questioned by the same committee. David Kelly, bleeding in the

Oxfordshire woods, felt soreness in the wrist he had cut, and a pain, like a heavy weight, in his chest. He felt weary, bitter, embarrassed, disillusioned – and beyond all of that, he felt something deep like grief. There was fear too.

He wished for unconsciousness. He was glad to be dying.

In the heat of this unusual July Tom Roland thought he remained awake; couldn't sleep. But when he considered carefully he recognised there were things in his head, recent happenings, which could only be dreams. Though awake, he must be slipping into sleep to catch a quick dream, like a marathon runner calling without stopping at one feeding station for a drink, at another for a snack, and racing on. So the dark figure who had come to him must have been a dream. "I've been waiting a long time for you," Tom had said.

"Sorry to have kept you waiting," was the reply. "Ready?"

He found the torch on the bedside table, and the waiting notebook and biro. Reading glasses – yes, here. He put them on and, lying on his left side, wrote down what had been given to him. It was almost formless, though now and then, even at this early stage, he noticed a rhyme here, another there, which in the end would define the ends of lines and the overall shape. He had seemed to hear the whole thing as a running rhythm, a series of connected sounds that shaped themselves almost into a melody that continued the lines written so many weeks ago and memorised. When he had a first draft down he lay back and fell into a deep sleep.

When he next woke the illuminated numbers of the bedside clock showed 3.35. He had slept soundly for an hour and a half. He could remember nothing of what he had written – not a word. This was something learned long ago. If an idea or a line came to him in the night he had to force himself to wake – enough, anyway, to make a note of it at once or it would be lost.

He got up, made himself a mug of tea and took it, together with the notebook and biro, to the little table in the sitting room. The window was open wide and the sound of the river came up to him as he turned on the lamp and began to read what the devil had given him. He could see at once where this draft took off from the half a poem brooded over so long. He went to work on it while earliest light began creeping in to the eastern sky. By the time it was full morning the lines were taking their proper shape. He felt an extraordinary, calm contentment. He had waited so long for this – so patiently, sure that it would come. He worked on, only polishing now. In the end there was nothing more to be done. It was finished.

He sat staring at it in the growing light. Strange that his man from Porlock should have come back. No – rather, it was strange he should have gone away, and come back. Tom's devil. It occurred to him he'd forgotten to ask was there a price? There had been no mention of one, so he supposed none was due. It was a gift. How extraordinary! Maybe a bill would be sent later.

He read it over, only needing to glance now and then at his own writing –

> Famine was somewhere, somewhere else
> Two bullets in the head;
> Far from his care tall stadiums
> Cast shadows on the dead;

But Tom in the land of Big Ideas
Grew full of sensitive weathers,
Counting chickens before they hatched,
Banking on feathers.

A hot rain falls on the rolling earth,
In office the Dog's obeyed.
For men whose brains breed weakling chicks
Coops are made.

A cold wind blows on the rolling earth,
Poor Tom's a-cold in his brain:
The chicken is plucked that sang heigh-ho
The wind and the rain.

He was satisfied – thought he was pleased. And he saw in these new lines a title for the whole poem: "Banking on Feathers". He would offer it somewhere. Perhaps that high-brow literary mag – something beginning with A – that Sam Nola had brought back from Oxford. Or the *T.L.S.*, why not?

Yes – to hell with it! – he'd try the *T.L.S.*; send it after a week or so, when he'd given himself time to get used to it and feel sure about it.

Right, then, the *T.L.S.* He'd give them a chance to do themselves a favour!

Sam was woken by Ruth in what she called "little brother's big bed". She was looking out the window at the moonlit garden. "It's the foxes. Look."

He pulled himself up beside her, put an arm over her shoulder and peered out. He could see the young foxes rolling over like two dogs having a pretend fight. One stopped to scratch and the other chased its own tail.

"I heard Percy growling downstairs. He must hear them."

"Or smell them."

They kissed. She ran her hands over his cheeks and down his arms, around his back. "Men in their forties have such lovely skin."

"Fifty's just around the corner."

"I'm not far behind you, Sammy."

"You're forty-two, for God's sake. And probably eternal – aren't you?"

"Probably."

He ran a hand lightly over her breasts. There was a long, palpable silence.

"Golden lads," she murmured. "How does it go?"

"Golden lads and girls all must . . ."

"Like chimney sweepers come to dust . . . Oh."

The "Oh" was in response to what he was doing with his fingers.

"You like that?"

"Mmm."

She slid down on to her back, pulling him with her.

The Prime Minister in first class, plugs in his ears and a mask over his eyes, was trying to catch some sleep in the hours between Washington and Tokyo. But excitement kept him awake, going over in his mind his speech to the joint houses. It had been a triumph. He had been annoyed at first at the White House asking to see the speech in advance, and wanting modifications. It meant the stuff about trying to involve Syria and Iran in a resolution to the Iraq question had had to come out. Barely a mention, despite the fact that Alastair had alerted the press to expect it. That would have been Cheney getting his oar into it. He would have thought it too conciliatory – and perhaps it was. Cheney wanted Syria thumped. Iran too – especially Iran – "Now, before it's too late."

But then when it came to the speech it hardly mattered what was in it. With all the jumping up and down they did, one standing ovation after another, there was hardly space to develop an argument. And how wonderful to be so appreciated, so loved! Not like at home where your own party turns on you and you have to look to the other bastards for appreciation.

He drifted towards sleep, seeing the eager faces, feeling the warm hands reaching out to touch his sleeve . . .

But the warm hand on his sleeve was Alastair's. "Sorry to disturb you, Tony."

The Prime Minister pulled the mask down and unplugged his ears. "What is it, Al?"

"Seriously shitty news from the office."

"O.K. Let's hear it."

"Walter Mitty's topped himself."

"You're . . . No, you're not . . ."

"Joking? No."

"Walter Mitty" was the name they'd given to the weapons inspector David Kelly, who had told the B.B.C. they had cooked up the case for going to war.

"Took himself off to the woods and slit his wrists. Wrist, actually. The bastard's so bloodless it only took one. That's tomorrow's front page, Tone. Your speech will be somewhere inside."

He sat up, sighing heavily, and rubbed his hands over his face. What to do? "Will you do me a statement, Al? Something I can say when we get off the plane at – wherever it is."

"Tokyo. It's Tokyo, T. Yes I'll do that. You'd better get some sleep – you're buggered aren't you?"

"Don't know that I can. Anything else?"

"Only Manningham-Buller. The 'we've radicalised every young Muslim in Britain' dirge."

"Soothe her down if you can, Al. We don't want her leaking stuff like that. That's the lot?"

"Yes . . . No. Well, there's . . ."

"What?"

Al put his head close to the P.M.'s ear. "N313P." It was the number of the Boeing business jet the C.I.A. used for "extraordinary rendition" of kidnapped prisoners, sometimes through Britain. There were beginning to be sightings, reports, questions.

"I don't need to know this, do I?"

"I don't think you do. No." Al straightened up. "Like a drink? Cup of tea? Bicky?"

The Prime Minister shook his head and pulled the blanket up over his shoulders. "Nothing thanks Al. Just write me a few words about Kelly. Nice and neutral, you know? We'd better sound as if we care."

Ruth could get away for one night every now and then. Two seemed to need plausible explanation and made her nervous. But there was what in New Zealand would have been called a bach – one of a dozen or perhaps twenty flimsy beach cottages, hardly more than huts, on the road between Whitstable and Faversham. Reuben had taken women friends there – called it his "getaway, bolthole and rumblepad" – and now it was Ruth's and Sam's. There was what the maps designated as the "Saxon seawall", originally an earth barrier, massive now, heightened and reinforced over centuries and recently, in some sections, with concrete. On its landward side were deep marshes, and beyond those, farms which were what it must first have been constructed to protect. On the seaward side wooden groynes ran out at intervals of fifty or a hundred yards, protecting stony beaches from winds, tide-rush and storms. Over miles of mud-flats patched with green weed the tide advanced to within twenty metres of the makeshift cottages and then almost at once, and visibly, began its retreat, ultimately all but emptying the enormous bay. At low water the lug-wormers trudged out with their digging forks and buckets, Wordsworthian figures in the haze, harvesting bait for commercial long-line fishermen. Flocks of gulls came and went. White cranes flew in, their aerodynamically inconvenient beaked spears pointing ahead. At full tide the sea was often shadowy with schools of small fish that flashed silver through the water, or broke the surface, as they were harassed and herded by larger predators below. On warmer days Sam bathed and Ruth watched, cheering or mocking as he plunged or, shivering, hesitated. Even a hundred yards out the water came only to his thighs, but he claimed to have once swum out to where it was over his head. They slept on a futon on the floor, ate picnic lunches, and dined at local pubs – the Sportsman close by, the Three Mariners further afield towards Faversham. It was somewhere to go and be alone together, undisturbed. It was silent at night; and from earliest light you could look away into the far distance (that was the great bonus when you came from London), across the sea or its vast absence, until a headland emerged away to the left out of the haze and straight ahead, the ghostly-white giant wind turbines did their semaphore (or were they shouldering arms?) on the horizon. Sam liked waking and lifting the curtains to look out across the green-gold of the short plants that grew up through the stones, over the dark mud, to the blue sea and the pale sky patched with pink and streaked with early jet trails. Neighbours in the line of cottages behaved with the discretion proximity most often enforces, willing to talk if the signals suggested talk might be welcome, or equally to behave as if the tide of human company had also gone out and there was no-one. Their immediate neighbour, when he was in, was always determinedly occupied. Even at leisure he was busy. He kayaked, swam, sailed, fished, with a different set of gear for each; or read books on kayaking, swimming, sailing, fishing on his little deck; or raked the horizon with binoculars, as if the only things to be seen were far away. Often Sam and Ruth were the only ones there.

At the end of that year Letty had completed her graduate course at Great Ormond Street and would soon return to Paris. Sam wanted her to know that he and Ruth were lovers. Perhaps she did know, or at least had guessed, but it had not been acknowledged between them. They were in Lamb's Conduit Street not far from the children's hospital, and heading for Ciao Bella where he'd booked a table for two.

Letty absorbed the information with a nod of the head. "It's not surprising. I knew someone would fall in love with you."

"That I would fall in love with someone."

"That too." There was no hint of disapproval, but she was curious. After they had been shown to their places and made their choices she said, "Ruth and her husband – he's very old isn't he?"

Sam laughed. "Yes, if you think there needs to be an explanation, Sir Frank is old. Very old. A fossil. *Un croûte*."

"*Une croûte*," she corrected.

"But he's a male.

"Yes, but '*croûte*' is feminine."

"So you can't use it of a man?"

"Yes, why not? If Sir Frank is '*une croûte*' that means he's . . ."

"An old fogey?"

"Yes."

Sam shook his head and raised his glass. "*Vive la langue française!*"

And no, she said, ignoring this mild mockery and returning to the point: it wasn't that she thought anything needed explaining. "*Pas du tout.*"

The waiter returned with bread, the wine they had ordered, the cutlery they would need. When he was gone Sam said, "I'm sure Ruth's very fond of him. But he's not well. There are a lot of things he can't do . . ."

"You mean sex."

"Well, a lot of things – walking uphill, climbing stairs. He gets about in a wheelchair. She's his nurse, you know? And yes, I suppose sex too."

"So you are Lady Chatterley's lover."

"If you like, Letty darling. If you insist. You can call me Mellors."

"Mellors. I think that's good."

"It's good for me."

"And for Lady Chatterley."

"And for her too, yes."

"Does he know?"

"It's hard to say what he knows. He hasn't been told and he hasn't asked. He's very civil to me in his noisy way."

"Noisy, did you say?"

"He's deaf so he shouts."

"Ah *oui*."

"And he has a very loud voice."

"Old and noisy."

They laughed. "You see," he said, "even your papa has to be an improvement."

She put a hand over his. "*Mon papa est hors ligne*."

"I'm not sure what that means, but I suspect flattery."

"It means you are very special."

He rearranged his cutlery. When he looked up he said, "I hope I haven't made my affair with Ruth sound . . ." He wasn't sure what word to choose.

"It sounds very nice," she said.

"I didn't want my new daughter to disapprove."

"She doesn't. She's pleased for you, Papa."

He nodded – a kind of thank-you nod. "I think I'm a bit scared of it."

"Of Sir Frank?"

"No no. Not at all. Of *it*. Of myself."

She squeezed his hand again. "Don't be scared. People only die of love in books."

He laughed. "I love you, Letty and for sure I won't die of that. It's life-enhancing. How am I going to do without you when you go back to Paris?"

"I'm going to miss you too. We have to stay close, with just the Channel between. That's what this is for."

She pushed a small parcel across the table. When he opened it he recognised a BlackBerry. He'd never had one – had mostly avoided even an ordinary mobile phone, not wanting to be more available than a landline and e-mail already made him.

"You're very kind Letty darling, but I haven't the faintest idea how to use these things."

"I'm going to teach you. Lesson number one is now."

THE CLUSTERFUCK

10

TAVISTOCK SQUARE

THE DAY AFTER TOM ROLAND RECEIVED WORD FROM THE *T.L.S.* that it was accepting his poem he was blown up on a bus in Tavistock Square. It was July 7, 2005, the day the G8 conference opened at Gleneagles in Scotland. No-one knew what Tom was doing in that place at that time. Almost two years had passed since he had sent the poem and he'd long since given up any hope of a positive response, or any response at all. In the old days, when he'd been young and hopeful and sent poems to Alan Ross for the *London Magazine*, there had always been a reply within a week or so, often just a rejection slip saying "THE EDITOR REGRETS" though usually with a few extra words, hand-written, sometimes encouraging or with suggestions of things to be avoided or changed. Once only there had been an acceptance – two poems, one a sonnet, the other a little love poem to Hermione called, in fact, "A Little Love Poem to Hermione" together with a clerihew in French written after a holiday there –

> *Les Baux*
> *c'est beau*
> *mais Beaulieu*
> *c'est mieux.*

There had been a few other poems published in those long-ago days, one in the *Listener*, another (of a vaguely leftist tendency) in *Stand*. The one in *Stand*, written at the time of the Vietnam war, was the latest to be published, after which fatherhood, paid employment, boardroom boredom – nothing so lurid as "shades of the prison house" but rather (as he liked to say) "life in all its pallid pastel shades" – had closed upon Tom Roland. Not that there were no poems; they came, sometimes like summer flies, pestering him; and when they didn't he was depressed and felt worthless. But confidence, belief in himself and in them, the products of his own hand and brain, was gone. Perhaps his diabetes had something to do with it. He wondered what daily doses of insulin were doing to his mental powers. And then there was alcohol. He had never been alcoholic – or anyway had declined to adopt the (as it seemed to him) self-important label. But there had been times when he'd abused it; and times of something close to dependence.

In recent years a poem now and then had gone out on offer – the rest had gone immediately into the bottom drawer, or the drawer above the bottom drawer now that the bottom one was full – the region he inwardly referred to ironically as "the Archive" comically as Bolgia One and Bolgia Two, and in bankers' terms as the first and second tranche.

As for the ones offered, these were not so much rejected as swallowed whole, "disappeared" (in the active not the passive sense), dropped from the editorial helicopter over the ocean like leftists under the juntas in Chile or Argentina. Editors these days had given up on the old-fashioned courtesy of an acknowledgement. Tom thought it might be an effect of courses in Creative Writing. There were now so many, and young people in unprecedented numbers were being "taught to write" and encouraged to offer their work for publication. He had heard about publishers' slush piles where unwanted and "un-agented" work was thrown, only glanced at or, very often, unread. That was where he supposed his poem had gone – into the black hole of the *T.L.S.*, on to its infinite "slush pile", the literary pauper's grave; and though he still liked the poem when he ran it through in his head in the night, still thought it one of his best and thanked the Devil, Monsieur le Noir, or whoever that dark figure had been, he knew, or thought he knew, he would never see it in print.

Then, after a year of waiting, and another of giving up on the idea that he was waiting, had come the letter which he felt changed his life; altered his view of himself and his plans for the future. It was in his pocket the day the bomb went off. It was, Hermione believed, what must have taken him away from his usual course on the morning of July 7. The letter came from Mick Imlah, the poetry editor, thanking him for his poem, telling him they would be using it soon, and enclosing a proof which he had at once marked and returned. It had been such a shock, such a boost, Tom had begun to think seriously about retirement from the bank. He and Hermione had talked about it late into the night of July 6. Perhaps after all he was not such a hopeless case. Ideas still came freely enough, and words and images. Perhaps – how could one know? – the best lay ahead. He could retire and give himself to writing; give it the time and thought and application it deserved.

She encouraged him. The bank hours were long, they didn't need the money, and everyone agreed he should long ago have been away from the trading floor, where stress burned out much younger men. Now he could assure himself that retirement would not be directionless, boring and unoccupied. There were cases, he had himself told her of several – U. A. Fanthorpe, for example – of writers who had begun late in life and made a go of it. Succeed or fail, it wouldn't matter, he would have a new aim, a new enterprise.

So all this must have been on his mind that morning when he set off apparently for work and didn't go there. How he came to be on a bus in Tavistock Square she didn't know, but it was, as everyone would say, "the wrong place at the wrong time". It was the last of four explosions that morning; the other three were on the Underground. Fifty-two people had been killed or would die, thirteen of them on Tom's bus.

On the morning of the explosions there were rumours – something had happened on the Underground. A power surge was what Sam heard first. Someone had seen a helicopter – possibly police, but it looked more like army – hovering over Piccadilly. When Sam's private line rang in the office it was Ruth, checking that he was alright. "There's been an explosion on the Tube."

"I didn't know. Yes, I'm fine thanks darling. Box of . . . you know?"

At just that moment Willard Bukowski came in to tell him there had been not one bomb but two – the second just reported.

"There's been a second," he told Ruth. "On the Piccadilly line."

"Don't come home on the Tube."

"I don't imagine it'll be running."

"I'll come for you."

"No don't do that. I'll find a way – taxi, or hitch a lift."

"Well, take care."

"I will. You too Ruthie."

When news of a third bomb came he called Letty in Paris to tell her he was safe. He didn't get her, but left a message. Half an hour later she sent him a text. She'd got his message and told him, mimicking him mimicking her, "'old on to your 'at, Sam-pa, and don't take risks'.

As the morning went on the staff gathered around television sets, drifted back to their desks, but kept returning. The three explosions had occurred on the Underground between 8.30 and 9.00; a fourth about an hour later on a bus. There was some small talk about who could, or who might, be held responsible for this, and what the consequences might be; but the politics of it was mostly avoided. Sam allowed himself to say that his daughter in Paris was safe, "Thanks to Chirac". No-one was disposed to argue. Mostly people worried about getting home.

Around midday the P.M. issued a statement from Gleneagles. He would be coming down to London to get reports "face to face with police and emergency services". The bombs, he said, had been timed to coincide with the G8 conference, and he thought it was "particularly barbaric" that this outrage had been unleashed on a day when they were "meeting to try to solve problems of poverty in Africa and the long-term effects of climate change". Britain and the world could be assured that he was determined "to defend our values and our way of life".

No mention of Iraq – no suggestion the one might be because of the other. "He's doing his outrage thing," Sam said to Willard Bukowski as they stood side by side watching.

Willard said nothing. He was a loyal American. He knew that tone when he heard it; had grown to recognise it in the past few months. "Just smile and say nothing" was his policy. Willard smiled and said nothing.

Late in the afternoon Sam set off for home. The Docklands Light Railway was running as far as Tower Hill. After that there was nothing – neither Tube nor buses, and the only taxis he saw had passengers already. He walked through Eastcheap, King William Street, past St Paul's and on through Holborn and Oxford Street. The streets were full of people walking. Tired at the end of a day's work, they trudged silently along. Now and then there was an exchange between strangers, and an outbreak of cheerfulness. No-one complained. Everyone was "being good about it", being patient, making allowances. Sam could see how it must have been in the Blitz. Yet this was London of a new century. These were not just "the bulldog breed", the English, the Brits. They were multi-coloured and multi-lingual, and there was the same stolid acceptance. It must be London, its collective character. Or maybe just humankind, faced with a crisis and coping.

Halfway along Oxford Street he called Ruth at Reuben's house and suggested she meet him at a Greek restaurant on Moscow Road. When he reached it half an hour later she was waiting at a table by the window. By now he had received anxious messages from Pete and Geoff in New Zealand and replied with reassuring ones; and there had been another exchange with Letty in Paris. All this on foot, and through streets that still sounded to him, when he ran through their names, like a map of the old Monopoly board of his childhood. Same names but a new, strange world of sudden death and instant communication.

Ruth hugged him. "I'm so relieved to see you."

They gave their orders, and Sam unleashed a weary mixture of politics and indignation – mostly against Tony Blair for the smooth interweaving of truth and lies; for the self-justification and self-righteousness; for the pretence that these bombs had nothing to do with Iraq – as if they had indeed been set off as a protest again the Gleneagles summit. "He's afraid of the Madrid effect."

"Of course."

Of course? He heard her tone as if she'd been delicately mocking him – but perhaps she wasn't. He asked, "Am I being a bore?"

"Not at all."

"Too impassioned? Too serious?"

"These are serious times."

There was a pause before he said, "I used to admire Reuben's detachment. You have it too." He was remembering Reuben saying he didn't care about being lied to so long as he knew it was a lie.

She said, "There's a force out there might have killed you, and it didn't – so hooray!"

"I'm pleased too, honey – believe me." His tone was ironic now, as he thought hers had been – but that was all. He could imagine them falling into a habit of quarrelling, as Charles and Githa were doing, as he and Ngaio had done.

In a moment they were talking about other things. He had moved to a flat in Maida Vale. It was on the second floor of a mansion block in Lauderdale Road, with two bedrooms, two bathrooms, a kitchen big enough to include a table, a spacious sitting and dining room with a balcony overlooking a street lined with plane trees. Not all the rooms were furnished yet and Ruth was helping him make choices.

Their main course arrived and they were eating it when a call came. It was good old "smile and say nothing" Bukowski with the news about Tom Roland.

Tom Roland hadn't died. He was in the upper section of the bus and it was there the bomber exploded his device. Tom had been near the front where a number of people survived. He had tumbled into the street. He suffered cuts, abrasions, a broken leg, cracked ribs, and concussion. He was taken, unconscious, to University College Hospital. His wallet identified him and after a lapse of some hours Hermione was called and taken in a wailing police car to his bedside. That day and the next, as full consciousness returned, Tom had no recollection of the explosion, none of being on the bus or how he came to be there. Even the letter of acceptance from the *T.L.S.* was only faintly recalled, so the shock of pleasure was given a re-run, and the poem itself had to be re-read and re-remembered.

He read it over slowly, and marvelled. "So I wrote this," he said.

Hermione assured him. "You did, darling. You said the Devil gave it to you."

"Ah yes I did. That's right."

"You called him Monsieur le Noir."

"Monsieur le Noir. I like that. He did well. Let's hope I see more of him."

"So long as this is not the price."

"The price?"

"You know – don't they say the Devil exacts a price?"

Tom didn't seem to mind that thought. There was a sort of shrug of the shoulders and then a wince because it gave him pain. "Never thought I'd make the *T.L.S.*" He closed his eyes, thinking about it. "Remember all those years ago when that nice little hand-written note came from Alan Ross accepting my poems."

"He invited you to lunch."

"He had a little prefab office at the back of a house – somewhere in Thurloe Place. He took me to his favourite Italian restaurant. Stephen Spender was there – they were old friends. We had pastas and drank a bottle of that Italian pink bubbly –

Lambrusco. He said it was really a picnic wine, but he loved it – had it with lunch every day. Afterwards, when we were out on the street Spender's bus went by, going slowly around a corner and Stephen jumped onto the platform – fell into the bus and then got up and waved to us so we could see he wasn't hurt. I must send him a note about this. He'll be pleased for me."

"Stephen Spender?"

"No darling, he's dead. I meant Alan Ross."

"He's dead too, Tommy."

"Is he really?"

"We went to his funeral. Three or four years ago." When he still looked puzzled she said, "In Sussex."

"Of course. So we did." Talk of a funeral shifted his thoughts. "I heard someone say there were others hurt. Killed, were they?"

"Yes. But you don't need to think about that just now, Tom."

"Was it very bad?"

"Four bombs altogether."

"Not as bad as Madrid, was it?"

"Not on that scale, Tom."

"Tell me. Give me the numbers."

"Well, fifty anyway. And nearly eight hundred injured."

"Jesus! What in God's name do they imagine they're doing?"

He seemed to doze for a few minutes, and then opened his eyes, remembering something. "Did you ever hear of a singer called Judy Campbell? Apparently she was famous during World War Two for singing 'A Nightingale Sang in Berkeley Square'. He told us . . ."

"Who, Tom?"

"Alan Ross. He told Stephen Spender and me that she'd been

his girlfriend, and she actually sang that song to him in Berkeley Square."

He hummed the melody, and drifted towards sleep.

Sam and Charles have crossed the Rainbow Bridge and are walking along the Port Meadow tow path heading for the Trout where they will drink a pint or two for old times' sake while looking down at the water rushing by. The sky is pale and high, the air clear and fresh. Autumn has moved past its "season of mists and mellow fruitfulness" without having quite achieved winter. It is good walking weather, dry underfoot. They find themselves briefly among a herd of cattle at the water's edge. They and the animals more or less ignore each other, the humans finding their way through and around, though Sam, putting a hand briefly on a passing haunch, enjoys the feel of the warm furry pelt under his palm, and the smells of bovine breath and bovine effluent.

They go past the poplars at Binsey. Long ago, Charles points out – not in the last century but the one before that – an unhappy priest, Gerard Manley Hopkins, wrote a poem lamenting that these trees had been cut down. "And now look at them."

They are high and healthy, rustle-rattling in a light breeze in the way poplars do.

Sam says, "And God said to the poplars, 'Talk among yourselves,' and they did so, and God heard that it was good."

He is only recently returned from taking Letty on a flying visit to New Zealand. It was for the wedding of Kevin and Ngaio, and to introduce Letty to her half brothers and her grandparents. He and Charles talk about that in a shorthand of place names and people names that need no gloss because they are the common ground of their early years. Charles, Sam notices, is eagerly interested but also resistant – fascinated and fearful – the expatriate who doesn't want the wall he has built between his beginnings and where he is now eroded. So they touch on the subject and leave it; leave it and return. How was the weather? (lovely, early summer); Where was the wedding? (Waiheke Island, in a vineyard); How were relations with the ex? (nervous, but not too bad) – all of this brief, touch-and-go, and then they are away, off on a different tack altogether, Charles explaining that his new academic interest, the one he hopes will give him a new book, is in the second half of the nineteenth century, when Britain's late *Imperium* looked for a war in which to assert and confirm its glory, and stumbled instead into the mud and mayhem of World War One. Rupert Brooke's sonnet, "The Soldier" was what it was supposed to be like – heroic. Wilfred Owen's "Dulce et decorum est" was what it was like in reality – sordid.

But it's the half century up to the Great War that especially interests Charles. "It was a time of storytelling. Not just Kipling. There was Wells, Stevenson, Chesterton and Belloc, Conan Doyle, Rider Haggard, Conrad. They dominated. That's what I want to write about. There's a special kind of confidence."

"Ah yes," Sam says. "Confidence. The mystery ingredient."

"Forster's in there too, though he's different – arrives a bit later, and uneasy about everything. He's on the fault line."

They have stopped and are watching the Godstow Lock filling for a passing houseboat. Sam says, "When I was living in Islington all those years ago I read a lot of Forster. I admired him; but then I developed a taste for the big Americans . . ."

"Bellow?"

"No, it was Mailer."

"Ah, Mailer. And of course, you were writing . . ."

"My thriller." Sam laughs naming it. "*Damn Your Eyes*."

"Good title. What happened to it?"

"Lost in the post. I'm sure I told you that."

Charles laughs. "Oh yes – the agent stung to death by Argentinian bees. You made that up of course."

"Central American. It's what I was told."

They walk on in silence, and then Charles asks again about the New Zealand visit. Sam tells how he hired a car and drove Letty with Pete and Geoff down to meet their grandparents at Papamoa, stopping off at Rotorua on the way so Letty could see a geyser and some boiling mud. Charles doesn't ask about the Rotorua stop. He just says "Papamoa . . ." and Sam knows he is seeing a many-miles-long line of white sand, a blue sea with waves breaking.

Now the silence they observe is the inner one of enjoying the walk and the random insignificant thoughts that come with it, putting one foot in front of the other, leaving the poplars behind, passing the line of strange, seated river creatures in oilskins with very long rods, rubber waders, nets and bait boxes, who are trying to catch fish so small the two walkers wonder – have often wondered and asked one another – why they bother? What is the mystery here?

They are outside the ruins of Godstow Abbey, going past its crumbling wall, when Sam remembers Tom Roland, and mentions that he's recovering from his injuries, has retired from the bank, plans to write more poems but is "waiting for the return of his Devil".

Charles has read the poem in the *T.L.S.* and thought it was "Not bad. Adroit," he says. "That ballady sort of thing – not easy to do it well."

Sam says, "When Willard Bukowski called with the news I was with Ruth in a restaurant. I felt such a surge of anger, and then I didn't know who to be angry with – Bush and Blair, or the bombers. And then I thought, fuck it, I'm angry with them all, because they're all religious, and they think their pieties justify acts of violence."

Charles nods and utters an affirmative hum which seems to mean, not quite "I agree", but something like "I hear you".

By the time they reach the Trout and buy their beers and take them out into the garden where peacocks are strolling about, parading their astonishing green tails, they have returned to the subject of Kipling, and the Great War that killed his only son, and a poem he wrote about it which Charles likes so much he has it by heart, and quotes above the sound of the stream rushing over the weir.

> "Have you news of my boy Jack?"
> *Not this tide.*
> "When d'you think that he'll come back?"
> *Not with this wind blowing, and this tide.*
>
> "Has anyone else had word of him?"
> *Not this tide.*
> *For what is sunk will hardly swim,*
> *Not with this wind blowing, and this tide.*
>
> "Oh dear, what comfort can I find?"
> *None this time,*
> *Nor any tide,*
> *Except he did not shame his kind –*
> *Not even with that wind blowing, and that tide.*

Then hold your head up all the more.
This tide,
And every tide;
Because he was the son you bore,
And gave to that wind blowing, and that tide!

Sam is moved, even though some part of him thinks he shouldn't be; or at least that his feelings about the poem should be mixed. "It's good," he says. "Sad." And they observe a silence that is a kind of respect, until Charles recalls something else about Kipling. "He said something really nice about our home town – remember?"

"He did." And together (half-ironic, but in unison now – as they were all those years ago in Auckland) they chant, "Last, loneliest, loveliest, exquisite, apart, / On us, on us the unswerving season smiles."

"Did it smile?"

"Mostly. There was some rain, some wind, a lot of sun – a bit of everything. The usual Auckland mix."

"And you got on alright with Ngaio's new man?"

"Kevin? When I was leaving we shook hands. I said 'Die you bastard.'"

"And?"

"He said, 'You too, cunt.'"

Charles laughs. "So you parted friends. That's good."

11

BAGHDAD

THE MATTER OF REUBEN LEVESON'S WILL, OR RATHER the lack of one, and the fact that there was a great deal of money and significant property which in the end would form the total bequest, meant that probate, and decisions about inheritance, were taking a long time. Documents were needed; and once found and supplied, there seemed always a subsequent request for more, or other. If Ruth, assumed to be the only beneficiary, had urged the lawyers to get on with it, things might have moved more quickly; but she was in no hurry to see an end to the process, happy to use uncertainties as an explanation for the time it was taking, and meanwhile to have her brother's house in Notting Hill as a place where she and Sam could meet. Mrs Teagle was quietly assumed into an understanding of their liaison. Nothing was assumed about the gardener except that he was a man of so few words, discretion of a kind (principally silence) could be counted on.

André Kraznahorkai's envelope had still not been unsealed when Sam, dealing with another matter on Interbank America's behalf, came on a reference to a company registered in the Cayman Islands and calling itself "Hawkeye Holdings, a subsidiary of Eaglegold Inc." It was a hedge fund dealing in very large sums of money. It called to Sam's mind Reuben's nick-name for Mr K. He and Ruth agreed over dinner that evening that it was time to look into the Swiss account. They were ready, or tried to be ready, to find it empty.

The bank was Credit Suisse and there was nothing very complicated about gaining access. The account held more than six million U.S. dollars.

They rechecked. There was no mistake. It was even possible to trace an initial deposit of $3,270,000 and watch how it had grown by a series of three-monthly disbursements from Eaglegold, whose insignia, the Habsburgs' double eagle, sat where, in documents of André Kraznahorkai's younger days, there would have been the hammer and sickle. He must have enjoyed the irony of that – and his hedge fund was scoring.

Sam, who was still, but only slowly, getting used to the size of the bundles of money being made in the brave new world of banking, said, "A healthy return," and laughed.

"Even in death," Ruth said, "my little brother goes on making money."

Sam was also making money – not on that scale, but more than he had ever made before. The salary was good; but it was the bonuses pushed his bank credit up to levels he tried to take for granted but couldn't be other than faintly embarrassed by. He was learning more all the time about the mechanics by which banks were earning so much on what was called "the sell side" of the financial markets. It was something to be marvelled at.

In some part of his mind he worried – but less about whether it was "right" than about how long it could go on.

He paid off his mortgage on the Maida Vale flat, bought himself good clothes, ate in good restaurants, became a Friend of the Royal Opera House and of the E.N.O., and gave himself expensive holidays. He thought about a club, decided he couldn't see himself at the Savile or its like, and thought about the Groucho, or Soho House, which Ruth told him were more informal; but enquiries left him unsure he would be welcome in either, and he gave up the idea. He helped his sons in New Zealand, and tried to help Letty in Paris, though she was resistant, saying the French government and health system were looking after her very well. Still in pursuit of competence in French he was discovering a Paris he hadn't known before, elegant, arrogant, expensive and hard to resist. There, as in parts of London too, he felt affluent, a person of consequence, or at least of "means", and though he disapproved of all this, and scolded himself, he enjoyed it. If there was an anxiety went along with it, a sense of precariousness, well, there was always anxiety – it was part of his temperament. And he had always known, since that long-ago O.E., that he would never quite belong or feel entirely at ease in England.

As the war in Iraq dragged on, costly in everything from human life to wealth that could have been so much better spent, he found himself trying to see it as the result of something large like Fate – an accident on a monumental scale. Bush and Blair of course, their wills, their mendacious, God-bothering egos, had a lot, had everything, to do with it; but they were themselves accidents, outcomes of events which might have been otherwise – the death of John Smith in Britain, the hanging chads in Florida. It was a way of damping down the indignation that otherwise burned you up and bored others who didn't feel it; and he began to approach, though not quite to achieve, something like the cool, the detachment, he'd admired in Reuben and now recognised in Ruth.

For Charles and Githa, on the other hand, Iraq was still a

subject that divided them. For Githa the revelations of torture in Abu Ghraib prison, and the eventual acknowledgement that there had been no W.M.D.s, had closed the argument. There was nothing more to be said. But Charles, still loyal to Blair and New Labour, found new reasons for the war. Blair (he argued now) had seen Neil Kinnock lose favour with America, and therefore with the Murdoch press, and when Murdoch had turned against him so had the public. That was Charles's line now: Blair was saving the Party. Yes, bad things had happened, and the reasons given for going to war had been less than accurate or honest. It was a pity, but poor Tony: he'd had no choice.

"So Iraqis die to save the British Labour Party?" Githa said, and the subject changed and was not allowed to return.

But Sam still caught echoes of all this from young Martin, who had begun to have a grasp on the lines of the argument, and who sided with his mother. He would say to Sam, "The boxing gloves were out last night."

"About . . ."

"The usual," and they would move on to something else. Some minutes later Martin might say, "Dad's insane, of course" – to which no answer from Sam, positive or negative, would have seemed proper.

No longer the little kid, but not yet quite the young man, Martin was still interested in the natural world that Oxford offered, but seemed in some ways to have exhausted it and spent more time in books. "He needs a spell in New Zealand," Sam told Charles, and saw his friend, the determined expatriate, close down on the suggestion.

"He's doing fine right where he is," Charles said.

"Of course he is," Sam said. "No worries, Edna."

Now and then Sam was persuaded to come to dinner at Ruth's house in Hampstead. "I want my daughters to know you better," she said. "I don't want you to emerge a complete stranger out of the shadows when the time comes."

"When the time comes" could only mean when the ancient husband, the grandee in the wheelchair, crossed the eternal threshold. Meanwhile, to be at a dinner party with him was a challenge Sam had to rise to. The twins, Cynthia and Lucy, seemed to go out of their way to put him at ease. Perhaps they knew, or suspected, what was going on in their mother's life and didn't disapprove; or perhaps it was just natural charm.

Sir Frank himself was a puzzle. Often he seemed to occupy a different space, the departure lounge; but now and then he came right back, even alert, with a penetrating light in the eye.

"You're Sam Nola," he said in one of these. "I think I hear a lot about you, don't I?"

"Do you, sir?" Sam said. "I hope it's all good. Or not too bad."

"Memory's not great, but I'm pretty sure if it was bad I'd remember."

"Yes I'm sure you would," Sam said, though the opposite seemed as likely.

"You and Ruth, you are . . ." Whatever he'd meant to ask, Sir Frank's question faded at the brink and he looked bewildered. Perhaps the question remained, but had coincided with the recognition that it couldn't be asked.

Sam thought of saying, "Ruth and I are friends" or "We're colleagues" but in that instant a better idea came to him. "Ruth and I are have been talking about going to Wimbledon. What do you think?"

Sir Frank's face cleared, brightened. "Excellent idea. Don't know why they hold it in June. Always rains. They have plans for a roof, you know? Centre Court. But why not just change the, ah . . . The whatsitsname?"

"Date?"

"Time of year, yes."

"Come on Daddy, time for dins." That was Cynthia (or was it Lucy?), shaking him up and beating him into shape like an old pillow, preparatory to wheeling him to the table.

"Don't," he said. "*Don't* – you're a brute, both of you." But he seemed more tickled than hurt.

Settled around the table, he said, looking at Sam again, "Ruth's young brother knew what he was about. Such a grip on these collateralised debt things."

Ruth said, "Sam worked with him, Frank."

"If we'd had longer working together," Sam said, "I suspect I'd have a better handle on the bond market now – or I would have got there more quickly. With the new man, Bukowski, everything moves rather sedately. But I'm a lawyer, not a banker."

"I have three sons," Sir Frank said. "None of them went in for banking. Joel's about your age. How old are you? Fiftyish? The other two are older. One's a doctor, one's a lawyer, and one's at the races." He laughed at his own joke. "That's Joel. Joel's at the races."

Sam said he had a daughter in medicine – a paediatrician in Paris.

"My Noah's in O. & G. Ladies' man. O. & G. and jazz. Gets the jazz part from me. You like jazz, Nola?"

Sam nodded, smiling. Should he mention his new passion for opera – or would that seem to be putting jazz in its place? And then there was the awkwardness of Wagner and anti-Semitism . . .

"Count Basie," a twin said. "Big bands – that's what Daddy loves. The big band sound."

"My kind of music," Sir Frank confirmed. "Autumn in Paris." And he made a humming sound which was perhaps the tune his head was nodding to.

At the end of the evening the old man, who'd been dozing in his chair, woke and called to Sam as he was leaving, "Next year in Jerusalem."

"Autumn in Paris," Sam replied, and gave him a thumbs-up from the door.

Late that summer Sam was able to take a week with Letty in Saint-Maximin. This time there was no flood, though almost on the same September day at the end of the first week the skies blackened, rain pelted down, there was war in the heavens, a night of continuous thunder and lightning. But it was gone at dawn, an overnight Old Testament reminder of what was possible, after which the days proceeded as they were meant to, a sunshine march onward to the harvest. So Sam saw the *vendange* that had been prevented in 2002 – the tall machines straddling the vines, moving down the lines, shaking the plants so hard it seemed surprising they would live to bear fruit another year. The grapes were off-loaded into large trailer vats and the air in the few kilometres between village and woods was heavy with the scent of crushed fruit, a sort of pre-fermentation wine smell, rich and delicious.

Suzy's had been sold and was now a high-class restaurant. The licence had been granted by the Mairie on condition that between the lunch and dinner sessions the place would be open for locals as a bar-café; but this was not what the new owners wanted, and though they remained open during the afternoons as required, it was with such bad grace, so disobligingly, the locals were being driven away. So now the bar hardly functioned, and the clientele for the restaurant were mostly foreigners or French visitors from the cities.

One evening Letty and Hélène went with Georges to a reunion of their old school, timed to coincide with the grape harvest. Alone with Simone, Sam mentioned things from their past. He wanted to know how much, and how well, she remembered. It was all so vivid to him, and it seemed important that she too should remember.

Did she remember their walking tour in the Wye Valley, when she'd told him she loved him?

The Wye Valley – yes.

What about the barge trip on the Thames when they'd had a massive quarrel?

She remembered the barge, and even the quarrel, but without details of what had caused it, or of things said.

"So you remember . . ."

What she remembered most was the fear when she thought she might be pregnant. And then the terror when she found out for sure she was.

"I thought you were on the pill."

"I was careless."

"You should have told me. We could have got married."

"No we couldn't."

"An abortion?"

"Never."

"I don't understand. I thought we were in love."

"There was the engagement to Gustav . . ."

He said again, "I thought we were in love."

"I felt such pressure. Family and friends . . . Gustav and I – we were supposed to be 'the ideal couple'."

She sat silent, as if trying to make herself think about it. "It was too much," she said at last, "and I was too young. He seemed more suitable than you. In fact he was. You came from outer space, Sam, and you wanted to go back there. I wouldn't have lasted in your country. And you in France . . ." She made a *pouf* with her lips. "The language . . ."

"I could have learned French."

"And practised law? No you couldn't."

He told her how he was learning French now, under Letty's guidance, and the progress he was making, the books he was reading – Balzac, Flaubert, with the help of glossaries, and some nice easy Simenon.

She said she was pleased for him. "*Alors,*" she said. "*Dis-moi quelque chose en français.*"

'No," he said. "I'm not going to speak bad French to you. I can *faire les courses* and ask directions and understand the answers, but conversation . . ."

She nodded and patted his knee, a mixture of affection and condescension. "What about your writing? When I knew you . . ."

"Nothing came of it," he said.

"Nothing at all?"

"After you left me I finished my novel. It got lost."

"How does a novel get lost?"

"In the post actually. Anyway I'd lost heart by then."

"So you lost heart rather than your novel."

They were silent again until she said, "I felt guilty about leaving you. And sad. But I had more to worry about than your feelings, Sam – or my own."

"And the marriage?"

"I suppose I missed you. Of course I did – I missed you, Sam."

He squeezed her hand. She returned the squeeze and then moved to put a small space between them. There was a moment's reflection before she said, "No it's true, it was a mistake. As I got to know Gustav better I found I didn't like him much – not in the way I'd liked you. And after a while he didn't like me. I began to notice how boring he was. And mean. He was a rich boy. That had been part of the attraction. Rich was good – it meant security – but he was a type. You know what I mean? You meet them often, the ones who could afford to be generous but are temperamentally incapable. And he had no ideas, nothing to say about the world at large. Nothing."

She sat glumly remembering. And then, in a different tone, "When Georges came into my life I grabbed hold of him with both hands and ran."

The talked turned now to Sam, to his life in London. Letty had told her his friends were rich Jews. Was it true?

He said, "My friend Ruth's husband is very rich. She is too probably – or she will be when she inherits her brother's money. And yes, they're Jewish."

"Letty says you're lovers."

Well, Letty would tell her mother that. "That's true." And then, "Of course."

"Of course." She laughed. "Is she nice? Are you in love?"

"Yes."

"Yes she's nice or yes you're in love?"

"I think both."

"You think? Aren't you sure?"

Was he sure? "No, both. Yes I'm sure."

"Good," she said. "That's excellent. I'm pleased for you."

Later, as they were wishing one another goodnight, he turned back at the door. "Your Georges – I like him very much. He's solid. Impressive."

"*Ah oui*, Georges," she said, looking over Sam's shoulder and out into the darkness of the olive trees. "He is the big man in my life."

Whatever she intended by that he registered it as a deft wound to his pride. He was a few paces from the door, heading up towards the little stone house when she called after him. "Sam."

He stopped and turned.

She said, "I'm never sure whether you're wanting to seduce me, or punish me."

He hesitated, on the brink of answering that he wasn't sure either. "Both," he said, and moved on up the path with a wave of the hand over his shoulder.

In the stone house, without lighting a lantern, he cleaned his teeth and got ready for bed. He heard Georges arrive back with Letty and Hélène, the young women talking excitedly, Georges a rumbling undertone. Sam picked up a word, a phrase here and there. It was true what Simone had said – he would never have learned French, not well enough to make it his working, everyday language. He had started too late, and in the wrong way, off the page rather than through the ear. He thought of Mr Kraznahorkai's idea that language began as song. Forget our past, it's not important Simone seemed to imply, but it was important to him, not only because together they were the parents of Letty. His past was himself and he needed to take hold of it.

Lying there his thoughts switched to Maja, his frequent companion in that region on the brink of sleep. He looked up at the bland clear sky and imagined her somewhere in the blackness between or beyond the stars. Soon he was dreaming of her – a dream so briefly shimmering and radiant it woke him again. Not that Maja had seemed different or less real. It was the dream itself that was beautiful, its intensity, like a promissory note from the stars that had already gone past the date when it could be redeemed.

It was in December that Tom Roland was at home standing in front of the television set thinking about journeys, being abroad, other landscapes and languages. The memory of a poem had set him off on this track. Or was it the other way around – the thought of travel that had made him think of the poem that began –

> When I was but thirteen or so
> I went into a golden land;
> Chimborazo, Cotopaxi
> Took me by the hand.

Tom, who liked rhymes and thought of them as hand-holds for memory, wondered why the third line hadn't been "Cotopaxi, Chimborazo" which would have made a rhyme with the first – but he was sure his memory was correct. He supposed it would have been because the poet hadn't wanted to commit himself to rhyming the first and third lines throughout as well as second and fourth. Second and fourth was going to be hard enough.

His eyes were on the television but he wasn't seeing it. He was thinking that with the cold weather already here he and Hermione should perhaps do what was becoming quite fashionable among their friends, and escape the winter by taking a trip to somewhere far away and warm – the West Indies perhaps – Martinique, Guadaloupe. Just saying the words over was like the poem, which had excited him so much in childhood he'd never wanted to know more than those names. Someone had told him Chimborazo and Cotopaxi were mountains in South America, but they could be anywhere. It was the sounds, and especially the sounds inside the framework of the poem, that made them special.

But travel: what about Cuba? Friends in the bank had gone there and found it charmingly raffish. Great fun they said, and you could take old Castro with a grain of salt – even admire the way he'd hung on so long defying the United States. Castro was a tourist destination in himself, still making interminable and sometimes ferocious speeches wearing army fatigues and carpet slippers. Or further afield – South Africa for example? Maybe a game park, where you could see the animals close-up. And Robben Island – that would be interesting: see the cell where Nelson Mandela was locked up for twenty-eight years. Twenty-eight – imagine it – and we never spared him a thought! Or the Nile. He'd seen something on television about a cruise on the Nile.

And then there was the window cleaner at the Interbank America building who had taken his wife on a cruise across to Florida and on through the Panama Canal, and then back by air – from Los Angeles, was it? He said going through the canal you could look over the rail from the deck and watch the jungle go by.

It was strange, Tom thought, to know that he could think of anything at all, any tourist destination, and more or less any hotel or resort, even quite expensive ones, for a stopover of a week or ten days, and know they could do it (flying business class, of course) and afford it. The time when they'd seemed really short of money was so long gone he had to struggle to remember it. They were affluent. Not rich; but affluence was the current reality.

The sky out there was grey and grey-black; the river, rushing seaward riding the outgoing tide, was grey-brown; the city in this light was like a dull mix of concrete and pewter and glass. And on television a man was being hanged.

Ushered towards his death by four men wearing black masks, he wore a large dark overcoat; he was dark-haired, ruggedly handsome with dark eyebrows and a whitening beard. He declined to have the bag over his head, and it was being arranged around his neck under the very large noose, as if a kindness to reduce rope burn when he dropped through the trap. There was a lot of noise, loud talk, shouting. Some of those around him or close by were hectoring him, abusing him. He seemed to be trying to focus on final prayers, final things a man says to his God as he goes to his death. He looked strong, unflinching, unbowed, dignified.

It was Saddam Hussein.

The recognition of what he was seeing – seeing only by chance because the set had been left switched on – broke into Tom's holiday thoughts. With it came a feeling of horror. "Oh no," he said to the empty room. "No no no, this is wrong. This shouldn't be happening. Quite unnecessary."

In Oxford Charles and Githa were also standing, also watching. A C.N.N. commentary cut in, saying the execution had possibly been rushed, brought forward because sectarian violence was out of control in Iraq and the Government hoped to "turn the page" into the new year.

"Oh God." Githa's was a sort of end-of-the-world sigh, as the image of the noose being adjusted around the neck returned. She whispered, not to Charles but to herself, "This is obscene."

Charles wished they were not seeing this. It was a long time since he and Githa had talked openly about Iraq. Not, anyway, since the report which acknowledged that Saddam had shut down his nuclear programme as early as 1991, and had possessed not a single W.M.D. He had talked about it sometimes to Ivan, but only when they were alone together, not wanting to subject themselves to the pressure there was everywhere these days to sound off about the liar Blair, to dismiss the moron Bush, to deplore the "war on terror" as a crime against democracy.

Githa's hand was at her mouth and her eyes were wide. Charles said, "I don't favour capital punishment. You know that."

It sounded weak. Why didn't he keep his mouth shut, just let the difference between them stand? Why should husband and wife always agree? Even as he thought this he was suppressing the urge to say more.

She glanced at him once and her eyes returned to the screen. The condemned man was hobbled, hands tied behind his back. There was an English-language commentary, a low-key explanatory monotone. Saddam was responding to the one or two who were telling him he would go to hell.

"The hell is Iraq," he said. And then clearly, so it would be heard, "And Palestine is Arab."

Now the noose was in place. He was over the trap and ready. He seemed to be reciting the Shahada.

Charles was looking at Githa as he heard the trap open and the man fall through. She was weeping angry tears. He put a soothing hand on her shoulder. "Don't." She shook it off. "Don't touch me."

12

GROUND ZERO

THROUGH 2007, AND ON FOR A BRIEF TIME INTO 2008, Sam felt secure. He had made a new life for himself, a second life, London-based. He neither rejected nor wanted to forget New Zealand; but he no longer felt bound by it, or to it. There was a sense of escape, relief, expansion; of breathing freely in a larger room, with a larger window that looked out on a human view rather than just "the foam of perilous seas". This was reflected in his dreams, so even the ones about childhood that had tinges of nostalgia could sometimes turn from happiness to anxiety, a shut door that wouldn't open and let him out, or sometimes a door with no handle and overgrown with creepers that wouldn't let him in.

Professionally his confidence was increasing, even though some of the things he had to deal with – the "instruments" by means of which the banking world was finding new ways to create credit and make profits – were so complex they made his head ache and his teeth hurt. He struggled with them, the credit default swaps, the collateralised debt obligations, and tried not to let anxiety creep in. Were they safe? And should he care if they were not? He remembered Reuben Leveson's enjoyment of dark prospects, and tried to foster in himself a similar cheerful indifference.

In August American shareholders brought an action against

Bear Stearns for the collapse of sub-prime backed hedge funds. In September there was a run on Northern Rock (something that hadn't happened to a British bank in 150 years), and it was taken into public ownership by the Bank of England. He told his colleague Maureen that he sometimes wondered whether Inter-bank America might collapse.

"Why on earth would you think that?" she said.

"Bear Stearns," he said. "Northern Rock."

"Not possible," she said. "They won't let it happen."

By "they" she meant, Sam supposed, the Government – or governments. It was what she'd said all that long time ago when they'd seen the movie "Nine Queens".

"For a socialist," he told her, "you have an unusual faith in the capitalist system."

"Well, aren't we in charge of it?" she said. And when he looked sceptical she asked, "Doesn't Northern Rock make my point?"

In his personal life he was content. There were worries about his sons caused by nothing more than intermittent silences, offhand responses and the uncertainties of distance. But e-mail messages went back and forth, and it appeared both were doing well and in no need of him.

Ngaio and Kevin were silent, invisible, and that was not unwelcome. Letty in Paris was content with her Corsican-born Marcel Saint-Jacques. As for Sam himself and Ruth – they were making one another happy, cruising through the days they contrived to spend together, and the nights. Sam felt fortunate, loved, admired for what he was and what he did.

"I'd like to have your child," she told him.

He smiled and kissed her. He liked the idea, and that she should want it, and was glad to be sure it wouldn't happen.

At work Willard Bukowski, who had been one of Interbank America's many vice-presidents, was now managing director of their section, and with that change came a promotion for Sam to executive director. It sounded grander than it was; but it pushed up his salary, and also his bonuses and his expectations. Partly because of that, and because for the moment he was spending so much of his after-work time at Reuben's house in Ladbroke Road, he put his Maida Vale flat up for sale and made moves towards buying a house in Kingswood Avenue, looking straight across into Queen's Park.

2007 was the year when he got to know something of New York. He was sent first for an "offsite" – a training and bonding exercise meant to keep the bank's two sides of the Atlantic on the same page, as Willard liked to say. It was not the first he'd experienced of this kind of corporate exercise; but there was something new about this one, as if they were there not just to reinforce faith in their employer and one another, but in the broader cause of banking itself, and in the bond market.

Later that year he had to return, partly to learn about even newer credit structures, and to work on one deal in particular – a complicated transaction which would drag on for many weeks. He sometimes asked himself was there anyone on either side who had a complete understanding of the documents. There were the quants who had drawn them up, and the rest who took them on trust because it was known this kind of thing "worked". It put him in mind of the biblical text about seeing through a glass darkly, with the promise that the time was to come when the glass would be clear. Like the Second Coming, clarity seemed a long way off.

He did the best he could, got on top of most of the complexities, and meanwhile became proficient in New York in the way a tourist does, pleased to be able to name places, streets, restaurants, and eager to talk about them when he was in London. He went with mixed feelings to visit Ground Zero. He still remembered that day, watching on Sky the two planes fly like spears into the sides of the towers; and later the buildings, first one then the other, like mortally wounded giants tottering and collapsing. But before the collapse there had been the horror of people falling, some, it seemed, choosing to jump, even in pairs holding hands, rather than suffer the pain of burning to death up there; the hurtling bodies bouncing off a glass screen reinforced so nothing coming even from that height could smash through it; and the distance they had to fall so great there was time for a voice to be heard saying "There goes another" and for the camera to hunt for it, find it and focus on its tumbling over and over before the thump of the impact – all of this against a background of sirens, dust, paper and plastic swirling in the winds through the canyons, voices of fear and warning, astonishment and even sometimes excitement, people running away, stopping to look back, hands at their faces.

He remembered too an argument in Oxford between Charles and Jake. Jake had said 9/11 had given him a feeling of *Schadenfreude*. It had been a bloody nose for America, a sort of Asterix blow against the might of Rome. Charles had been shocked, called this "disgusting". Githa had tried to arbitrate. 9/11 was a horror, she'd said; but what a coup, and on what a scale! You couldn't approve, but you had to marvel.

Looking back on all that now, Sam could see Jake's point more clearly because these had been years of the war in Iraq – the war that Condoleezza Rice had said was "doable" and which had been dreamed up, in part anyway, as America's retaliation. All it had produced was more death and destruction, more waste, more anger and appetite for revenge. Much of the sympathy for 9/11 had melted away in those years. For the individual victims pity remained. But for George Bush's America, sole superpower and self-appointed world policeman that had unleashed Shock and Awe on Baghdad in 2002, there was next to nothing left. The sympathy fund was exhausted, the goodwill account overdrawn, the vault empty. What was meant as revenge for 9/11 had become its retrospective warrant, almost its justification.

These were Sam's reflections as he walked the famous streets and gave proper thought to those hurtling bodies, and to the ones that had remained up there locked into the wreckage of burning planes and towers. He avoided the "somber and respectful experience" offered by the "Ground Zero Museum Workshop Tour ($29.99 – 5 min by subway from the actual site)" but contented himself with looking at the place itself, with its still evolving plans for what kind of permanent memorial was to go there. It was a big space, still a construction site really, with a good deal of boarding, many flags, many memorial messages and photographs from family and friends ('Luv you frever Mikey – Nat" "Miss you always Hon – Dadda.")

Reverence and flags and a deep hole: perhaps Ground Zero was the real heart of America.

Even in the great city, and partly as a relief from banking law and the big challenging world of every-damn-thing that Ground Zero represented, Sam kept up his efforts with the French language, urged on by Letty and reporting progress to her by e-mail. It was there, looking up from time to time and out over the Washington Square Park with its Arc de Triomphe-style monument, that he worked his way through Balzac's *Père Goriot*, and felt exhilarated at reaching the end, not just because it *was* the end and represented such an advance in his level of French (though again he'd used a school's edition with a glossary and notes), but because of the end itself, in which the young hero Rastignac's sense of the corruption of French high society has just been confirmed by the meagre funeral of old Goriot, robbed and neglected by his two daughters. Rastignac climbs to a high point above the Père Lachaise cemetery, sees Paris spread on either side of the Seine with its lights coming on, recognises the part of it, between the Place Vendôme and Les Invalides where flourishes the *beau monde* he has hoped, and failed, to penetrate, and resolves, not to run away from it, not to return to the purity of Angoulême and the provinces, but to try again. He sees it as a challenge, even a war. His failure, and what he has learned, will be his training for the future; and looking at that distant prospect he says to it finally, "*À nous deux maintenant!*"

Literally it meant "To us two now". The note in Sam's edition offered two possible translations: "It's war between us now!" or "Now I'm ready for you" Whichever way you read it Rastignac was not giving up, not turning away from the bright lights and the corruption, but going back to do whatever he had to do to flourish there.

"It came as such a shock," Sam said in his e-mail to Letty. "Not at all what I expected at that moment. No 'I've learned my lesson now'. Just the determination to try again. Greed, ego, youth, and balls – how Balzac! I loved it."

Only a few days after the start of this second New York visit, Sam called Willard Bukowski to tell him just how opaque this particular negotiation was proving to be, and to pass on broader anxieties. He tried, without being too direct, to convey his sense of its insecurity. "These sub-prime deals, Willard, they feel unsafe. You know? – risky."

"Risky?" Willard was a Wall Street man with a faith in the business Wall Street did. "Hey Sam, come on, we deal in it don't we? Risk is our business."

Mentally Sam added "Risk is our business" to Gordon Gekko's "Greed is good," and "Lunch is for wimps".

He said, "More than 80 per cent of these loans have been rated triple-A."

"You don't like that?"

"I don't believe it. I don't find it credible."

"And how am I supposed to weigh your hunch against S&P's rating?"

"Their hunch against mine, you mean."

"They're the experts, Sam. That's what we employ them for."

"You know this deal is worth five hundred million."

"You're new to big numbers," Willard said, "so you scare easily. That's good. It means you're . . ."

Sam cut across him. "You know A.I.G. have stopped insuring securities with sub-prime tranches."

"Is that a gun in your pocket, or are you just pleased to see me?"

Sam paused, drew breath, and started again. "Willard I'm a lawyer not a banker, so what do I know? But I'm hearing gossip over here . . ."

"Gossip," Willard repeated. "Yes?"

"Serious gossip. Not just idle chat in the men's room and at the water cooler. These guys are anxious. They know something's wrong, something bad's going to happen, is happening, but they can't agree what to do about it."

"Worry goes with the territory, Sam."

He thought of telling Willard that Warren Buffet had called derivatives W.M.D.s, but was it true? Had he really said that? It would be dismissed as hearsay. He began again: "I heard a lecture . . ."

"Academics," Willard said.

Sam persisted. "His name's David Einhorn. I thought you must be an admirer. You signed off two thousand dollars for me to hear him."

"I thought that was a charity dinner."

"It was a charity dinner, but with a lecture."

"What did that do for your digestion?"

"O.K. Willard . . ."

"What do you mean, 'O.K. Willard'?"

"I mean if you don't want to listen . . ."

"I'm listening."

Sam sighed. "It was a warning, that's all – about the kind of thing we're all getting into. It was serious, well argued."

"Good. So it was worth the money. I hope the food was O.K."

"It was a warning," Sam said again, "or that's how I read it, and I've passed it on."

"Thank you."

There was a long silence, until Willard said in his "caring boss" voice, "You're working too hard, Sam. Slow down. Take a break. Go to a movie."

After this conversation, and perhaps because of it, Maureen O'Donnell was sent to give him back-up. He didn't need her (sometimes two heads were not better than one), but he was glad of her as someone to talk to, congenial company. He thought at first she was seriously committed to what they were there to do; then that she had been primed by Willard to bolster his confidence in it. Soon, however, she dropped the pretence and entertained him with jokes about the men they had to work with, especially the ones with multiple names passed, like the names of kings, from generation to generation, indicated by a II or III – even in one case a IV. The truly important among them, the ones who dealt in billions rather than millions, tended to cool, upholstered modesty except when it came to talking about the means of getting to work – helicopter commutes across the water, or Learjets from Chicago or Boston. But there were sometimes signs of strain – keys fiddled with, pencil points jabbed and broken, voices raised.

Sam and Maureen were lodged not far from one another in Greenwich Village, he in a well-appointed but rather stark apartment belonging to the bank, she in a cheapish but clean hotel. Together they discovered, in the immediate or not far distant neighbourhoods, eating places, movie houses, and one or two off-Broadway theatres.

Maureen liked to drink what were called malt-liquor forties and smoke – dope, as it had been called in Sam's student days, but it seemed New Yorkers had gone back to calling it "pot" – though "shit" was also favoured, and it seemed almost any noun could mean marijuana if the context and tone of voice (a sort of wheezy indrawn breath) suggested it. Sam went along as protector while she bought the stuff on the sidewalk outside a local place called Three P.s (Pizza, Pasta and Pastrami), from a child-size man in a hood, while another, larger but not much, also in a hood, leaned over and nudged shoulders with her saying, "You don' wan' buy that shit, Dude, this shit's better."

One evening, when they'd eaten pastas and were sharing a bottle of wine, she asked about the young woman who had come weeping to the office.

"My daughter," he said.

"That's what she said." The smile suggested Maureen still didn't believe it.

"And you thought?"

"Your girlfriend, of course. Nice. French, judging by the accent."

"Come on, Maureen, she's half my age."

"So? You think you're too old to have fun?"

Sam asked something that had been on his mind but which, without this exchange, would almost certainly have remained there. "Do you ever think about going to bed with me?"

"Never," she said.

They stared at one another. She'd been too quick. There should have been a look of surprise, a moment while she thought how to reply.

"What about you?" she said.

"Yes, often." This wasn't true either. Now and then would have been closer.

"Oh well," – a tone of apology now – "I don't." And after a pause, "I guess, sometimes maybe. You know – as one does."

"Speculatively."

"Yes."

"*What if* rather than *would like to*."

"Yes."

"Dreams, mere dreams," he said. "That's Yeats – more or less."

"Yeats? I don't . . . Do I?"

"A poet. Anyway New York's not a Yeats kind of city. It's an O'Hara city. Another poet."

"Dead or alive?"

"He was killed in 1966. A dune buggy ran him down on Fire Island."

She giggled. It was the pot having its say.

"We should go there," he said. "There's a ferry. I'll read you a poem O'Hara wrote about Billie Holiday. About New York, really. It's called 'The Day Lady Died'."

"The day Lady Di."

"Died."

"Yes but I was thinking of . . ."

"I know – Lady Diana. That would have to be 'The *Night* Lady Di . . .'"

"Died."

"Died, yes."

"So go on then."

"What?"

"Read it."

He pretended, elaborately, to search his pockets. "I don't have his poems with me at this moment, Maureen." He laughed; they laughed together.

"Are you high?" she asked.

"No." He shook his head and thought about it. "Drunk maybe. Not even drunk. Just . . . I don't know. New Yorked."

"New Yorked," she said. "I like that." But she was thinking about something else, staring at his shirt. He looked down. Had he spilled something? She reached out and touched it. It was cotton, pale blue with small white spots and a white lining inside the collar which showed when he wore it, as now, without a tie. He thought it rather stylish, though it was not a shirt he would have chosen for himself.

"That's so odd," she said. "Reuben Leveson used to wear a shirt just like that."

"Funny that," he said. He held one leg up and pulled up the trouser exposing a black sock covered in a pattern of small spots, red, orange, yellow, green, blue. "Ever see these?"

She blinked. "Have I?"

"You've heard of wearing dead man's shoes – I'm wearing dead man's socks."

"And dead man's shirt. That's obscene, Sam."

"His sister gave them to me. And, by the way, my long-ago lachrymose morning caller was, and is, my daughter. Her name's Leticia Clairmont. Letty."

"Your 'long-ago lachrymose morning caller'? Jesus, Sam!"

Whether or not they had told one another the truth about thinking of sharing a bed, they certainly thought about it now. For the next thirty-six hours they thought about little else, even when they were doing their masters' business. It was a dazed, salacious interlude, a lubricious romp which at the end of two days had exhausted itself, and them. Soon they were agreeing it had been nice but would be best forgotten; or if not forgotten, certainly best not repeated or spoken about.

They went to a play together at an off-Broadway theatre. It was set somewhere in the Austro-Hungarian Empire after the end of World War One. An old soldier, a Jew, finds a cement bust of a late emperor in his cellar. He dresses it in a blue tunic with some stage medals and puts it up in front of his house. He puts on his own old uniform, and each day, going out to do his shopping, and returning home, he salutes it. This strange ritual comes to the notice of officials of the new regime, and he is ordered to desist. He doesn't. To him the empire and its authority still exist, and the new nationalism is unreal. Slowly the wheels of the new authority grind into action and destroy him.

"What was all that about?" Maureen said as they walked away, huddling together against a cold wind off the Hudson River.

"It was about . . ." Sam hesitated. He wasn't sure. "About loyalty to an idea, maybe – and the consequences."

"And being a Jew."

"That too. That especially, I suppose." As they trudged along the edge of the park he told her Maja's joke about the Jew and the lotto ticket.

Maureen laughed.

"A friend told me that in a note she left before she killed herself."

"Killed herself? Really? Why?"

"Why the joke, or why did she kill herself? The joke was because she thought of herself as the Jew. She seems to have felt she'd never had the courage to buy her ticket, so life could hold no promise."

He had never told anyone about that note – not Letty, not even Ruth. Maureen's ear seemed like a neutral one. "I was in love with her," he said.

"You were?" Maureen asked, leaning forward as they walked and turning to look at his face.

Was he? Had he been? Or was he trying to impress her? He wasn't sure; doubted himself. It was a relief to have said it to someone who by tomorrow, or next week, would have forgotten. She would be more likely to remember the dead man's shirt and socks.

*

The wrestling with the new C.D.O. deal, its many painful pages of detail, and its several participants, went on as the weather got cooler. Sometimes little foretastes and flurries of snow floated down the canyons, through high branches that were giving up the last of their bronzed or yellowed leaves, and over the rhyming lines of yellow cabs. No more games of outdoor chess in Washington Square. People no longer sat on the benches but hurried through in scarves and hats, hunched against the wind. The ones sleeping rough in doorways crammed more newspapers into their bags and cardboard boxes. The handout queues grew longer, the people in line more pinched and miserable. Sam sometimes thought that if he could have taken all these millions of dollars they were creating opaque structures to manipulate and contain, and scattered them from tall buildings over the cold thoroughfares, he might have been more usefully and meaningfully employed.

The news was full of the battle for the Democrat nomination, and there was excitement as the senator who had voted against the Iraq war seemed to edge ahead of the one who had voted for it.

In the end the deal was done, the contracts agreed and signed, and there was a celebration dinner at a posh Manhattan restaurant, San Pietro. Maureen's name was not on the guest list and Sam insisted she be added.

"I thought she was your girl Friday," the organising secretary said.

"She's one of the team," Sam said.

After that they returned to London, Maureen to announce her engagement to Stig Ardelius, Sam to move into his new home looking out on Queen's Park, and to take possession of a new car he had ordered; both to the promise (was it a promise, or just something assumed?) of a larger end-of-year bonus. Sam's car was to be a Prius, "green", expensive but better for the environment than ordinary cars. He knew he would hardly use it in London; but at the weekends sometimes he would get out into the countryside, drive Ruth to Whitstable, maybe even take it over to France and drive in Europe. He was looking forward to being a driver after all these years away from it.

On the flight back the hostess gave the names of the captain and his deputy on the flight deck, and of her colleagues in the cabin.

"And my name," she concluded, "is Hope."

"Amen to that," Sam said.

At Heathrow baggage claim he and Maureen stood together, knowing that Ruth and Stig, though quite separately, would be waiting on the other side. "D'you know your Wittgenstein?" he asked.

"Of course." She punched him on the upper arm, hard. "Who is he? Another poet?"

"He's a philosopher. His most famous statement goes something like, 'What cannot be spoken about we must pass over in silence.'"

"Good one," Maureen said. "He must have been getting up to tricks." At that moment she saw her bag and darted to grab it up from the carousel. Sam saw his own not far behind but let it pass. It could do another circuit. That would give her time to get out and away ahead of him.

She reached up to him and kissed him quickly on the mouth. "Bye, Sammy. Have a nice life" – and she was gone.

13

THE BRANDENBURG GATE

DECEMBER IN LONDON WAS WINDING-UP-THE-YEAR TIME,
party time. Charles and Githa, whose difference over Iraq had been
buried without a headstone, came down and stayed in the Queen's
Park house, bringing Martin this time (a bigger lad now, taller than
his mum), while Sam crossed by Eurostar to spend two nights in
Paris with Letty, who told him she was pregnant, and to meet
again Marcel Saint-Jacques, father of the child *in utero*.

Back in London Sam was taken by Charles, with Ivan Pem-
berton, to an end-of-year party at the Royal Society of Literature.
In the press of famous name-tags and faces he listened while
A.N. Wilson, wearing a crumpled linen suit and cycle clips,
explained to Hanif Kureishi just where in the Inferno he thought
Dante would have placed Wagner. "It would have been unfair,"
Wilson was saying, "but rather beautiful, don't you think?"

Out in the street afterwards Sam invited Ivan to bring Sophie
with Charles and Githa to the housewarming he was planning at
Queen's Park.

A day or so later Ruth persuaded him he must come to a party
with the Vogel family, a Hampstead houseful that included Sir
Frank's three sons and their wives and children. Greeting him
at the door, she kissed him. "Don't mention Bear Sterns. We think

Frank's lost a lot of money and we're not telling him."

"Won't say a word. How's your hedge fund?" He meant the Swiss account, the access codes now with Ruth.

"Oh God, darling, I have to talk to you about that."

"Losses?"

"When I last looked it was climbing."

One of the twins appeared behind as he took off his coat. "Cynthia – this is Sam, remember?"

"Hi Sam." The young woman held out her hand and Sam took it and kissed her cheek. "Hullo Cynthia."

"I'm Lucy," she said.

Ruth said, "No you're not," – and then looked hard. "Are you?" To Sam she said in a tone of amused apology, "I should have called them Goneril and Regan."

"Or Regan and Regan."

"Lucy will do," the twin said.

"In Stockholm," Sam said, "they'll be celebrating St Lucy – the saint of light."

"Saint of light," the twin said. "I like the sound of that."

It was a big noisy crowd. Sir Frank, pushed in by an Asian nurse in a blue-grey uniform and greeting people from his wheelchair, didn't at once recall who Sam was or where they'd last met.

But "Of course," he shouted when Ruth reminded him. "The Count Basie fan from Corsica. 'Autumn in Paris'. I love it."

Sam's housewarming party came a week or so later on December 20. Charles and Githa were there again from Oxford, and Letty and Marcel from Paris. Letty's pregnancy was obvious now; but Sam wondered whether Githa too might be pregnant. Was the little raja, who was no longer little, but had once talked about his mother's "biological clock" to have a sibling after all? Sam didn't ask, and would wait to be told.

Jake and Jan Latimer came, bringing Elvira Gamble who was rehearsing in Jake's new play about the Trojan Wars. She was accompanied by her new friend, a young (possibly ten years her junior) out-of-work American actor whom Jake had referred to on the phone as "the Donut" The couple stationed themselves at one end of the room, as if to be seen, Elvira tossing her hair like a pretty racehorse at the starting gates, the Donut staring into the distance as if he could see through walls into a noble future.

"Why do you call him the Donut?" Sam asked Jake, *sotto voce* and already refilling his glass.

"It's his brain," Jake said. "I used to call him the Adonis but then I talked to him."

Ivan and Sophie Pemberton looked in briefly on their way to somewhere else. Willard Bukowski had been invited, and surprised Sam by arriving with Mrs Manoly – Mary from Derivatives. Were they now a couple? Tom and Hermione came, Tom limping from his injury and now using a stick. Maureen and Stig Ardelius arrived late with two other couples from Credit Products. When Sam greeted them Maureen looked suddenly rattled. It was the only time he had ever seen her blush.

Simone phoned to wish Sam well in his new home, and chatted to Letty. A New Zealand couple, neighbours from Summerfield Avenue, came, bringing a wine, Sleeping Dogs from Central Otago. The local Baker and Spice had done the catering. Sam and Letty had chosen the wines, some from the Duchy d'Uzès and Collines du Bourdic, others from New Zealand.

This was the day when, in Wall Street, Morgan Stanley acknowledged a $9.2 billion loss which its C.E.O. seemed unable to explain. It was rumoured to have been a single trade – or a single strategy, the work of one trader. How was risk on such a scale even possible? The sum was so huge no-one seemed able to make sense of it. It was talked about, but what was there to say? It was mean-ingless – an "out-of-this-world" number. An aberration, everyone agreed – a "one-off" surely.

Willard spoke of it to Sam. "This is big stuff. Very big. Terrify-ing, actually." The words seemed to come out of the side of his mouth.

"Risk is our business," Sam said, and Willard frowned as at a quotation dimly recognised and meant to embarrass.

"There are limits," he said.

Sam refilled his glass. "Drink up Mr B. It's bonus time."

Ruth came to the party, but not for long. Sir Frank, she explained, now knew about his Bear Sterns losses; and worse, the day's news about Morgan Stanley had reached him before they could protect him from it. "He's upset," Ruth explained. "These things shake him, and he's so frail."

"More losses?"

"Oh God yes. Huge."

"Are you worried?"

"No. I mean yes, I'm worried because it affects his health."

She and Sam stood side by side. As he looked about the room, seeing his guests – his and Ruth's – enjoying themselves, he felt as if after years in which he'd been holding his breath he could now at last breathe normally.

Ruth leaned towards him, nudging him with her shoulder. "You look happy Sam."

He kissed her cheek.

Tom and Hermione left early. Tom was showing signs,

Hermione said, as she waited for him outside the bathroom. "It takes so little these days. Another drink and he'll be dancing. I need to get him home before he keels over."

"I thought he'd given up."

"Well yes, but..."

Sam had called them a minicab. He was to spend Christmas with them, but two days later Hermione rang and cancelled. Tom was back in hospital. There were heart problems associated with his diabetes. There was to be a procedure, possibly a stent, and monitoring.

Ruth would be spending the day with her family. They were Jews, but British, so Christmas was celebrated. It seemed too late for Sam to make other arrangements. He thought of Nastasya in Stockholm, not seriously but with a certain nostalgia, remembering the sense at that time of obstacles overcome, of making his way on his own, unaided – and of physical pleasures that had been, like virtue, their own reward. He had a card with her phone number, but didn't call.

I'm a man alone, he thought. He had come so far since the break with home and family. It was never going to be easy and it hadn't been, but he was O.K. He would be fine.

So he spent Christmas alone, though a lot of the morning passed making phone calls. He walked many miles that day, through quiet streets, through parks and along the river. The air was crisp and cold with now and then flurries of sleet. The night's frost hadn't quite thawed, and in shadow the grass in the parks was crisp underfoot. The crows were loud and theatrically sinister, playing their part in the Christmas panto. Doors suddenly opened on colours and noise, music, voices (especially of children), and then closed again. It was a tinsel world, rather lovely, as if London had taken the short step back to being the city Dickens had recorded – or perhaps invented.

He might be a man alone; and maybe he didn't belong in this city – or not yet; but it was the right place. For now, it was where he wanted to be.

It was early in May that Tom Roland's heart failed. He was making his way home along the South Bank when he saw outside the Globe a man who reminded him of his night visitor, Monsieur le Noir, author, instigator or "onlie begetter" of the poem which had now appeared in the *T.L.S.* It was not that Tom believed in any simple way in the reality of this person. He knew it was a dream, an emanation from within himself. So he knew, or thought he knew, that this passer-by would be the possessor of a name, an identity, a residence and a history all his own and nothing to do with Thomas Roland's. But the feeling of a mysterious and known presence, both beneficent and dangerous, was so strong, the pull so powerful, Tom found himself turning about and following.

The man was walking at a brisk pace. He went up onto the Millennium footbridge, stopped to look around at the scene, and down to where Tom was labouring in his wake; then set off across the river in the direction of St Paul's.

It was hard work climbing from Bankside onto the bridge, and Tom lost ground. He was halfway across the river when his breathing changed from panting to something more sinister. It was a new kind of breathlessness. He took deep breaths but seemed to get no air; and at the same time a weight pressed down on his chest, which felt like a cold shaft, empty of everything except pain. He staggered and fell to his knees. People walked around him and walked on. He looked ahead and seemed to see the dark figure stop and look back at him and wave a kind of farewell – or perhaps it was a salute.

But in the hospital Monsieur le Noir visited him again in the night. Next day Tom told Hermione about seeing him on the bridge and about the visit when the person in black promised him another poem. "Get better first," he said, "and then we'll see what I have for you."

Tom died that afternoon.

The funeral service was held in St Mark's church, just up from Prince Albert Road. Years before, when Tom and Hermione had lived in Camden Town and Hermione was still preserving the habits of an Anglican childhood, it had been her church. It was not far from Regent's Park Zoo, and Sam was sure during quiet moments and pauses in the vicar's valediction he heard a lion's roar and the howl of a wolf or wild dog.

Maureen was there in the crowd. He noticed her shoes first – high heels of a kind she mostly didn't wear to work, and with little triangular gaps which showed part of her neat toes. It came back to him from that brief torrid time in New York that she had small elegant feet. It was something he'd registered, never brought to consciousness but now remembered. His eyes ran up over the long, well-shaped legs and body in a pale green linen suit.

Maureen turned now towards him and saw him looking her way. She waved out, across the churchyard, he returned the wave, and they kept a space between them, as if by silent agreement.

On a table just inside the church door there was a framed photograph of Tom looking portly and jolly, and beside it, on a small book-stand like a picture frame, his one book of poems, *Floating*, the signed numbered copy Sam had found and had given him for Christmas three or four years before. Hermione wept greeting friends and relations. Sam hugged her and shook hands with son and daughter, Claude and Bridget.

The service was Anglican-informal. There were nice words spoken by family and by banking colleagues. Willard did his best and sounded once again as if he was writing a reference or a promotion report. Tom would get an afterlife bonus; or an upgrade of a place or two nearer the heavenly C.E.O.

After the tributes came a duet, probably Strauss, Sam thought, played by Bridget on the violin and Vaclav on the cello. Vaclav had a way of closing his eyes and pulling breath audibly in through his nose as he drew the bow across a particularly delicate note, as if afraid he might damage it. Sam looked down at his knees and suppressed a laugh, remembering Tom describing this to him once, imitating it, explaining that his secret name for his son-in-law was Vlad the Inhaler.

While they played and the congregation reflected, Sam remembered the Ern Malley line Tom had struggled to quote over that distant Christmas dinner: "I am still the black swan of trespass on alien waters" – after which had come Tom's nose-dive towards the table and roll to the floor, ending the celebrations ahead of schedule. Sam at the time had felt himself to be the black swan of trespass, and the waters to be alien. But that was the very day when Letty's message had been waiting for him at Gloucester Terrace, and after that, slowly, London had begun to open its doors to him.

But now they were being reminded that Tom Roland was a poet. This was something everyone seemed to know and respect and so no-one was going to be surprised when the informal part of the service ended with his son reading Tom's poem that had appeared in the *T.L.S.* – "a mordant piece" Claude said, "perhaps oblique, even obscure. It seems to be a poem about Dad himself, full of ironies and self-mockery: Tom the poet mocking Tom the banker, perhaps.

"Dad was modest about his poems," Claude went on; "or shy, anyway. But I think he would have been glad to have this one read today – as an acknowledgement of what he liked to call his 'secret service'. Respecting the place and the occasion," he concluded, "the poem's one f-word has been replaced, as it was in the *T.L.S.*, by something more anodyne."

And he read –

BANKING ON FEATHERS

Some Toms sing for their supper,
One was a piper's son,
Some grow old and howl on the heath –
This is the story of one:
Clever Tom who hatched in his head
Ideas like chickens he sold for bread.

Bolt your window, bar your door,
This I never told before;
That wind against the house-wall hurled
Cold with the coldness of the world
Will shout a moral if it can.

This little chicken went to market,
This one he kept in his head –
Their welfare was Tom's precious care
And his care, well-fed.
Tom's neighbour's coop caught fire,

237

He doused his own with water;
Tom's neighbour's wife fell ill –
He praised their daughter;
And gently, steadily over the scene
The rain fell down and kept it green.

Famine was somewhere, somewhere else
Two bullets in the head;
Far from his care tall stadiums
Cast shadows on the dead;
But Tom in the land of Big Ideas
Grew full of sensitive weathers,
Counting chickens before they hatched,
Banking on feathers.

A hot rain falls on the rolling earth,
In office the Dog's obeyed.
For men whose brains breed weakling chicks
Coops are made.

A cold wind blows on the rolling earth,
Poor Tom's a-cold in his brain:
The chicken is plucked that sang heigh-ho
The wind and the rain.

After that came the blessing – "in the sure and certain hope of eternal life". How, Sam asked himself, could "sure and certain" be followed only by "hope". Either you were "sure and certain" or you "hoped". For himself, and when the matter in question was life after death, he didn't even hope.

As they filed out following the coffin on its way to the waiting hearse, the Seekers singing "The Carnival Is Over" came from the speakers. It was a song Sam hadn't heard for years, and there was something about the melody, and a sort of break in the woman soloist's voice, that caught at your throat and made you think, Poor old Tom – and poor old everybody, because the Carnival was always coming to an end and it was always sad.

Outside in the fresh green spring day he joined the queue to hug Hermione and say his few words. "Do you think it was alright?" she asked.

"It was lovely. And the poem . . ."

"I don't think Vaclav quite approved of the Seekers after Strauss."

"'The Carnival Is Over' – that was perfect . . ."

"We went to a funeral once that ended with that and Tom wept and said it was just right, so I thought . . ."

"You were right, Hermione, it was."

She was still holding on to him when he saw, over her head, the hearse very slowly begin to move away. So Tom was going to the flames alone. Sam hoped he'd been embalmed. "Tom's going," he murmured, and turned her gently, still holding her by the shoulders while they watched as the heavy black vehicle rolled away into the traffic.

Sam was walking down Parkway afterwards, on his way to the Tube, when his mobile rang. It was Ruth. "How was it?"

He told her.

"I have to go to Berlin. Will you come with me?"

"Berlin? How exciting. Why?"

"Don't ask. It's a surprise."

"A surprise . . ."

"Will you come?"

"When, darling?"

"When, darling," she mimicked.

She was becoming impatient. Here's not to reason why . . . "I'll come," he said. "Of course I will. I'd love to. When?"

"Tomorrow?"

"Can we get flights?"

"We can. I'll tell you more tonight. *Ciao*, Sam. *Ciao, ciao*."

He took the Northern line going south and had gone all the way to Charing Cross, before deciding he was not going to the bank for what was left of the day. He got out, found the Bakerloo platform and took the train to Queen's Park. He didn't go immediately home but walked around the park on the pavement outside the railing, pacing it out, counting. He had plans to run here in the evenings, to get fit again. Once round that perimeter would be . . . what? A mile? Less? He was timing himself. It took just under fourteen minutes at a brisk walk. Whatever it was it was going to offer more space close at hand than he'd had at Maida Vale, but still nothing on the scale of Kensington Gardens.

He went in through the gates. At one end was the Nature Walk with its pictures of the animals and birds you might see if you were lucky. Squirrels of course; but also the frog, the fox and the field mouse. Then an array of birds, some perhaps theoretically possible (a woodpecker? a blue tit?) but improbable, surely. There was also the witchy possibility of a bat and a toad.

Most of the animals he saw in fact were human – and their dogs, which were also human. Squirrels rippled over the grass, stopping to jerk and twitch, undecided, before rippling on again. Crows strode about with a "Masters of the Universe" air, looking to rob the squirrels of their best finds. Bored nannies, and fathers doing "quality time" talked into their hands while their charges tottered about and fell backwards on the grass, or stared up round-eyed out of prams and pushchairs. There were six tennis courts, a sort of coffee bar, a bandstand, two outdoor table-tennis tables, an area for golf, with greens for putting, and big enough to practise your drive if your drive wasn't big – and then just the open field, said to have been once the training ground of Queen's Park Rangers F.C., where kids now kicked balls and adults would sit or lie in the sun when summer came. The iron-fenced infants' play-ground ("Adults admitted only if accompanied by a child") was full of minute but furious activity, accompanied by shouting and weeping. A fight was going on about turns on the flying fox. At the end furthest from the Nature Walk, the Quiet Garden, with its beautifully kept flower beds, was quietly occupied by sad old men. The hands of three t'ai chi exponents sliced the air into planes and curves.

Sam felt and fought off what he had come to identify as "the London oppression". He didn't yet know the area well; but he knew that only a mile away was Kilburn High Street with its raucous ugliness and pockets of undisguised distress. He had visited it once or twice and returned home entertaining the fantasy that its denizens, hated by the Tories and abandoned by New Labour, might come pouring down the tree-lined, litter-scattered streets dancing the carmagnole to set up a revolutionary council here in Queen's Park for the requisition of all the nice middle-class homes round about, and a redistribution of wealth – perhaps with a guillotine in the bandstand. Why were the "less well-off" so easily persuaded that they had what they wanted, or as much of it as they deserved; or that what they wanted was in sight, only a thousand, or a hundred thousand, hours of boredom, bad health and bad housing away? Human order was more mysteriously durable than disorder, but the enemy was always at the gates.

Stopping under the trees he rang Willard Bukowski and told him his cardboard eulogy for Tom had been very good. "You always do these things so well."

"You think so? There's not a lot to say about poor old Tom."

"Not a lot, but you said it – brilliantly."

This was coming on rather, but Willard didn't seem to doubt he meant it. "Thanks, Sam. Very kind of you."

Sam said, "I've been going over that problem I mentioned..."

There was a silence while Willard struggled to remember.

"With Berliner Volksbank," Sam prompted. There was no problem with Berliner Volksbank – or no more than with any other.

"Ah yes," Willard said. "Stress testing, was it?"

"I need to go to Berlin."

Willard should have asked, couldn't it be sorted by phone. "Up to you," he said.

Sam said, "Thanks Willard."

"Ah, Sam . . ." Was he having second thoughts? Sam waited. "You could put in a routine call at our Berlin branch. Always good to let them know we're thinking about them."

"Of course. Will do."

"I'll let them know to expect you."

They flew from London City Airport and Ruth had a car waiting for them at Tegel – a shiny black limo and a driver in a dark suit and tie who drove like the wind, but well. Berlin was bright with new green – parks with lawns and trees, parks that were almost woods, tree-lined streets and boulevards. And then they were into

242

and through the area around the Bundestag, spectacular modern architecture, building after building, much of it constructed since the Wall had come down and the seat of Government had moved from Bonn. It was not in the spirit of Albert Speer, grandiose to the point of absurdity – "thousand-year-Reich" absurd; but it was not modest. Deutschland was not now quite *über alles*, but it had flourished in defeat – or this corner of it had.

They crossed the Spree and on into an area that had a different feel to it, as if more of the buildings, some anyway, had survived the massive destruction of the war. The car pulled up in a busy street and the driver hurried to get their bags from the boot. Ruth spoke to him in German, something about an arrangement for returning to take them again to the airport. Sam reached for his wallet but she waved it away. Whatever was due was paid, or would be later.

They wheeled their bags off the busy sidewalk into a courtyard, beautifully decorated in heraldic designs in variously coloured brick and ceramic tiles. This courtyard led to a second which gave on to a third with a tree at its centre, small shops at ground level, apartments with balconies going up four floors.

Their apartment was on the first floor. Ruth went out onto the balcony and he heard her having an exchange in German with a neighbour.

"You didn't tell me you spoke German," he said as she returned indoors.

"I didn't? Well, I suppose you didn't ask." She pecked his brow and fell backwards on the bed, one arm out wide, the other behind her head. "You want to fuck in Germany?"

He did, and they did.

That afternoon he called the Berlin branch of Interbank America and took a taxi to Charlottenburg. He was taken for coffee and cake by two young executives from Mergers and Acquisitions who treated him with respect, though they must have known there was no special significance in the visit or a more senior person would have been assigned to it. Both spoke English, one fluently, the other hesitantly, both giving to English "o" vowels the rather posh sound typical of German speakers. He sat with them out of doors in a pleasant side street off Kurfürstendamm. As the talk narrowed to banking matters it was clear that some of the New York angst had reached them, but their interests, and their sense of where the serious action was taking place, went eastward – oil and gas mainly, but other things too – aluminium, copper, wheat, fish. Hitler (not that the H-word was uttered, or even hinted at) had gone in the right direction but in the wrong way. Huge loans were needed and were being made, in hundreds of millions, and with corresponding profits. They talked about covenants, securities and disclosures; cash-flow models, waivers and indemnities – showing off perhaps, wanting at least to make a good impression on London.

The coffee was good, the cake excellent, the talk lively. They offered to take Sam to a club in the evening, with hints of mild riot and safe sex. He declined with thanks, and with jokes meant to show that he was not against fun, just too busy on this quick visit for bare breasts and pole dancers. They parted on good terms. A car was provided to take him back to Ruth.

That evening when he and Ruth were eating in a café not far from the apartment she told him she had studied German at school and university. "My grandparents thought it was learning the language of the enemy. My father thought that was a good thing to do; my mother wasn't so sure."

"Is that how you see it now?"

"Germany as the enemy of the Jews? No more than anyone

else. Probably less, they're so ashamed of their past." After a moment she said, "Reuben used to say Israel was the enemy of the Jews – but he liked to say extravagant things. Things he wouldn't be held to."

They were returning when Sam asked whether they were in East or West Berlin. She pointed to the tram rails. "When you see rails you know you are in the east. The D.D.R. at least kept a few things worth preserving."

She paused at the street entrance to their courtyard and pointed with her toe. Set into the pavement were three small bronze plaques, each only three or four inches square, and the engraved words so small you had to bend right down to read them. Each read "Hier wohnte" and then a name, the date "1943" and "Auschwitz" It was a reminding stab, small and precise. He imagined these people in the black-and-white world of the 1940s, each with a small suitcase of permitted "belongings".

"These two," she said, pointing again, "were my great-aunt and great-uncle. The other was their daughter." He felt reproached, though he knew that the feeling was all his own and not her doing. Somehow the guilt was shared and extended to the whole of humankind.

She explained that the apartment had been appropriated by the Nazis and then had become the property of the D.D.R., so had only been returned to the family after the two Germanies were reunited. "Reuben used it. We hadn't decided what to do with it. Now it's mine." Probate had been established at last, so everything that had been Reuben's was hers.

That night they slept under a quilt with the windows onto the balcony open. There was a chill in the spring night air. The sky was clear and there was a moon. In the morning they had breakfast in a café on one of the courtyards – "Hof VI" which was both the courtyard's number and the name of the café. She had made an appointment, she said, for 10 a.m. at the Brandenburg Gate and Sam was to accompany her.

They set off on foot – half an hour's walk, she said, which took them through a warren of smaller streets, then a market under the S-Bahn, and finally down Unter den Linden. At the Brandenburg Gate tourists were milling about, photographing one another under the heroic charioteer with her four horses, who had once held aloft the eagle of war now replaced by the dove of peace.

"Our friend will be standing under the gate," she said. "You will have to identify him, because he and I have not met."

Sam thought afterwards this should have told him straight away who it was he was to look for but it didn't – not until he recognised the tall figure with the neat beard and longish hair slicked down at the back over his collar: Hawkeye from Hungary! In his suit and tie among the milling informality of the tourists he looked out of place.

"André." They shook hands. "I understand you and Ruth Leveson haven't met."

Mr K. embraced her, held her at arm's length and then they embraced again. "I loved your brother," he said. And then, "Reuben, he was my brother also, if I may say."

"You may say," she said, her eyes moist.

"Come," he said. "I rent office quite close. We can talk. Prague is still home for business, but I keep small space in Berlin. Small foothold, I think."

He took her by the arm and led them back a short distance to a building of spectacularly up-to-the-minute design, and security to match. "Voice recognition," Mr K. said; and then he spoke by intercom to explain that he was accompanied by friends.

One floor up they settled over coffee, looking down into a sunken courtyard through an irregular glass screen designed in the image of an immense spider's web, its struts fine steel.

The coffee came with croissants and pains au chocolat, which they admired but didn't eat. "For breakfast," Mr K. said, "hour is late." Could they speak German, he asked, since he had noticed Ruth spoke it well? His German, he explained, was so much better than his English, and it was important to be precise.

So what followed was not clear to Sam in every detail, although he was pretty sure he understood it in outline. A point had been reached (possibly because probate in Reuben's estate had been settled in her favour) where the investment in Mr K.'s hedge-fund had to be withdrawn or renewed. It seemed she was being offered the choice of taking some millions of dollars now, or reinvesting.

Ruth asked Mr K. what he would advise and Sam was sure he said he preferred not to advise.

She asked what he thought her brother would have done and he said he could not, of course, be sure, but he thought Reuben would have reinvested. In the pause that followed while she thought about it he added in English, "Is risk of course."

She said she thought he was right about what Reuben would have done, and that was what she would do.

A leggy blonde Berliner who had been hovering now produced papers prepared, it seemed, in anticipation of this outcome – though there may have been an alternative set also ready. They were signed, there were handshakes and hugs, and they returned to coffee and the English language.

"How is your wife's pastry shop?" Sam asked.

"This year pastry shop makes profit," he said, clearly pleased for his wife. "In Budapest, small business is good."

"Business is not good in banking," Sam said.

"It can be good," André corrected. "Crashes still to come no doubt. But for hedge funds, bad can be good if right person is making decision."

Sam thought of that enormous Morgan Stanley loss – 9.2 billion – still an incomprehensible number. And yet he'd heard it said in New York that a very small group of the cleverest hedge-fund managers were turning losses like that into profits.

Ruth said, "My brother used to say it was the computers made the decisions."

"Computers, yes," Mr K. said. "Very important, it's true. But algorithms are workers. Hedge-fund manager has to know when to . . . you understand?"

"Take control?"

"That is what makes difference."

"Well, you seem to be getting it right," Ruth said.

"Karl Marx is good teacher."

"Marx?" She was surprised. "Marx didn't do much for the Soviet Union."

Mr K. smiled. "Stalin was not Karl Marx. Stalin was repression and collective and five-year plan."

QUEEN'S PARK

2008 WAS THE YEAR OF THE CLUSTERFUCK. THROUGH spring and summer it had been rumbling and threatening like the warnings of an incipient earthquake. Gradually people in the banking world began to show signs of nervousness. Was it right to be anxious; or was anxiety dangerous because it could lead to panic? By the middle of the year the big investors who had proceeded according to the "big-picture scenario" which said that the property market, and its close-but-complex relative the bond market, despite hiccoughs and modest retreats, always went up (U.P., meaning Unlimited Potential, had been the name of a real-estate firm in Sam's home town), were scuttling, always too late, to find a way of "shorting" on their investments. Honest (dumb and honest) toilers at the coal face like Willard Bukowski, who had proceeded on the same assumption, and had refused to recognise what was happening until it was . . . happening – these did little, because there was little they could do; or they did nothing, for the same reason.

By March the earlier intimations about Bear Stearns were confirmed with its collapse. Summer passed into the autumn of real anxiety and the winter of dismay. Early in September the huge

American mortgage corporations, Fannie Mae and Freddie Mac were pulled back from the brink by interventions from Washington. A week later Lehman Brothers went into Chapter 11 receivership. On Canary Wharf that morning, as Sam went to his office, he had to make his way through and around journalists and news cameramen gathered outside the Lehman Brothers building, trying to catch shots through windows of the meetings at which the workers were being told their fate, or grab interviews from the stunned young executives – they were mostly young – emerging with the square cardboard boxes they had been supplied with to clear their desks. Across the hundred or so yards of water that was called Middle Dock, recruitment agents had set themselves up at the green-canvas-shaded coffee tables, taking names and details. They, and the journalists too, were the horde of gulls that follows the fishing fleet inshore, scooping entrails cleaned from the catch and thrown overboard into the wake.

Before the end of September the Bank of America had taken over Merrill Lynch; Lloyds had bought out H.B.O.S.; Goldman Sachs and Morgan Stanley had converted their status to "bank holding companies" so they could access help from the U.S. Federal Reserve; Bradford and Bingley had been nationalised . . .

Sam asked how Interbank America was faring and was told it was secure, but the blood-letting had begun, and a few days later became a haemorrhage. First in ones and two, soon in sixes and sevens (Maureen O'Donnell among them), staff were laid off and sent down with their cardboard boxes to evade (or not, as they chose) the waiting journalists, and to join queues at the recruiting agents' tables. Right at the end of the month Willard came into Sam's office and closed the door. He stood with his back to the wall, stiff and awkward. "Sam, this is very hard for me."

So this was the wolf (in sheep's clothing) come to eat M. Séguin's goat. Or should it be seen as the release to new pastures?

Sam pointed to the square box on the floor already packed. "Don't ask me to feel sorry for you, Willard. You'll live through the pain of this."

"I'm so very sorry. We value the work you've done for us."

This was the man who, when Sam had expressed anxiety about those clusters of mortgages and how they were rated, had told him he was working too hard and to go to a movie – but Sam didn't remind him.

Willard handed him a large envelope. "This is the stuff about your severance package. Forms to be filled out, and so on."

Sam shook it. "Doesn't rattle."

Willard's smile was wan. "Might be my turn next."

"I don't think so, Mr B. This is the *Titanic*, isn't it? You'll find a place in the lifeboat."

Willard turned away and moved to the door, then returned to shake Sam's hand. As handshakes went it rated low – both damp and limp. "I wish it could have been . . . You know?"

Yes, Sam knew.

"And when you need a reference . . ."

"Sure. Thanks Willard."

Willard eased himself back to the door with a sideways motion. As he was sliding out he said, "Take your time, son. No rush."

"Son" didn't need time. He was packed and ready. For two days now he'd been glancing at that box which, without prompting, he'd begun to fill with papers he would want to take with him. This had been done, not in fear, but in anticipation, sometimes almost in hope. As he'd stared at it he'd thought of the stone cottage behind Simone's house in Saint-Maximin; the cheap hotel in Bandol where he'd stayed with Letty; Ruth's Berlin apartment not far from Hackescher Markt. These were places where he'd made notes and felt the excitement of what it might be like to write a novel again – something better, more to the point, more to his own taste and closer to his own experience (he'd never committed a murder – nor solved one) than *Damn Your Eyes* had been. There were places in New Zealand too – many places. For Sam, places signified stories. He liked telling himself stories, and always saw them as happening somewhere. The where was part of it.

Walking out through the offices carrying that box was faintly embarrassing, and he left quickly, down by lift and out on to Canada Square, head down through the smaller crowd now of journalists, leading with shoulder and elbow, angling this way and that, avoiding their questions and their cameras, not even stopping to register with the seagulls on the other side of Middle Dock. He took the grand escalator down into the Wharf's wonderful extension to the Jubilee line, with its sliding glass doors that didn't open until the train was in, so any despairing banker of a mind to cast himself in front of an incoming train would have to go to a more plebeian station to do it. No entrails on the tracks at Canary Wharf! How soon would he be back? Maybe never. Maybe soon. It was good to feel uncertain, and not to be troubled by it.

At home there was an e-mail message from Letty. Her baby had been born and would be christened Orféo Sam Saint-Jacques. The attachments were two colour shots of a very tranquil, wise-looking baby with slightly bruised eyes, and the sounds of his first cries in the delivery room, while a male voice, possibly Marcel's, murmured that he'd been born at "*deux heures du matin*", gave a heart rate, something about his eyes opening, and that he was "*magnifique*". Then there was the sound of a tiny person's breathing, like a panting puppy, and in the background Letty's voice, full of astonishment and pleasure.

Sam was fifty-two and wept his first grandfather's tears. He called her mobile, left a message full of love and congratulations, and made himself coffee. There was something – the death of the banks, the birth of this grandchild – that made him think of *The Winter's Tale* again. His Perdita had given birth – but it was more than that.

He got out the text and spent half an hour hunting for it.

That night he dreamed about Mrs Barton's cat and the Gloucester Terrace flat where the whole adventure had begun. Paddington was on the Bakerloo line, only four stops from Queen's Park. He would set off as if for work, but would get off there instead, and pay a visit.

Walking up from the Underground and through Paddington mainline station he was invaded by a sense of Englishness, of England, not as home but as a second home – another, a different, an alternative almost mythical place, but also his, because there was a sense in which he had grown up with it. It was the peculiar reverberation under the vast arch, the press of people each on a slightly different path, the announcements coming on the intercom, their accents, their lists of place names that could still come to him as if they belonged in a book, unreal but comfortable, rather lovely in fact. Sometimes, when one or more of the trains about to pull out was warming up, there was so much noise you could sing full voice and only someone who passed within inches would hear you. He sang now, his favourite Sinatra song, about flying to the moon, and to Jupiter and Mars, with the refrain "In other words, hold my hand; in other words, baby, kiss me".

He went out of the station past the statue of Isambard Kingdom Brunel, seated and holding his top hat against his knee; past the line of black cabs, up on to Eastbourne Terrace and down past the restaurant, once called Spices, now Thai River.

Mrs Barton answered his ring at the doorbell, buzzed him in when he said who he was, and was waiting at the door of her flat to greet him, her black face shining with pleasure.

"Mr Nola, hullo stranger, long time no see. What brings you back?"

He told her he had dreamed of Trinnie. "She'd caught a rat and wanted me to admire it."

"Oh she don't do that," Mrs Barton said. "I think if she saw a rat, she'd run. Come in, luv. Now you're here you'll have a cuppa won't you?"

While the kettle was coming to the boil, the biscuit tins explored and cups and saucers set out he sat and held out a hand to Trinnie. She was looking older, almost past her use-by date, and she approached the hand with caution, but soon accepted that he was indeed someone known to her, arching and turning sideways to rub against his trouser leg. He picked her up and she felt frail, as if her bones were only a loose and approximate arrangement inside her skin. "I did warn you about relativity," he told her, standing at the window and holding her half over his shoulder.

Across the street he saw that the office he'd watched so assiduously from one floor up was now closed. An interior folding metal grille was drawn across the street-level window. There were no curtains in the first-floor flat and no furniture, or none he could see.

"Your neighbour over the road's gone," he said when Mrs B. returned with the teapot.

"Mr Joyce? His business collapsed you know."

"Mr Joyce. I never knew his name. Not James, I suppose."

"No," she said, as if it had been a serious question. "I think it might have been Robert. The man in the paper shop used to call him Rob anyway."

She said the business had been in gift hampers. They took the orders over there in the office and made arrangements for shipping and delivery. There was a warehouse somewhere in West London where the hampers were assembled. "That's closed too. It's to do with this trouble with the banks everyone's talking about."

She poured the tea, pausing to give the pot an admonitory shake when the stream from its spout wasn't dark enough.

"Some of their 'ampers was lovely," she went on. "Pricey – but they put them together so nice, in a basket with bright ribbons and coloured cellophane and that. Made your mouth water just to read the brochure. Two years running I sent one to my favourite cousin in Trinidad – and then he died, sudden. They like English things out there, don't they?" She pronounced running "runeen" – it was one of the slight deviations from London that hinted at origins further afield.

"I suppose they do," Sam said. And then, "He had a girl in the office."

"That was Belinda. Very nice young lady. She's on the checkout at Marks and Sparks in Whiteleys now."

"Oh dear, that's a bit sad."

"Well you have to take what you can get these days, don't you? And she looks as if she's expecting."

"Expecting, I see. There's a husband is there?"

"I'm not sure about a husband," Mrs Barton said. "But there has to be someone doesn't there?"

"Biologically speaking, yes indeed."

"She was gone from over there a year ago – before the business collapsed. He ran it on his own at the last, and he gave up the upstairs flat. Used to sleep in the office."

"Hard times," Sam said. And then, "There was a time when Belinda – was it? – and Mr Joyce seemed to be getting on rather well."

Mrs Barton giggled, covering her mouth. "Until Mrs Joyce took a hand."

"Ah, Mrs Joyce. I always imagined there must be a family somewhere in the country."

"Wife and two daughters. They do horses and that sort of thing. Probably won't be so much of it now."

They sipped their tea. "I lost my job yesterday," Sam said.

"Oh Mr Nola, I'm sorry to hear that. I didn't think that would happen to you. Heavens! What will you do?"

"I'll have a small R. and R. and then look for another, I should think."

"But you've got your own place, haven't you? That's what matters – a roof over your 'ead."

"Yes," he said. "I have a roof."

"I told you about my boy Rod?" She hadn't, so she told him now. Rod had only had two ambitions, to play professional football and to sing in a rock band.

"To be rich," Sam said.

"Well it would have made him rich and famous, that's true. But he loved it, football and music, that's what he loved, and he was good. They called him Silky . . ."

"You sing beautifully yourself," Sam said. "I used to listen to you."

"Kitchen and bathroom," she said. "I didn't know you was listening. You should've said."

"He's out of work, is he?"

"Rod? No, he's got a job with the hotels. They call it front of 'ouse. But his wife, Thena, she's Greek Cypriot and she doesn't like it here. Hardly speaks any English and wants to go home. And my girl Norn, she's a nurse and she's going to marry an Indian. He's a nurse too."

"The melting pot," Sam said.

"That's what they say isn't it, but half of us is meltin' and half's not, if you know what I mean."

He wasn't sure he did, but he nodded as if this had been a wise observation and he agreed with it.

As he stepped out into the sunshine of Gloucester Terrace he remembered he had nowhere to go, nothing to do. It was a light-headed moment like giddiness to a child, exciting but not altogether pleasant. He strolled down to Queensway. At White-leys he went in and at M. & S. selected a bottle of New Zealand wine and a bottle of water from France. There were not many customers. He looked for Belinda at the check-out and took a moment to be sure which was the young woman he'd watched from across the street. As Mrs Barton had said, she was obviously "expecting".

"Hullo Belinda," he said giving her his blue basket.

She blinked, said "Hi," checked the articles and told him what they came to. "Plastic bag?"

"Please." Reaching for his wallet he said, "I used to live across the street from Mr Joyce's office."

"Did you?" She scooped up his coins and tried, but not very hard, to appear interested.

"I had a flat in Mrs Barton's."

"Oh yeah? Nice."

He took the bag and put the two bottles into it. "I hear the business is closed."

"Mr Joyce's – is it? I didn't know." She swept back her hair from her face with both hands, arched her back as if it was hurting, and looked out into the echoing concourse. Her eyes returned to his, asking either nothing, or whether there was something else he wanted to say.

"A bottle of wine," he said, "and a bottle of water. I'll see if I can turn the water into wine, and then I'll have two for the price of one."

She smiled, not unfriendly but not eager to talk. "Not quite," she said. "You had to pay for the water."

Ah so she had a brain then – he was glad. "Bye," he said, and walked out into the sun.

That evening he called Ruth. "I must see you. I've got news – good and bad."

She couldn't leave the house – Frank was dying. "It's ghastly here, Sam. Frightful. But do come, darling. We can talk outdoors."

It was a clear night with an almost-starry sky and a big round moon. She met him at the door, kissed him and took him out into the garden. There was a fountain trickling just audibly over rocks watched over by a little female figure in marble, and a rose-covered pergola with a bench. It was the same figure, the same fountain, that Reuben had installed in his Ladbroke Road garden, as if in imitation. Lady Luck, perhaps.

They sat there, the stillness of the late September night broken at regular intervals by the growl of a jet plane going over, and the occasional police or ambulance siren in the down-below distance.

"Tell me about Frank."

"He's in a coma and it's only a question of how long. The doctor thinks tonight."

"I'm sorry, Ruth."

"Yes it's sad, even though I've been expecting it for months. But you know . . ." She stopped, and started again. "We've been together a long time. He was quite dashing, you know."

"Of course," Sam said.

"And it's hard on the girls. I've sent them away for the night – they're with Noah's children."

They sat for a while in silence, holding hands.

She said, "I always thought the death rattle was something that happens at the last moment and then you're dead, but really it's the sound of someone in a deep coma fighting to breathe. It goes on and on. I didn't know that. It's so awful. The whole house is full of it. And the smell of death – death and chemicals. You know that phrase 'to give up the ghost' – that's what you want the dying person to do. To stop fighting – but the body goes on trying to stay alive. Long after the mind has given up, the body persists. Like a habit – I've never thought of that, have you? – that living's a habit."

"An addiction," Sam murmured. "A dependency." No he hadn't thought of it like that, and was quite glad of the thought, even though the image of the body clinging on was distressing.

Another pause, another jet going over. "Once I tried to kill a wounded hedgehog . . ." She was weeping now. He put an arm around her shoulders and she said, "At least he doesn't know how bad things are . . . His fortune's gone."

"Truly? You mean . . ."

"All of it. Noah thinks so."

"How much was that?"

"I don't know. Fifty million."

"Fifty." He said it aloud to be quite sure.

"The boys are upset. Especially Joel. Noah and Gerhardt are O.K. They have good jobs and they've looked after their own money. But Joel . . ."

Sam remembered Sir Frank's joke: "One's a lawyer, one's a doctor, and Joel's at the races."

"There's this house to be divided up. And Maiori sul Mare. And the yacht must be worth a bit."

"And for you?"

"Oh I'm alright, Sam."

He supposed she was. It had been established that she was her brother's sole heir.

After a while she'd stopped crying. "Tell me your news, Sam darling."

He gave her the bad news first. She was comforting about the loss of his job – said what could be said, which wasn't much. "What will you do? You won't . . ."

He thought he knew what she meant, but waited.

"You'll find another job," she said. "You've proved yourself here."

He said, "I'm a grandfather" – and he told her about the message, the images, the sounds from the delivery room, the murmuring doctor, the heartbeat, the little panting puppy and Letty's voice in the background.

"Oh Sam, I'm so pleased for Letty – and for you, darling. Orféo Sam Saint-Jacques. Doesn't that sound splendid? Rather aristocratic. I like it that it's Sam, not Samuel. It's more compact – tucks in so neatly."

He quoted the line he'd hunted for and found in *The Winter's Tale*: "Thou met'st with things dying, I with things new-born."

"It's true," she said.

"I was thinking of the banks dying, not of Frank."

"Well either way, it fits. But it's not all bad, Sam. I haven't kept you up to date – you've been away, and I've been distracted by Frank's ill-health. But Reuben's investments . . ."

"The Swiss account?"

"Our Mr Kraznahorkai's hedge fund has gone wild."

"Losses?"

"No, gains."

"Big?"

"It could be as much as twenty-five. Even thirty."

He laughed. They laughed together – couldn't stop; but then steadied themselves, knowing their laughter shouldn't be echoing up from a moonlit garden into the house of a dying man who had just lost his fortune. But there was something so bizarre about it, so delicious, so meaningless. Fifty million lost, twenty-five gained? They were numbers. Against a background of losses counted in billions they were, each of them, quite a small fortune, one going out the other coming in, not in trunks full of silver and gold coins or gold bars, or even in suitcases full of banknotes, but in numbers on a screen. It was fairy-tale, it was myth, but it was real; and the banks, those great castles that had created these possibilities, were shaking now, as if in an earthquake, their towers wobbling, threatening to come down. This was *Götterdämmerung*, "the twilight of the gods". Loge the fire-god was at work – except that Valhalla was "too big to fail" and panicky governments were hurrying to prop it up.

He looked into her eyes in the moonlight. She was smiling – they both were – and the pleasure came more from the sense of an absurdity than from the money. He said, "If you weren't so rich, I might think I should ask you to marry me."

She said, "If I weren't so rich, I might think I should accept" – and they both laughed again.

There was the sound of the door opening and footsteps on the path. It was the nurse. "Mrs Vogel, doctor says you should come. I'm afraid Sir Frank is . . ."

"Yes, of course. I'm coming."

The nurse went in again.

"You go Sammy. I'll call you later this evening, or in the morning. I'm going to need you."

He took her to the door. "*Bon courage*, darling."

She went in and he walked to the edge of the garden that ended in a kind of belvedere looking out across the suburb, and beyond over the great bowl of London, glittering and humming with life. He thought of Balzac's Rastignac resolving that he would not go back to the virtuous provinces; and he said over to himself the sentences which he had by heart in the free translation he had made of them just to show Letty the progress he was making:

"Down there was the beautiful world he'd hoped to enter. It murmured like a hive, and it was as if already he could taste its honey, as he said, 'You and I are not finished yet.'"

*

That night when he had driven back to Queen's Park in his new Prius and was cruising the streets looking for a parking space he saw there was a black motorbike up on the pavement across the street from his house. He drove by, slowly. A tree in the pavement on his side cast shadow on his house but he could see no sign that his doors or windows had been disturbed. It was a terrace house, so no easy or obvious way it could be approached from the back. He slowed almost to a stop as his headlights passed over the bike's number plate:

661

BAK09

Even when Jean-Claude had been ranging up alongside Simone's Mégane Sam hadn't taken note of the number; but this one did look as if it might be French. There was the usual small circle of gold stars on a blue background representing the E.U., and what might have been the letter F below it – or was it a D? Deutschland? And surely Jean-Claude had given up long ago.

Sam drove around the block and found a parking space in Summerfield Avenue. He got out, locked, and walked back around the corner, watchful, alert. The bike was still there, with no sign of an owner.

A hedge surrounded his small front garden which contained one tree not tall enough to reach the upper-floor windows, some potted bushes and window boxes, and a wisteria running up a trellis beside the windows. There was a break in the traffic and he heard his own footsteps on the pavement.

He walked very steadily, deliberately, as a man would walk if he thought he knew exactly what was waiting for him and was calm, confident, with steady nerves and a strong right arm. As he came through the gate he saw there was someone sitting in the shadows on a bench which did not quite conceal the council-supplied rubbish bins.

The dark figure sat there looking up at him from the shadow.

"Jean-Claude?"

It didn't move. And no, it was too small to be Jean-Claude. He went closer. It was . . . was it?

"Maja?"

"Back from dead, Sam."

"Yes," he said, "I see that. If you're not a ghost."

"No, not a ghost. Here, feel . . ."

He took the cool hand she held out to him and sat down beside her, still holding it as if he were a doctor taking her pulse. For the second time that day he quoted, "Thou met'st with things dying, I with things new-born."

She squeezed his hand. "You always have quotations."

"Not often so apposite."

"Opposite?"

"Apposite . . . Never mind."

He remembered her message that had said, "You live in the world, Sam, so surprises, including good ones, have a chance of finding you." Was this a good one?

There was a strange high-pitched bark from across the street. "Fox," he said.

She said, "Sam, I have to . . . to explain."

"Yes, if you like. I mean . . . Well yes, an explanation wouldn't go amiss."

She took a breath and shifted slightly sideways, as if to face him. "When I wrote you a farewell letter I really did mean to shoot myself. Really truly, Sam. It was what you call firm resolve. Trouble is I could not wait until I have . . ."

"Shot yourself," he prompted.

"You see?"

"Yes, I do see that. Of course. You had to write your letter first." He was laughing quietly. "Must remember that, if I ever . . ."

"I am serious."

"I'm serious, Maja, believe me. Just because I'm laughing doesn't mean . . ."

"So if I send the letter and then lose nerve . . ."

"You've created a problem."

"Yes. I am very sorry."

"Don't apologise. So – and Aunt Rosa . . ."

"My letter went to her so she thinks I am dead. Then I phone and say, 'Rosa, sorry but this is Maja. Very sorry Rosa, but after all I don't shoot myself.' You see?"

"You told her the plan had changed. Was cancelled."

"Yes."

"She was pleased of course."

"She is angry with me for grief I cause her, but yes, soon she is pleased."

"So what about the letter to me?"

"I tell her please keep it. If Sam comes back to Zagreb give it to him. Better if he thinks I am dead."

"Why?"

"I don't know, Sam. Just it's better."

"You wanted to make me unhappy?"

"Or angry. Something. I wanted to make . . . What is the word? Impact?"

"Well, that was achieved."

"You and me together – I wanted it finished. Like in the movies – The End."

He said, "You don't like loose ends."

"No, I don't like them."

He knew better than she did how loose the ends were now – how large the sense of a disruption. But he was feeling something rather different. It was like a plunge into a cold stream, the shock of it, the sense of refreshment, the wish to do it again.

He took her face between his hands, kissed her lightly, quickly, and looked again. "I'm glad you don't look different."

"Why should I look different?"

"In your letter you said you'd thought of a face-lift. Why?"

She shrugged. "Sometimes I am a bit mad."

"How did you find me?"

"Long time ago Rosa gave me name of your Interbank America, so it is not difficult. And Sam . . . I'm sorry." She took his hand again. "Rosa died."

"Ah." He absorbed that. "When?"

"Is a fortnight now."

"No-one told me."

"I am here to tell you." She hesitated, finding the words. "In person. You see?"

"Yes, I see. Thanks, Maja." He stood up, took a few steps around the garden. "Had she been ill?"

"No, she was well. She went to look at land she inherits. She loves that place – very much. She's talking about going to live there. I don't think it is likely – but it gives her something to dream."

"So what killed her?"

"It was stroke – sudden – bang dead. Best way I think."

266

"Well, if you have to die . . . yes." He sat down again and they were silent for what seemed like minutes, until he asked, "Is that your motorbike?"

"Motorbike?"

"Across the street."

"I came by taxi. From St Pancras."

"Ah. I thought . . ."

"Why would I have motorbike?"

He shook his head. "No you wouldn't. Of course not." After a pause he said, "You must come in. See my house." But they didn't move. A jet went over, a black cab went by, and the fox barked into the silence that followed. "I lost my job at the bank," he said.

She nodded, unsurprised. "I have no job." She laughed quietly. "No home, poor, unemployed – but I am a free woman."

"Feels good does it?"

"Feels good, yes. For now."

Someone shouted goodbye from a nearby house and the sound of a door banging shut echoed in the street. A moment later the motorbike started up and roared away down towards Salusbury Road.

Sam said, "You know the sign they have on the main road north of Auckland – did I ever tell you? 'Welcome to Northland' in three languages – Maori, English and Croatian – 'Haeri mai', 'Welcome' and '*Dobro došli*'. It's because of all the settlers up there who came from your part of the world. From the Dalmatian coast in fact."

"That sounds nice, Sam. One day you could take me there."

He stood up, taking his keys from his pocket. "We'd better have a cup of tea."

ACKNOWLEDGEMENTS & PERMISSIONS

The story told on pp. 131–2 about the door-to-door salesman is derived from one told in *Groblje manjih careva* ("The Graveyard of the Little Stars"), by the Croatian writer Zoran Malkoč, which I heard the author read in Rijeka at the Festival of the European Short Story, June 2010.

My thanks to the city authorities of Zadar for the award of a brief residency in 2010.

Thanks also to Guy Clayton for advice on technical (banking) matters.

"Why Brownlee Left" taken from *Why Brownlee Left* © Paul Muldoon and reprinted by permission of Faber and Faber Ltd; "Poetry of Departures" taken from *Collected Poems* © Estate of Philip Larkin and reprinted by permission of Faber and Faber Ltd.

C.K.S.